MY BEST FRIEND'S MARDI GRAS WEDDING

BOYS OF THE BAYOU

ERIN NICHOLAS

ISBN: 978-0-9998907-9-0

Editor: Lindsey Faber

Cover design: Angela Waters

Cover photography: Lindee Robinson

Models: Daniel Smith and Hannah Fitzpatrick

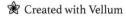 Created with Vellum

1

There were naked breasts everywhere. Literally.

It was Mardi Gras on Bourbon Street in New Orleans.

So yeah, lots and lots of naked breasts. And naked other things.

And Josh Landry didn't care.

For possibly the first time in his life.

Okay, that wasn't one hundred percent true. They were naked breasts. But as he handed yet another woman a strand of beads, Josh was already pushing past her.

A nearly identical strand of plastic beads smacked him in the face a moment later.

What the fuck? He looked up at the balcony where a group of drunk frat boys were throwing beads down to the street. Another one went whizzing past his ear. Jesus, they weren't supposed to wind up to throw the things. And did he look like he had tits?

Josh took a deep breath. He liked Mardi Gras. Mardi Gras was great. Mardi Gras was a hell of a good time.

Until it had made him a huge sap.

And celibate. He couldn't forget that.

He hadn't been with a woman in a *year*. His friends were past concerned. They were convinced he had a brain tumor.

But that was all about to end. He was going to be with a woman tonight. *The* woman. The one he'd met last Mardi Gras. The one who he hadn't even slept with and yet couldn't stop thinking about. The one who was supposed to be here tonight at the same spot where they'd met last year.

Well, they were if they were both still interested. And single.

And able to get to the fucking bar.

This was his fourth trip down Bourbon on this particular mission and it would be his last, dammit. He was bartending at Trahan's until one a.m. and he'd taken a twenty-minute break every two hours to walk this path—okay, scratch and crawl his way along this path—to get to Bourbon O's to see if she was there. Thank God his bosses were good friends of his and gave him a lot of slack. Leaving a bar, *any* bar, in New Orleans short staffed on Mardi Gras was a dick move.

He emerged from the crowd on Dumaine onto Bourbon. He knew better than to try to walk up the entire length of the most popular street in the city, but there was a point where he had no choice but to join the insane mass of revelers.

He was sure the crowd wasn't any bigger this year than any other, but he'd never noticed, really. Because he'd never resented them before. He was a bartender. He loved a party. He joined right into all of this usually. He loved New Orleans and seeing new people come and experience the city. Mardi Gras was his favorite time of the year. Until now. Because all of these drunk-off-their-asses revelers were between him and the woman who had occupied his thoughts for nearly twelve full months.

But of course he was going to keep making this trek all night. Until he found her or the clock struck midnight and officially ended Mardi Gras. Because the fact that he had to fight a Mardi-Gras-in-New-Orleans crowd for eight blocks from Trahan's Tavern on St. Peter to Bourbon O on Bourbon was like a man being willing to swim the Nile, climb Mount Everest, and cross the Sahara for true love. That was fucking romantic as hell. He was finally living up to the Landry name when it came to matters of the heart.

He laughed and shook his head. It had been bound to happen eventually. You couldn't live with the Landrys and Morelands for twenty-eight years and not become a starry-eyed imbecile.

He just really wanted this story to have a happy ending.

She had to be there.

Josh growled at a group of fifty-somethings that had just stopped in the middle of the street to pose for a selfie.

"Oh, would you take our photo?" one of the women, wearing a *Birthday Girl* sash and tiara, asked. It had to be her fiftieth birthday, if not sixtieth.

The fact that she'd braved Mardi Gras to celebrate the milestone actually impressed Josh. Mardi Gras on Bourbon Street in New Orleans was not for the faint of heart.

And regardless of the fact that these people were holding him up on his mission, how could he say no? They were hardly the *only* ones in his way. And he was not just a born-and-bred Louisiana boy who believed that Mardi Gras was an experience everyone should have at some point in their lives. He was also a French Quarter bartender and, well, a big believer in having a hell of a good time whenever he could. How could he not encourage these women with their bright-orange *Angie's Birthday Bash* T-shirts? They were all clutching Hand Grenades, the powerful drinks served at the Tropical Isle bar, and he could tell these weren't their firsts.

He gave the birthday party a big, good-ol'-boy grin. "Okay, girls," he said. "Let's do this," even as someone slammed into him from the back. He gritted his teeth.

It was part of his calling in life to make sure people left New Orleans and the great state of Louisiana with huge smiles, fond memories, and commitments to get back as soon as they could.

Just like the woman he'd sent back to Iowa a year ago with a huge smile and a commitment to get her pretty ass back here as soon as possible.

Like tonight.

She should be just down the block, in fact.

That sent a shot of adrenaline through him, and he hurried to get the women positioned for the photo. Four phones were thrust into his hands and Josh sighed.

The women giggled and the five friends gathered around birthday girl. He made sure to angle the photo so that the Bourbon Street sign over their heads showed up in the photo. "Okay, one-two-three." He shot three photos on each of the first three phones.

But as he finished the countdown on the fourth phone, the six women—who were old enough to be his mother—lifted their shirts and flashed him their breasts. Their naked breasts.

He blew out a breath. But took the photo. He'd spent Mardi Gras in New Orleans every year since he'd turned eighteen. This wasn't the first—or last—time he'd see breasts he didn't mean to see.

Josh handed them all beads. "Looks like you girls know what you're doin' down here," he said honestly.

They all laughed again and Angie took her phone back

from him. She checked the photo and showed the other girls. They all grinned and nodded. Josh shook his head.

"I gotta go," he told them. "But...be good, okay?"

"Good?" One of the women wrinkled her nose. "Really?"

"I didn't say to *behave*," he told her with a wink. "I said be *good*. At whatever you're doin' tonight."

She nodded her head with a big grin. "Got it."

He laughed and turned to continue working his way through the crowds to Bourbon O, the bar where he'd met Tori last year. He'd been working there at the time. Over the past few years, he'd poured drinks in six of the bars along Bourbon, but Bourbon O was his favorite. And it was by far the nicest. If a bar had strong liquor and live music, they could get away with being just this side of nasty on Bourbon. Tourists didn't care. In fact, the "dive bar" ambiance seemed to be almost expected. But Bourbon O was a step—or ten—above most on the street. Not that Josh hadn't had fun and made really good money at those "dive" bars. He'd just worked his way up the street as his reputation for being great at the important combination of bartender, bouncer and bring-'em-back guy grew. He flirted when that was called for. He talked sports, or fishing and hunting, or any other topic that was appropriate if *that* was called for. He could also listen to anyone cry over nearly anything as long as they had a drink in their hand. He was great for business, period.

And he was now working for two of his best friends. Gabe and Logan Trahan owned Trahan's Tavern over on St. Peter. It was off Bourbon—several blocks off Bourbon, in fact—but they did very good business. The tavern sat on a corner just across from Jackson Square and had more than their fair share of tourist traffic and local regulars. Of course, Logan and Gabe were like Josh—good at flirting, having intellectual conversations, or sympathizing, depending on the situation. And until they'd met their wives, they'd done their part in "entertaining" the female tourists in the Quarter too.

Now, though, it all fell to Josh.

He grinned. Okay, maybe not *all* to him, but he did his best to "help out."

At least until he'd met Tori.

Josh picked up his pace down the street as images of the gorgeous brunette who'd sat at the bar at Bourbon O for nearly four hours last Mardi Gras flashed through his mind.

Please be there.

He was one block away and finally allowed himself to acknowledge the fact that Tori might not be there.

One year, two weeks, and six days ago...

"I WANT TO SEE YOU AGAIN." His hands cupped her face and he took her mouth in a slow, deep kiss. "Tell me I can see you again," he said against her lips.

"I live in Iowa."

But the way she melted into him like she was a pat of butter and he was a hot piece of cornbread told him that she wouldn't mind doing...all of this again.

"Yep. And there are roads in between here and there, Tori."

She moaned softly, the sound he'd imagine she'd make when presented with a huge slice of chocolate cake she didn't think she should have. But wanted.

"It's really hard for me to get away. It's really hard for you to get away," she reminded him.

"But not impossible."

Okay, it was close to impossible. He had two jobs, one for a business he was a partial owner in, and a big, overly involved family that expected a lot from him. She was a veterinarian. The only one in the little farm town in Iowa where she lived. A lot of people depended on her not just to keep their pets healthy, but also to care for the animals that were their livelihood. This weekend away was her first in two years. And it was only three days.

She blew out a breath, running her hands up the sides of his neck and into his hair. "I wasn't expecting any of this."

"Me either." That was a huge understatement. He'd certainly noticed her the moment she took the stool across the bar from him, but there was no way he could have expected the connection, the way she made him laugh, the way he wanted to make her laugh.

It had been two days. They hadn't even gotten naked. They'd just sat and talked and flirted and laughed. For hours. And he wanted a hundred more days with her now.

She sighed as he kissed the side of her neck. "This is just the romance of New Orleans," she said.

"And I was the first Southern boy who grinned at you?"

She laughed. "You've been the first a lot of things but no, not that."

He gave her one of those Southern-boy grins. Southern boys couldn't help flirting with pretty Yankees. And pretty Southerners, for that matter. But it was especially fun to give the girls who spent their time above the Mason-Dixon line a taste of Southern charm.

"I just think maybe I'm getting...swept up in things. This is all so different from my usual weekend." She laughed softly. "My usual life. I'm probably going to get off the plane in Des Moines and realize that this was all just...like a dream. And I'm guessing the second another girl takes that stool and asks for your specialty, you'll forget my name."

That made his gut clench. No way would he forget her.

He blew out a breath. "At least tell me you're going to give me your phone number so we can keep in touch. And I can work on talking you into coming back down here."

She looked at him for a long moment, then rose on tiptoe,

and pressed her lips to his. Then she stepped back. "I think the spell will wear off, Josh. I really do. And I don't want to be sitting at home, waiting for you to call, and then be heart-broken when you don't."

"I will."

She gave him a little smile. "And if you do, I won't know what to do with it. With you."

"I can give you a very long list of things you can do with me."

There was a flicker of heat in her eyes even as she shook her head. "I know you will want to call. I believe you. It might last for a while. But, I think that..." She sighed. "We both have lives. Very different lives. It's probably better to leave it at that."

Maybe that would be better. But he didn't want to do that. At all.

He probably shouldn't say what had just come to his mind. But he was going to. Because he came from a long line of very passionate, romantic, slightly crazy people. And this idea was all of those things.

"Meet me next year."

She frowned, clearly puzzled. "What?"

He nodded. "We'll give it a year. And then, if we're still thinking about each other and want to see each other again, we'll both show up at Bourbon O on Mardi Gras. If we're both there, we'll know."

She stared at him. It was a wild suggestion. But it was...safe. If one of them showed up and the other didn't, no harm, no foul. If neither showed up, the world would go on. There were four million things that could keep them from getting together again. But there was the...possibility of it.

He wanted at least that much.

That was extremely romantic. His dad would be very proud. So would his mom. And his grandma, grandpa, aunts and uncles... yeah, the family was going to love this story.

They would, of course, also all be the assholes giving him shit if she didn't show up next year. But that was a risk he was willing to take. The Landry family lived by the motto that the only things worth doing were the things that made your heart pound.

"That's—" Tori shook her head.

"Come on. At least agree to that much. Give me this crumb," he said, grinning and stepped close to her again. "Let me cling to this for now. If it really does fade as soon as your plane takes off, then so be it. But at least this way there's a chance if it doesn't fade."

She laughed. "Okay. Fine. Next year. Mardi Gras. Bourbon O."

He kissed her long and deep. Then said, "I'll be there."

She'd just smiled.

SHE HADN'T BELIEVED HIM. But she'd played along. He'd realized that even at the moment.

Now he was dodging beads and boobs, making his way down Bourbon, on his way to see her.

And there was a very good chance she wouldn't be there.

Fuck.

His family was going to give him so much shit about this.

———

THIRTY MINUTES EARLIER, two blocks away...

TORI WAS SUPPOSED *to be* the Best Man.

If she was, she would be having drinks at some place called Trahan's right now. Tori didn't even care what they served there, only that it would be *off* Bourbon Street. And she'd be talking to

Andrew and his friends. And *not* babysitting Paisley and *her* friends. All of whom made Tori want to stab her eardrums with the tiny colored plastic swords that were skewered through the pineapple chunks at the top of their drinks.

Correction—all of whom made her feel like someone *was* stabbing her eardrums with tiny plastic swords.

The subjects of their conversations were bad enough—how could anyone talk this much about shoes?—but the talking also *never stopped*. And then there was the giggling. And the squealing. Holy shit, the squealing.

It got louder and more frequent the more of the icy, pink and green drinks the girls consumed.

Andrew owed her big time.

It was interesting that the guy from out of town was celebrating *off* Bourbon, while the girl who had grown up in New Orleans was the one getting shit-faced on the infamous party street. Paisley struck Tori as more the mint-juleps-on-the-front-porch type than the doing-shots-and-flashing-her-boobs-for-beads type.

But she'd become that second type tonight. On Tori's watch.

Thanks, Andrew. At least he was going to be the one dealing with Paisley's puking later. And her hangover tomorrow. Tori couldn't imagine the Southern princess hungover. Yikes.

Tori took a tiny sip of the pink concoction she held. And grimaced. She was a beer girl, when she drank at all. This was, obviously, meant to be consumed quickly and after several other drinks.

But this was one of *those* places on Bourbon. It had the neon-on-steroids lights, the crowds of people, the overpriced-but-loaded-with-liquor drinks in collectible glasses that you'd never want to see again after spending the early morning hours kneeling next to the toilet.

What the hell were they doing here? Paisley was a rich girl. Classy.

A loud, screeching squeal went up from the herd of girls standing a few feet away and Tori rolled her eyes. Classy-*ish*. Apparently Paisley didn't go out partying like this with her friends on a regular basis, and the rum and lights and festive atmosphere were getting to her. And, of course, the fact that people kept pinning dollar bills to her chest. It was a tradition, apparently, that if you saw a bride during her bachelorette party in the Quarter, you pinned money to the little clip she wore on her shirt. Or, in Paisley's case, the very low-cut, tightly fit, strapless dress she wore.

Oh, and then there were the masks. The masks were such a huge part of Mardi Gras that Paisley's girlfriends had insisted they all wear them tonight. They were meant to obscure your identity and make it easier to just let go and revel in everything crazy and sinful.

Paisley's was a bright pink, glittery thing that matched her dress—including the sequins—and covered everything but her mouth. No one would know she was the daughter of Robert Darbonne, the past and very beloved Mayor of New Orleans and a current United States Senator. It was the main reason that Paisley's father had agreed to let her take the bachelorette party down to Bourbon tonight. Her mother thought a tasteful cocktail party would be more appropriate. So they were doing that. Too. Tomorrow night. But Paisley's bridesmaids—minus Tori—had insisted on taking her to Bourbon for a traditional bachelorette party. For better or worse.

Paisley had grown up in the Garden District of New Orleans in a real, honest-to-God mansion on St. Charles Street, the only child of her politician father and nationally renowned neurosurgeon mother. Paisley was a princess. At least as far as Tori could tell. She dressed the part with lots of designer labels and flashy styles. She certainly acted the part too, making lots of demands and clearly expecting people to ask "how high" even before she said to jump. She was the most spoiled person Tori had ever met.

And she was marrying Tori's best friend, Andrew.

In four days.

Tori was in New Orleans, a part of the bridal party for a woman she barely knew and didn't like, for an entire week-long wedding extravaganza.

And the Darbonne family didn't do "nontraditional" things like letting a woman be the groom's first attendant. So Tori was the *ninth* bridesmaid—the *last* bridesmaid—standing up on Paisley's side of the aisle.

Tori took a bigger drink of the strawberry slush in her hand —and instantly regretted it—as Paisley stuck her chest out for a group of guys to pin bills to her dress and give her congratulations. Though "congratulations" really sounded a lot like "how about I make you wish you were staying single."

Tori wished Paisley was staying single. That was for sure.

Not that anyone—especially Andrew—knew that. As far as he knew, Tori was happy for him and his bride-to-be. That was mostly thanks to the fact that Tori and Andrew didn't often see each other in person. He'd been living in Louisiana and she'd been in Iowa for the past six years.

Tori sighed as she thought about how things had changed between them. That was why she'd been so happy that he'd wanted her to be a part of his wedding. "You're my oldest friend, Tori. You know me in a way no one else does. Of course you need to be a part of my wedding." Those words were why she'd said yes to standing up at a wedding she didn't really want to happen. She didn't have a lot of close friends and none like Andrew, who she'd known since kindergarten and who had always liked her in spite of her weirdness.

She missed him. Andrew had grown up next door to her, literally, and she couldn't remember a time when she'd gone more than a day without talking to him even when they were both at Iowa State. It wasn't until he'd gone to law school at Tulane that they started to talk less. She'd been in vet school, so they'd both been working hard and the time between phone calls had stretched, sometimes to a couple of weeks at a time.

But it had been okay. Mostly. They had texting and Snapchat and Skype.

Until he'd met Paisley.

She'd swept him off his feet. A political science major, Andrew knew all about Paisley's father, and the promise of a dinner with the famous, mostly-beloved Louisiana politician who they'd been courting to run for President—yes, of the United States—had been more than enough to get Andrew wrapped around Paisley's dainty, perfectly manicured finger.

He hadn't come back from that first dinner as the Andrew Tori knew.

"Oh my *God*, Paisley!" Jenna, one of Paisley's bridesmaids, exclaimed as she finished her drink. "This is the most fun *ever!*"

Tori felt her eye twitching.

The girls were loving this because of the attention they were getting.

Tori guessed that bachelorette parties always got a lot of attention from the men on Bourbon. Where else could you find entire herds of young, beautiful, tipsy women who were out for nothing but a good time?

Oh yeah, pretty much anywhere else in New Orleans on any other day of any other week.

Tori almost took another sip of her drink, but then remembered that she hated everything about the slushy pink mix of... whatever. She lowered it and sighed as she watched Paisley look at her phone, grin widely, and then show it to her friends.

Andrew had just texted her a photo of him making a kissy face.

What the hell had happened to Tori's best friend?

Paisley was exactly the opposite of everything Tori would

have expected Andrew to fall for. She spent more time on her hair than Tori spent going from waking up to walking out the door. Paisley had studied early childhood development in college but had no intention of teaching. Or working with kids at all. She was clearly trained and intent on being a politician's wife. And, maybe worst of all—no, *definitely* worst of all—Paisley didn't like animals. She *said* she was allergic to both dogs and cats, but Tori thought it was really more that she was a terrible person.

Tori again lifted her glass, thought for a second about just chugging it so she'd at least have some liquor in her system, opened her mouth, and then thought better of it. She lowered the glass again. Dammit, she wanted a beer.

She never thought people were *terrible*. She didn't like every person she'd ever met, of course, but mostly she gave people the benefit of the doubt and...avoided them as much as possible.

Animals really were superior to people, in almost every sense, and spending her days taking care of everything from cats to cows, and even one alpaca, made Tori exceedingly happy.

She watched Paisley's friends gather around her for a selfie. They didn't ask her to join in and she had no desire to. She knew that Paisley was putting up with her because of Andrew.

No, scratch that. She knew that Paisley absolutely did *not* want her here.

Why Andrew had told Tori that, she had no idea. Why he thought that she and Paisley should hang out tonight, she had no idea. Didn't Andrew know Tori better than this?

The two women had absolutely nothing—other than Andrew, she supposed—in common. That had been painfully clear when Tori had come to visit Andrew for Mardi Gras last year. Things had been tense and cool between the women, and Tori had ended up spending a lot of time alone while Paisley monopolized Andrew as if they didn't see each other every single day.

Of course, that had led Tori to Bourbon Street on Fat Tuesday last March, which had led her to Bourbon O, the bar five blocks from where she was right now, which had led her to Josh Landry.

So she should probably be *grateful* to Paisley.

Tori sighed again, but happily—maybe wistfully—this time.

Tonight was Mardi Gras. *The* night. The only night she really cared about being in New Orleans. The night she was supposed to meet Josh Landry back at Bourbon O. If she wanted to. If he wanted to. If they were still thinking of each other.

And dammit, she wanted to.

She was definitely still thinking of him, and when Andrew had announced that he and Paisley were getting married the weekend after Mardi Gras and asked her to come, Tori had immediately decided to come for the festival and stay for the week-long extravaganza that was going to be Paisley Darbonne's wedding. Not Andrew and Paisley's wedding. This thing was all about the bride.

Most women had one day. *Maybe* a weekend. Not Princess Paisley. The week before the wedding was filled with activities and meals and tours all designed to make the wedding in her hometown into something of a destination wedding for all of the Iowa guests.

Tori hadn't gotten to New Orleans until today, but she would have waited and shown up on Friday if it wasn't for Josh Landry.

And now she was five blocks away from the place they'd agreed to meet up.

Just the fact that Josh had suggested this had been making her heart pound for nearly a year. Whenever she thought of it, anyway. It wasn't like she thought about him constantly. Just once or twice. Every day.

But this kind of stuff didn't happen in her life. Her life was very...normal. Other than the occasional set of bovine twins or an injured mare, there were very few dramatic flares in Tori's life.

So what the hell was she doing even thinking about running down Bourbon Street to the bar where she'd first met Josh? They'd only spent about six hours together total and that hadn't even been all at once. She'd sat across the bar from him as he worked for two nights. The first had only been for about an hour. The second had been for five hours. Five hours that had flown by. They'd only talked. And laughed.

But, as she was leaving each night, he'd come after her. And kissed her.

The best kisses of her life.

Seriously. They were easily the best four out of the twenty-three she'd had.

And then he'd asked her to come back a year later. After two nights of just talking. And four amazing kisses.

That had all been enough to get him to ask her to come back.

That was just...wow.

And she was right here, after all. *On* Bourbon Street. On Mardi Gras. She could just pop in and see if he was there. He was maybe even working tonight.

"Victoria!"

She cringed as Paisley called to her across the bar. Paisley refused to call her Tori, no matter how many times Tori told her to.

"Yes?"

"You have to go and stall Andrew, okay?"

It wasn't a big place. Why did the girl think she needed to yell like that? Tori moved around the group of people between her and the perky blonde socialite with the hope that if she was standing closer to her, Paisley would lower her voice a little.

"Stall him?" Tori asked.

"Yeah, the girls and I are heading to the Hustler store," Paisley said. Loudly. "But we're supposed to meet them in like ten minutes. I need a little more time." She winked from behind her pink sequined mask with the tiny bit of tulle attached like a veil to one corner.

Well, helping Paisley pick out sex toys or lingerie for her and Andrew was *not* on Tori's To-Do list tonight and hell yes, she'd love an excuse to meet up with the guys somewhere besides the craziness of Bourbon Street.

She'd enjoyed it last year. It had been a part of the whole I'm-so-not-in-Iowa-anymore whirlwind she'd experienced. But Paisley had insisted that Andrew needed to attend her grand-mother's family dinner. Family only. Left out and pissed off that she'd nearly had to sell a kidney to afford her hotel room on Canal Street, Tori had stubbornly headed to the French Quarter on her own. It was freaking Mardi Gras. She wasn't going to sit in her hotel room alone.

But as soon as she'd stepped out onto the crazy, loud, crowded, holy-crap-there's-nothing-in-Iowa-like-this street, she'd had a mini panic attack. It wasn't safe. What the hell was she doing? So she'd ducked into the first place that had no neon in its windows. Bourbon O. She'd taken a seat at the bar and ordered a drink as she pulled her phone out to search for a local taxi company. Then she'd looked up and met Josh Landry's gaze. He'd grinned at her. And she'd put her phone away.

And now, here she was in New Orleans on Mardi Gras again...and irritated on Bourbon because of Paisley *again*.

But if she went and found Josh, he'd make her grateful for the turn of events all over again. She couldn't help that thought.

Her trip to New Orleans had turned out to be amazing last time. Maybe it could be again.

"I will definitely go find Andrew," Tori said, setting her glass down and pulling her phone out to find out where Andrew was.

"Oh, they're on their way to Bourbon O," Paisley said. "It's just up the street."

Tori lifted her head and stared at her. She would have had Paisley repeat the name of the bar if the other girl wasn't completely incapable of talking softly. Tori had not misheard her. Andrew was on his way to the very place Tori wanted to be.

"Great. I'll meet them there." She tucked her phone into her back jeans pocket, her heart thundering.

This was a great chance for a little time with her best friend. She'd come in that morning and had been promptly caught up in getting settled at the plantation—of course Paisley was having her wedding at a plantation—and then heading for Bourbon.

Tori and Andrew hadn't had any alone time just to talk in over a year. Even when they got on the phone together, Paisley was there in the background.

So yeah, she and Andrew needed some time alone to catch up and talk. And, yes, Tori needed to hear and *see* in his eyes that he really wanted to marry Paisley.

But she was going to be meeting him at Bourbon O. Where Josh Landry might be working behind the bar. And if he was, and she walked in, he'd think she was there for him.

And she would be.

She definitely would be.

Would he be happy to see her? Shocked? Would he *remember* her?

Suddenly her stomach plummeted down to somewhere around her pinky toe. Why had it never occurred to her that Josh might not even remember her? But that was *very* possible.

The guy met hundreds of people every single weekend. And the guy was obviously a player. What were the chances she was the only out-of-towner that he'd charmed and laughed with? How many times had he used that suggestion to send a woman off with a soft smile and thoughts of how romantic and amazing he was?

But dammit...now she couldn't *not* go to Bourbon O. Andrew would be there. And even if Paisley hadn't sent Tori to meet him, she wanted the chance for a few minutes alone with him. In the chaotic sea of people on Bourbon Street.

"How long do you think it will take Andrew to get to Bourbon O?" Tori asked Paisley.

She shrugged. "Trahan's is several blocks over, and with this crowd? It could be a while." She giggled. "But getting up to Hustler is going to take us some time too."

Okay, so it might take Andrew a while. Whereas Tori was just five blocks away. Sure, she'd have to get through the crowd too, but she had a few blocks head start. Which meant, she could pop in there, see if Josh was working, see if he recognized her and if he acted thrilled...or like a serial killer stalker had just shown up...and then duck back out if it was the latter. She could catch Andrew on the sidewalk and talk him into another bar instead.

With a deep breath, she stepped out onto the sidewalk and started down Bourbon without another glance at Paisley.

It was slow going for sure. Tori scowled as she jerked back to avoid a guy's elbow and a set of beads flying from somewhere overhead. Then she was hit right in the cheek with a strand of pink beads the color of Paisley's dress and mask tonight. Tori frowned up at the balcony full of drunk frat guys. No, she wasn't going to show them her boobs. Or anyone else her boobs.

Unless it was Josh Landry.

2

She dodged a group of women dressed in bright orange T-shirts that read *Angie's Birthday Bash*. She also, barely, managed to get around a twenty-something girl who looked ready to hurl, just before she threw up all over the back of the guy in front of her.

Tori slipped through the crowd, gritting her teeth when someone jostled the guy in front of her, spilling some of his beer onto Tori's shoe. She rolled her eyes when two girls flashed Tori their boobs—she didn't have any beads to give them anyway. And she managed to not run over, or get run over *by*, the stroller that a young couple was pushing up the middle of the street. A *stroller*. With a little boy who couldn't have been more than a year old.

For fuck's sake, people.

But she did not avoid the next group of women in matching T-shirts. These were purple, though, and read *Mardi Gras Sucks.* They were handing out lollipops. And collecting donations for the homeless. Wow, you really did see everything on Bourbon Street. Tori handed over two dollars and got two suckers. She tucked them into her pocket, laughing.

And then, suddenly, she was in front of Bourbon O.

She took a deep breath as she looked up at the sign.

She would probably hate New Orleans and everything Mardi Gras if Josh Landry hadn't leaned on that bar and said, "Welcome to N'Awlins," as he slid a drink to her.

One year ago...ish...

"What's this?"

"New Orleans specialty. All the tourists love it."

"How do you know I'm not from here?" she asked, picking the glass up and taking a careful sip.

She wrinkled her nose at the sweet, fruity taste.

He laughed. "You don't like hurricanes?"

"Is that what this is?"

"Yep. Invented right down the street. But ours are better."

She shook her head. "Can I just have a beer?"

He looked surprised. "Really? And insult this born-and-bred Louisiana bartender by asking him to pour a simple *beer*?"

"You're against beer?"

"I love beer."

"Then what's the problem?" she asked, tipping her head.

"Part of my mission in life is to make sure everyone who comes across my path loves Louisiana a little more."

"And your beer here sucks?"

He laughed. "Not exactly. But when you're in the Big Easy, you gotta soak up the atmosphere and history and the stuff you can't get back home."

That "stuff you can't get back home" thing caught her attention. It wasn't like Iowa was devoid of hot, funny, charming guys. But...she couldn't get a New Orleans bartender like him back home, that was for sure. She narrowed her eyes. "Okay. I'll give you another chance. Some New Orleans specialty but not a hurricane."

A flicker of amusement danced through his eyes and he nodded at the challenge. "You got it, Indiana." He started reaching for supplies.

She laughed. "Close, but not quite."

"I don't think it's Minnesota or Wisconsin," he said, pouring ingredients into a shaker.

"Nope. Neither of those." She studied him as he shook the ingredients all together, particularly the sexy grin behind the short beard and the arm with the muscles and a tattoo peeking out from under one sleeve. She hadn't even been paying attention to what he'd poured into the shaker.

"Kansas?" he asked.

"Nope. Still close."

"Iowa then."

She felt her eyes widen. "Yes." It had taken him four guesses...well, kind of two. He'd known she wasn't from Minnesota or Wisconsin. "I'm impressed."

He grinned and poured the drink into a martini glass. "I talk to people, mostly visitors, every day, all day long. I'm good with accents."

"I don't have an accent."

He passed the drink over. "Whatever you say."

She rolled her eyes. "So the accent thing is like a super-power or something?"

"Or something," he agreed. "I have several...gifts, as a matter of fact."

"No kidding." She was amused by his blatant flirting. She was certain bartenders in the French Quarter made good money, but it never hurt to give a little extra effort to the tips and she had to admit it was working. He was making her smile. Tonight, that was no small thing.

"Interestingly, my other *talents* have a lot to do with the girls I meet too."

She snorted at that, glad she hadn't yet taken a drink of the concoction he'd mixed her. "I have no trouble believing that."

"Already?" he asked, looking amused. "I haven't even really turned it on yet."

"Wow. Thanks for the warning."

He laughed, this time the sound lower and deeper. "Don't want to scare you off. I can ease in."

Damn, that sounded...dirty. In a good way. Not in the way she was used to getting dirty with the guys she knew. That kind of dirty was...well, actually *dirt* dirty. And mud. And blood. And...other things.

There wasn't much flirting in her life, really. She typically got to know the guys she met over the back end of a cow. Being a large animal vet in small-town Iowa wasn't the most glamorous career, that was for sure. But the guys, farmers mostly, of course, thought that her knowing about their animals—and being willing to put her hands in places a lot of men they knew wouldn't—was some kind of turn-on. Maybe not the places she was putting her hands, but her willingness to get dirty and get the job done. But after doing that for an afternoon, the guy usually just asked if she wanted to have a drink or if he could grill her a steak or if she was going to be at the street dance on Saturday. Grilling her a steak made from the brother of one of the cows she'd just manually impregnated had always seemed like an odd offer. And she'd only said yes once. As for street dances...yeah, she went to about half of them. But she never went *with* anyone. She'd grown up there, for fuck's sake. She knew all the guys. If she hadn't been in the same class, she knew *of* them. And their parents. And their grandparents. The milk they poured on their cereal in the morning probably came from cows she'd impregnated.

Her world was small. And a little weird if she thought about it too hard.

But, in any case, there wasn't a lot of flirting in her life. In fact, she spent so much time covered in animal *stuff*—from blood to crap to, yes, semen—that she rarely felt things like pretty or sexy.

Not so with this guy. He was looking at her like she was both. A lot of both.

So this was definitely different.

She finally took a sip of the drink. It was really, really good. "Wow."

"Ramos Gin Fizz. A specialty around here," he told her, looking satisfied.

"I'm a fan."

"Awesome. I'll keep plying you with those all night."

"How many do you think it will take?"

"Until?" he asked. But the way he quirked that one eyebrow told her that he knew what she was talking about.

"Until I decide that there's more of New Orleans I should sample before I go home."

Heat flared in his eyes. "Damn," he'd said softly. "Didn't know Iowa girls were so upfront."

Well, crap. She was a matter-of-fact person. She mostly dealt with rugged farmers who didn't beat around the bush and who needed to flat out know if their cow could be saved and if so, how much the bill was going to be. Frankly, sometimes the bill was too high.

Again, not a lot of flirting, of any kind.

Maybe she needed to dial it back a notch. She could be coy. Or cute. Or whatever the hell she was supposed to be.

Probably.

She tipped her head. "How do you know I'm not talking about beignets?"

He gave her a slow, knowing grin that made her tingle. Whoa. The last time she'd tingled it had been because she'd gotten too close to Mr. Lencroft's electric fence.

This wasn't the same. At all.

"*Are* you talkin' about beignets?" he asked. "Because I'll very gladly help you get all the...beignets...you could possibly need."

That little pause of his made her wiggle on her barstool. Yeah, they weren't talking about beignets. And she wanted exactly what he was offering to give her.

"Is your nickname Beignets, by chance?" she asked.

He laughed. Low and deep and she had to swallow hard.

"If you say you've never wanted anything as much as you want beignets, then it's gonna be."

She grinned. She never talked like this with guys. And she loved it. Tori picked up her glass again. "The way I understand it, I can't leave New Orleans without having Beignets."

He stuck his hand out across the bar. She took it. But rather than shaking it, he just squeezed and held on. "Hi, I'm Josh 'Big Beignets' Landry."

She laughed, feeling the fun and pleasure wash through her. "I'm Victoria Kramer. My friends call me Tori."

"Is there anyone calling you Tori in here with you tonight?" he asked, still holding her hand.

"Actually no," she said. "Not yet," she added.

The flicker of heat and interest lit his eyes again and Tori couldn't help the little thrill that shot through her. She might not flirt much—or at all—but maybe she didn't completely suck at it.

"*Tori*," Josh said. "I would really like for you to go over to that booth—" He pointed over her shoulder.

She swiveled to look at the empty booth in one corner. If she sat on one side, she'd be able to see the entire bar. If she sat on the other, she could hide away.

"—I would like for you to order whatever you want—food, drink, whatever—from Kara, the waitress who's covering that table. And I'd like you to stay until I get off work."

Tori looked up at him. "Why that booth? Why not stay here until you're done?"

"Two very good reasons," he told her, stroking his thumb over the back of her hand. "One, Kara has known me for about five years and can tell you all about me. Assure you that I'm a good guy. She can even bring Liz over to talk to you. Liz doesn't really like me, so you can be assured to get an honest answer from her about my flaws."

"You have flaws?" Tori teased.

"Two, according to Liz," he said with a nod. "I don't like ginger beer—which is one of our specialties here—and I do like brunettes, maybe a little too much."

Jealousy stabbed Tori in the chest before she realized *that* was ridiculous. She was brunette, after all. And she'd just met him. She was expecting...what? Him to have never been with another woman? Him to swear off all other women now that he'd met her? That was crazy. She smiled. "Liz isn't brunette?"

He laughed. "She is." He paused. "So's her daughter. Who is the one I hit on before I knew she was my boss's daughter."

Tori couldn't help her grin. "You work for a woman who doesn't like you?"

"She gets...exasperated with me," he said. "But I'm fantastic at what I do, so she keeps me around. And I stay because she runs an awesome business and treats her employees very well." He paused. "And I kind of like exasperating her."

Tori shook her head, still grinning. "You need someone to exasperate?"

"Oh, I've got plenty of those—a mom, three grandmas, a sister, aunts, a whole town full of girls I went to school with— it's just that I'm really good at it and Liz needs someone to keep her on her toes."

Tori nodded. "Got it." He had three grandmas and a sister. And an affectionate look on his face when he talked about exasperating them. That made her like him even more. "I'm sure Liz agrees."

"You can ask her."

"You really think I should ask your co-workers and boss about you?"

He sobered a bit. "You should definitely not take me back to your hotel without asking some people about me."

The idea of taking him back to her hotel room made her heart thump hard against her sternum and she had to take a quick breath. "How do I know they're not going to lie just to help you get lucky?"

"Good girl," he said. "Always assume guys are lying to get you into bed."

She laughed. "Well, I can assure you that most of the guys I spent time with are not trying to get me into bed."

He studied her face, then shook his head slowly. "Not true. I promise you."

Her heart did a little stutter. He was wrong. But that was really nice.

"Taking you back to my hotel isn't a good idea then, huh?"

He shrugged. "It is. But you have no way of knowing that. So you shouldn't do it."

Now it was her turn to study his face. He was gorgeous. But there was more than that. He had an air of mischief and, dare she say, sweetness about him. She had no doubt that he charmed women out of their panties on a regular basis, but she also had a feeling that he enjoyed the flirting and serving them their first Ramos Gin Fizz as much as he enjoyed getting them naked. Okay, *almost* as much as he enjoyed getting them naked.

He has three grandmas that he clearly loves and loves to tease.

He could be completely lying about that.

You could talk to his boss though.

Really? What am I going to say? Hi, I'm Tori, do you think sleeping with Josh is a good idea?

You could just take a chance for once.

I could also end up hacked into little pieces and shoved into the ice bucket in my hotel room.

Don't be ridiculous. He couldn't get all *of you into the ice bucket.*

She blew out a breath. She couldn't take a total stranger that she'd met in a bar on Bourbon Street back to her hotel room.

But she wanted to.

Josh was different. She didn't have to know him well for there to be something *very* appealing about him. Namely, that she didn't know him well. And he hadn't known her all her life.

He hadn't seen her wrestling a sheep down for a vaccination or up to her knees in mud or dodging a pissed off goat. He hadn't witnessed her punching Mike Trotter in the nose when she'd realized he was messing with her animals at the State Fair. Josh hadn't seen her slip in the afterbirth of a mama sow and end up on her ass in the pile of slop in the pen. He hadn't seen her burst out crying and run from the room when Allie Donally did a report about the inhumane treatment of animals in packing houses. He didn't know about the time she'd been picked up by the local cops for rescuing a bunch of dogs from an area farm and hiding them in her barn. He hadn't been in the truck when she and a group of friends hit a deer on the way to the river and she'd jumped out to check on the deer and then grabbed the shotgun and put the poor thing out of its misery when she found it still alive but dying.

All the guys she saw on a regular basis had been there for those events. They all knew her as the animal-crazy tomboy who preferred time alone on the farm and who was very socially awkward when she did go out.

Tori shook all of that off and focused on Josh. The guy who had no idea that she owned fourteen cats—and three dogs, two horses, two fainting goats, a geriatric pig, a stupid chicken named Cher, and a miniature cow. She lived on a farm. It wasn't like she had all of those animals in a trendy apartment in some big city. But...even she knew that was a lot of cats.

And it was because of those cats—kind of—that she realized she couldn't take a hot New Orleans bartender back to her overpriced hotel room on Canal Street. She wasn't that girl. She might want to be that girl. A little. When that hot New Orleans bartender was holding her hand and looking at her like she amused, and aroused, him. But when it came right down to it, she couldn't even deal with the guys she'd known her whole life. She didn't want to talk to them or eat with them. She was far more interested in their dogs and cats. Hell, even their chickens—and she pretty much hated chickens. The only guys she liked to talk to were her dad and Andrew. And now Andrew was gaga over a bubbly, blonde heiress who probably couldn't tell the difference between a Buckeye hen and a Plymouth Rock.

She really didn't understand men.

"Those wheels are really spinning in that pretty head," Josh said after a long silence. "You realizing that you could do a lot better than me?"

Tori gave him a little smile. She shook her head and reluctantly pulled her hand back from his. "Just realizing that I'm not really a gin fizz kind of girl."

Josh didn't say anything for a beat. Then he nodded. "I figured."

"Yeah?"

"I think that must be part of what I like about you."

She laughed softly. "Or is it just that I'm a brunette?"

He gave her a grin. "I shouldn't have told you that."

She laughed again and swiveled on her stool, sliding to the floor. She reached for her purse, but Josh stopped her. "Don't you even think about paying for that drink."

"You're not getting my number. I should at least give you a tip," she said. Was that flirtatious? Maybe.

He opened his mouth, then shut it, and shook his head.

"What?" she asked.

"There's nothing I can say here that doesn't sound like a come-on."

"No?" She grinned and handed him a twenty.

He handed her back nineteen-fifty.

"A fifty-cent drink and no tip or a free drink and a fifty-cent tip?"

He tossed the two quarters in the tip bottle on the bar. "Free three sips of a drink. Fifty-cent payment for the advice to stay the hell away from N'Awlins boys who drink too much bourbon and barely recognize nice girls anymore."

"You think I'm a nice girl?"

"I definitely do."

She was. She didn't realize she broadcast it quite so loudly, but yeah, she was. She nodded. "Sorry about that."

He gave her a smile. "Somebody's gotta go square dancing with all those nice farm boys up north."

She gave a little gasp, but she couldn't help her grin. "I've never been square dancing in my life."

He chuckled. "But I bet you've let a nice Iowa boy drive you around on his tractor." He wiggled one eyebrow suggestively.

She scoffed. "Not even once."

"No?"

She shook her head. "Don't need a boy for that." Tori slid her purse strap up on her shoulder. "I've got my own tractor to drive around. When I'm in the mood for...tractor driving."

There was a brief pause and then he laughed.

In a brief flash of sassiness, she winked at him. "But if you ever make it to Iowa, I'll take *you* on a ride."

"Damn, girl, that's tempting."

She smiled. "Thanks, Josh."

"For?"

"Being a good guy."

He gave a little shrug. "I'm already regretting it, I'll be honest."

With a smile, she turned and started for the door.

She'd just stepped out onto the sidewalk when she felt someone grasp her upper arm and twirl her around.

It was Josh.

"Wha—"

He cupped her face and covered her mouth with his.

Whoa.

It took her about three seconds to recover from her shock. She tilted her head to deepen the kiss, opening her lips under his, and stepped in until they were belly button to belly button.

He gave a soft growl that made heat curl through her and settle between her legs. She arched closer. He swept his tongue over her lower lip and then in along her tongue.

God, he tasted good. He felt good. He smelled good.

A far-too-short moment later, someone bumped into him from behind and broke them apart. Josh stood, still cradling her face, staring down at her.

"What was that?" she asked.

"Came to tell you to assume all the guys you're going to meet down here are N'Awlins boys who drink too much bourbon and don't recognize nice girls when they meet them."

"Most of these guys are tourists," she pointed out.

He nodded. "Even worse than N'Awlins boys."

She chuckled at that. "So just stay away from all the guys here no matter what?"

"Definitely."

"And the kiss?" she asked softly.

"That, I just couldn't help."

"Because you're a N'Awlins boy and all that?"

"Ah, girl," he said, his drawl getting deeper and longer. "I'm way more fun, and dangerous, than a N'Awlins boy."

"Dangerous?" She lifted a brow.

"I'm a bayou boy." The sexy grin said it all. Bayou boys were definitely cocky.

"And that's worse?"

"N'Awlins boys need liquor and beignets and jazz and the Quarter and all kinds of stuff. Bayou boys only need a little beer and the great outdoors."

"Is that right?"

"New Orleans has nothin' on the bayou, Iowa."

Him calling her Iowa even gave her tingles. "Just being outside is enough?" She could relate to that. There was no city that could ever compare to being outside on the farm for her.

"Yep. We've got stars overhead and frogs and crickets to serenade you and nice, quiet back roads where no one will bother you for days." He leaned in. "And humidity that'll make you want to strip right down to nothin'."

His voice was low and gruff and Tori felt like stripping right down to nothing right here.

"Mosquitos the size of small birds and alligators."

Josh chuckled. "All the more reason to stay close to a bayou boy who knows how to take care of all of that."

She smiled. "So going down to the bayou with you tonight would be fine, but I shouldn't take you back to my hotel room?"

He seemed to think about that for a moment. Then he blew

out a breath, leaned in and gave her a soft, lingering kiss that curled her toes, and then let her go. "Nah. Probably not."

Tori tamped down her disappointment. "It wouldn't be safe?" she asked lightly.

"Well, you might never want to leave. I'm guessing there are some people in Iowa who'd miss you." He gave her a little half smile.

She nodded. Yeah, it was for the best that she just tuck this memory away and not get hung up on a playboy bartender from Louisiana. Really, where was *that* going to go?

"In that case, quit coming after me when I go to leave, okay?"

He nodded. "Yeah. This time."

She started to turn.

"Probably."

She glanced back.

"Just don't..."

Her eyebrows rose.

"Don't square-dance with...too many guys."

"Too many?"

He shrugged. "I was going to say with 'anyone' but that sounded a little ridiculous."

She laughed. "I told you I don't square-dance at all."

He nodded.

She turned away again and took a step. Then heard him say, "And don't..."

Tori smiled, but hid it before she turned around. "Yes?"

"Don't go stargazing with anyone else. You want stars, I'll give you stars."

Whoa. What the hell was going on here? This was crazy. And romantic. And...crazy. "I've got stars at home," she admitted. "And crickets and frogs and quiet back roads."

He just stood looking at her for a long moment.

"And beer," she added when he didn't say anything.

Finally he nodded. "Good. That's good. You seem like the beer and back roads kind of girl."

She really was. But how did he know that? She looked down at her outfit. A summer dress and sandals. She could be from anywhere in these clothes. "Yeah?" she asked.

"It's in your eyes."

Those eyes went round.

He shrugged as if he didn't get it either.

"Well, you're right," she told him.

He looked pleased about that. "So go on, get out of here. Go back to your Yankee stars. And don't trust anyone with a Louisiana drawl or a plastic souvenir cup of any kind."

She laughed. "What about a bayou drawl?" She could definitely hear the difference.

"Yeah, *definitely* don't trust any of those. They'll get you hooked on sweet tea and crawfish pie and you won't even remember how to spell Iowa."

Yeah, that's not what she would be hooked on. Because she felt a little hooked already and there wasn't a crawfish in sight.

"Thanks for...whatever this is," she finally said.

He laughed. "You bet. And trust me, I don't know what the hell it is either."

That was maybe the best thing he could have said. He was letting her go and he didn't know why, but it was clearly *not* because he wanted to.

This was so interesting.

Tori finally turned and managed to get to the end of the block without him stopping her. She paused at the corner and looked back. He was still watching her.

Her heart thumped. But she turned and kept walking. All the way back to her hotel.

And the next night when she walked into Bourbon O again and Josh looked up, his gaze locking on hers in spite of the madness of the crowd that wasn't much thinner now than it was Ash Wednesday—supposedly a holy day— and his face broke into the biggest, most sincere grin she'd ever seen, she knew she'd made the right choice coming back.

Now...

TORI TOOK ANOTHER DEEP BREATH.

This was it.

She was going inside. She reached up to tuck her hair behind her ear and her fingers brushed over the mask she wore.

The mask she wore.

She was anonymous in this mask. Josh wouldn't even know it was her. Until she decided to tell him. She could go in there and see if he was working, even watch him for a little bit and *confirm* that she wanted to see him again. If so, she could take the mask off. If not, she could still hang out with Andrew and forget about her stupid fantasy about the guy falling in love with her after just a kiss. Okay, two kisses. Still...that was crazy.

She stepped through the doorway and into a crowd of people. Wow, there were just people *everywhere*. She'd stupidly been hoping that the classier bar and restaurant would have a smaller crowd. But she didn't know why'd she thought that. Last year had been the same.

Someone bumped into her from behind, then someone else crashed into her left side. A splash of the girl's drink hit the toe of her boot. Tori glared at the drunk redhead, but the girl didn't even realize she'd spilled. She was too busy making out with the guy who had swung her around, causing her to hit Tori.

Tori sighed. She couldn't blame the girl. Sometimes you just had to go with it. And when "it" was a hot Southern boy, you *really* had to.

She didn't know that this guy was from here, but in her head, every guy sweeping a girl off her feet was a bayou boy. She was clearly not here *just* for Andrew.

Fingering her mask again, reassuring herself that Josh would only know she'd shown up if she let him see her, Tori started for the bar.

Oh God, what was she going to do if he didn't remember her?

She swallowed hard and focused on the people behind the bar. Thankfully they weren't wearing masks.

The first person she saw was a guy about Josh's age, but it wasn't him. Neither was the next guy. There were also two girls. But no Josh.

She glanced around but only saw waitresses. Not that she could see every person in the bar, but she remembered Josh saying he was really good at his job, and his boss put up with him because of his talents as a bartender. Surely he'd be manning the bar on a night like this. If he was here.

If he wasn't here, working, then...would he be here to meet her? Would he show up just for her? Would he even remember asking her to come back?

Finally, unable to stand the way she was worrying, she pushed her way between two people at the bar and leaned in to get the bartender's attention.

"Hey, what can I get ya?" he half-yelled over the noise.

"Is Josh Landry working tonight?" she asked. Might as well just meet this head-on.

"Sorry. Don't know a Josh."

"He doesn't work here anymore?" she asked, surprised. That hadn't occurred to her as an option. Stupidly.

The guy looked over his shoulder and shouted, "Kara!"

Kara. Tori remembered the woman's name from last year. Not that there couldn't be multiple Karas in New Orleans...

"Yeah?"

"You know a Josh Landers?"

"*Landry*," Tori corrected.

"Landry!" the bartended yelled.

"Yeah, what about him?" Kara was pouring two beers at once and looked harried.

Tori felt a little bad. But this was about finding Josh.

"He used to work here?" the guy asked her.

"Yeah. Quit a while back though."

"You know where he works now?" the bartender asked.

"Autre!" Kara called back.

The bartender looked back at Tori. "Autre.'"

"Is that a bar here on Bourbon?" Tori asked. Damn, she'd have to brave the crowd on the street again. But she was willing. All the love songs talked about people being willing to walk five hundred miles and endure other hardships to get to the one they loved. Bourbon Street during Mardi Gras was absolutely a hardship. But Josh Landry just might be worth it.

"Autre's a town," the guy said. "Down by the bayou."

Ah, right. Of course. The bayou. As in not here. In New Orleans. Where she was right now.

Dammit.

"Okay, thanks," she told him.

"You wanna drink?"

"Um...a Ramos Gin Fizz," she said. She was suddenly feeling nostalgic about that night last year.

"You got it."

The guy mixed the drink, not looking even half as hot as Josh had doing it, and handed it over. She paid, took a sip, feeling memories of that night crashing over her—the smell of the hurricane Josh had given her first, the flip in her stomach when he'd grinned at her, the sensation that she'd just swallowed a mouthful of hot cocoa when he'd first said her name, the feel of his lips on hers, the warm and tight feeling in her chest when he'd asked her to come back.

She really wanted to see him. Okay, so he wasn't here tonight. Maybe she could still find him. She was here for nearly two whole weeks. How far was Autre? And how horrible would it be to show up and have him not remember her?

She took a sip of the drink and was again accosted by memories from a year ago. The sound of Josh's laugh, the way he'd drawled *I'm way more fun, and dangerous, than a N'Awlins boy,* the way he'd looked at her like he couldn't believe he'd met her...and wasn't going back to her hotel with her.

That could have definitely felt like a rejection, but it hadn't. At all. It had felt like he was doing it because he felt *more* than just attraction and lust.

Of course, she spent most of her time with cows, so what did she really know?

She turned away from the bar, trying to decide if she should try to wait for Andrew outside, or if her chances of finding him were just as good, i.e. horrible, out there as they were in here.

Tori surveyed the room as she took another drink. And suddenly froze.

He was here.

Josh. Josh Landry was here.

Her throat attempted to swallow her gin fizz at the same time she tried to take a deep breath and she sucked gin, half-and-half, and lemon juice partway down her windpipe. She started hacking and coughing. No one seemed to notice. Except him.

The guy with the wide shoulders and dark hair, wearing ass-hugging jeans and a black mask with gold trim turned to her. He started for her.

She was still coughing as her heart started racing. That was him. The mask covered his whole face except for his mouth and the sexy short beard, but everything about him was familiar. She'd definitely seen that mouth before. And he'd obviously recognized her.

"Tori? Is that you?"

Over the din of conversation around them, it was hard to hear him, but she knew he'd called her by name. He'd definitely recognized her. *Oh my God, he's here.*

She was wearing a mask too, she suddenly remembered, so she nodded quickly. "It's me," she croaked.

"Are you okay?"

She wasn't. She was feeling jittery and so damned happy to see him and more than a little relieved. She felt like she wanted to cry, actually. She also felt like laughing hysterically. Adrenaline. She knew that. On top of the stress of Andrew's wedding plans and Paisley and being on Bourbon Street during Mardi Gras for the past two hours when she was used to wide open spaces, dark and quiet, with no humans for miles. Everything about this night had her off-kilter.

She had no idea what to say. So instead of saying anything, she grabbed the front of his shirt, pulled him in, and kissed him.

It took her about three seconds to realize that this was *not* Josh Landry.

Tori started to pull back, but the guy wrapped his arm around her waist, his big hand splayed over her lower back, and brought her up against him. He opened his mouth and deepened the kiss, moving his lips over hers. She gripped his shoulders to keep from tipping over, though with the hold he had on her, that was a low risk.

It was...weird.

The kiss wasn't bad. It was actually an okay kiss. And there *was* something familiar about it.

But this was not Josh.

Yet, this guy had called her Tori. And he seemed fully comfortable being in her personal space. And he hadn't seemed overly shocked by her kissing him. In fact, he was *very much* going along with it.

She felt him groan slightly as he slid his tongue against hers and registered the fact that he was enjoying this. The feeling of familiarity continued as she breathed in, taking his scent in.

And that was when it hit her.

Andrew.

3

Tori shoved Andrew back.

He didn't go far, since he still had a pretty firm hold on her, but she was definitely staring up into the eyes of her best friend. No wonder he'd seemed familiar walking toward her. She should have known him right away. That just went to show how obsessed her mind had been with Josh. She'd *wanted* to see him and so the first male who seemed familiar automatically became him? Wow, that was crazy.

"What are you doing?" she asked Andrew.

"What do you mean?"

How had she not noticed his cologne immediately? It was as familiar to her as the smell of her farm. She internally winced. Okay, that didn't sound very flattering. But Andrew's cologne was as ingrained in her brain as the smell of home. But honestly, they were surrounded by so many people, so many smells, that until she was this close—and not thinking of Josh —she hadn't noticed.

"You're *kissing* me!" she exclaimed, pushing against his chest.

He gave her a little smile that was *absolutely* familiar. If only he'd smiled at her when he'd come up to her a minute ago. She would have known him for sure then.

Probably.

"Actually, *you* kissed me," he told her, still not letting go of her.

He smelled like beer. See? Andrew was a beer drinker. She could have been drinking *beer* with him and his friends tonight. And then she would have known what he was wearing and what mask he had on and none of this would have happened. This was actually Paisley's fault...

Tori's entire body went cold. Paisley. Andrew's *fiancée*.

She pushed him back again. "I thought you—"

"What the *hell* is going on?"

The screech was shrill enough that it stopped conversation for an impressively large circumference around them.

Andrew let go of Tori then.

Tori turned to face Paisley. The bubbly blonde bride-to-be was *not* looking so bubbly right now. In fact, she looked capable of homicide. And her chosen victim was quite obvious. Tori took a step back—right into Andrew.

His hands went to her hips, to steady her, but she could only imagine how it looked.

Not good, judging by the narrowing of Paisley's heavily made-up eyes.

"Hey, babe," Andrew greeted, stupidly not letting go of Tori. "Just a mistake. We're both drunk and—"

"*She's* barely had anything to drink," Paisley said, planting one hand on her hip and pointing her other index finger—with the very sharp-looking nail—at Tori. "She's not drunk."

"I thought he was someone else," Tori said quickly, moving away from Andrew.

She stepped to the *side* rather than forward, and closer to Paisley, but with the crowd there wasn't very far to go.

"See, mistake," Andrew said.

Tori nodded. "Total mistake."

"You didn't know who she was?" Paisley asked Andrew, one perfect eyebrow arched.

"Well..."

"Which means you were just kissing some *stranger* then?" Paisley continued. "How is that better?"

"No, I knew it was her," Andrew said.

Maybe he thought that kissing a stranger would be worse and this was the reassurance Paisley wanted, but, well, it didn't work that way.

Paisley burst into tears.

Oh shit. Tori took a step toward the other woman. "Paisley, I swear I thought he was Josh."

Paisley gave her a look that chilled Tori to the bone. She quickly took that step back again. And then another.

"Who the hell is Josh?" The question didn't come from Paisley though. It was from Andrew.

Tori looked up at her friend. "A guy I met last year."

"Last year?" Andrew frowned.

"When I was here. In New Orleans."

"He's from here?"

She nodded. "Yes. Well, near here. Autre." She said it as if she'd known that prior to asking the bartender a few minutes ago.

"You just randomly met him last year and now you're here thinking about kissing him?"

"We spent time together last year," she said. "And—" She shrugged. "Yeah, I *really* wanted to be kissing him tonight."

"What kind of *time* did you spend with him?" Andrew asked, looking annoyed and worried.

Oh, for fuck's sake. Tori looked at Paisley, who was still crying. She was now surrounded by her bridesmaids—which meant there were eight other women also shooting I-wish-you-were-dead looks at Tori—then back to Andrew. She raised her eyebrows. The look was supposed to indicate that he should probably be comforting Paisley. But he was still frowning at Tori.

"Just...time," she said, exasperated. "Talking. Laughing. Getting to know each other. And he was supposed to meet me here tonight."

"You never said anything about meeting a guy here last year," Andrew said.

No, she hadn't told her best friend about Josh. Because... there hadn't been much to tell.

But that wasn't really it.

Andrew had been so wrapped up in Paisley that Tori honestly hadn't thought he'd care.

And she'd wanted to keep the memories to herself.

That sounded silly, even in her mind, but it was true. It had all felt a little magical, almost dream-like, and she'd been afraid that if she talked about it out loud, and had someone say something like *do you really think this guy just fell head over heels for you in a night or two?*, she'd start thinking about it too hard and doubting and the magic would be gone.

"Just because I didn't tell you, doesn't mean it didn't happen," she said. Then she frowned. "Wait a second. Do you think I'm lying about him?"

Andrew shrugged. "I'm just saying that I haven't heard anything about this guy. And he's not here."

Paisley stepped closer to them, her eyes shooting daggers.

"And you *kissed Andrew* and then got caught. It definitely sounds a little suspicious."

"If I wanted Andrew, why would I be trying to convince him that there's another guy?" Tori asked her.

"Because you thought that you'd have time to tell him how you really feel and to convince him to run off with you, but then I showed up and ruined your plan. Now you're embarrassed."

Tori rolled her eyes at that.

Wrong move.

Paisley sucked in a gasp loud enough to be heard over the people around them who had returned to their conversations. Of course, ninety percent of the people around them were still watching this confrontation avidly.

"Look," Tori said before Paisley could speak. "Josh and Andrew are built a lot alike. I haven't seen Josh in a long time. I saw a guy who looked familiar and who's wearing a *mask*—" she added in her defense. "It was just a mistake. There's nothing going on with Andrew and me. We're friends. That's it. I would *never* kiss him."

"Hey," Andrew, the idiot, protested. "It's not like we've *never* kissed."

"You've *kissed* before?" Paisley said, her sobs forgotten in her outrage.

"That was eighth grade!" Tori said to Andrew. What was he doing?

"And tenth," he reminded her.

"Oh my God," Tori groaned. "None of that matters. That was forever ago." She turned to Paisley again. "I *swear* I thought he was Josh. I *wanted* him to be Josh. I wish right now that he was Josh."

Paisley sniffed. "I don't believe you. I think you've been in love with Andrew forever. I know you don't want this wedding to happen."

Okay, Tori could not, in good conscience, insist that she was thrilled Andrew wanted to marry Paisley, and she couldn't convincingly convince anyone that she was happy about this wedding. Which meant that she took just a beat or two too long to reply. "I just—"

"I don't believe you!" Paisley stamped her foot.

Looking for an ally, Tori turned to Andrew. "Andrew, you have to tell her that nothing's going on."

"Nothing's been going on," he said to Paisley. "I had no idea that Tori wanted to kiss me."

Tori felt her mouth drop open. Okay, he was drunk. But seriously? "What are you doing?" she asked him, stepping closer.

He shrugged. "If you have feelings for me, it's okay. It's understandable. I don't like the idea of you with some guy you met down here last year either."

"It's *okay*?" Tori repeated. "It's *understandable*? *Either*? Are you insane?"

He shook his head and swayed slightly. "You don't have feelings for me?"

"Of course I do," Tori said. But she added quickly, "Friend feelings. Affection. Caring."

"Love," Andrew said. "You love me. It's okay."

Tori glanced at Paisley. She looked like she was about to have a stroke, but she seemed to be waiting to hear Tori's response.

Tori took a deep breath. "Yes, I do love you, Andrew. But as a friend. Like a brother. I'm not *in love* with you."

"Paisley and I have discussed this and she says that we need to acknowledge your feelings for what they are so that they're out in the open where we can all deal with them," Andrew told her.

They'd talked about Tori's feelings for Andrew? Or what they thought Tori's feelings for Andrew were anyway. Tori frowned at the other woman. "What the hell does that mean?"

"I know that you've always told yourself that you only loved Andrew as a friend," Paisley said, suddenly looking cold and completely in control rather than steaming mad and out for blood.

Wow, that switch turned on and off quickly.

"I *have* loved Andrew as a friend," Tori told her.

"But when the person closest to you is suddenly closer to someone else, it can stir those feelings up and help you realize what they *really* are. You've always imagined a certain life with Andrew. Maybe in your head it was on neighboring farms or something," she said, the scorn for that idea clear in her tone. "But the truth is now hitting you—his entire life is different. His future is different. And it doesn't include you. And now that you're losing him, you're realizing that you're in love with him."

Tori felt a stabbing in her chest at the truth in Paisley's statement. Andrew's life and future *were* totally different now than she'd always imagined they'd be. Not that she'd imagined *them* as husband and wife, but she'd always assumed he'd be a part of her life, down the road, sharing things like holiday dinners and events like the births of children and the deaths of parents. She would take care of his animals and he'd help her wade through her dad's will when it came time.

And now all of that was...gone. It would all be different. Most of that would be nonexistent. If Andrew helped her with her father's will, it would be from a distance.

She felt tears stinging her eyes and pressed her lips together. Her throat was so tight that she couldn't argue with Paisley's assumptions.

Paisley stepped forward, reaching for Andrew's hand. She regarded Tori with a touch of pity, and a lot of triumph. "It's really important to be honest about how you feel," she said. "It's only fair to both Andrew and I. He needs to know where you stand. He can't assume. And it isn't fair to me to be asked to give you time alone together anymore. If you were just childhood friends, that's one thing, but you can understand why I would be concerned now."

It was Tori's turn to gasp. "So you don't think that Andrew and I can have a private conversation now because you think I'm in love with him?"

She saw exactly what Paisley was doing. The other woman was jealous of Tori and Andrew's relationship—a *friendship*, dammit—and history, so she'd come up with a way to justify keeping them apart. And a way to make it all Tori's fault.

"Exactly." Paisley said it coolly.

"So, you're absolutely convinced that I'm in love with Andrew and planned this kiss and some kind of jilted-bride scenario?" Tori asked.

"Yes, I am." She leaned into Andrew and ran her hand up his chest. "Fortunately, I'm completely sure of Andrew's feelings for me."

Tori wasn't sure about that. Why work so hard to keep him and Tori apart then? And maybe Paisley hadn't noticed the way Andrew had kissed Tori back.

Tori was *not* going to say that though. It didn't matter. He was drunk and she'd caught him by surprise and the kiss didn't mean anything.

"Come on, Andrew, time to go." Paisley started tugging him toward the door.

"I can't just leave Tori here," Andrew protested, taking a few steps with Paisley anyway.

"Oh, I think she'll be okay," Paisley said, glancing over her shoulder at Tori. "Apparently she found her way down here alone and met a 'friend' last year."

Andrew shot Tori an apologetic look, but he let Paisley lead him out of the building.

Tori watched the other bridesmaids turn and follow them out.

Then she blew out a breath.

Well...fuck.

She had, in fact, found her way down here on her own last year.

And even though he had stood her up, she was missing that "friend" more than ever right now. If he'd shown up, she could have proven to Paisley that she had no romantic feelings for Andrew. Having Josh sweep in in the middle of *that* debacle would have been *perfect*. Paisley would have had to acknowledge that Tori had not only been telling the truth, but she would have seen that Tori wasn't pining after the boy next door. The spoiled bitch would have seen that Tori could, by God, attract a hot, sexy playboy with panty-melting drawl who looked at Tori like she was his favorite flavor of *everything*.

Yeah, that would have been perfect.

But it hadn't happened. At all.

And it finally sunk in fully that Josh had not shown up for their rendezvous. Tori felt a knot in her stomach and a sadness that was far more intense than made sense. She barely knew the guy. It had been a year. There had always been the chance that one or both of them wouldn't, or couldn't, make it to this spot on this night.

But she still felt like crying.

So, now what was she going to do? The wedding had been on track for being an incredibly frustrating, awkward affair anyway. Now? Now that the entire bridal party thought Tori was after Andrew? Now that *Andrew* thought that Tori was in love with him? This had all the makings of the worst week of her life.

She could leave.

There was nothing that said she *had* to be here. There were lots of people who would prefer she leave.

But, no matter how stupid he was when he was drunk, Andrew was still her best friend. They'd been there for every major occasion in the other's life forever. If she missed his wedding, she'd always regret it.

Probably.

So she needed a way to salvage this. A way to prove that she did not want Andrew for herself. She just didn't want him with *Paisley*.

No, Tori, you can't think about that. If you break this wedding up, everyone will definitely think it's because Paisley was right. Andrew might even think that. And that will make everything between you and Andrew awkward forever.

She couldn't let that happen either.

She really needed to prove that the kiss had been about another guy altogether. A real guy. A guy that actually existed and had romanced her last year and had *asked* her to come back. A guy she *really* wanted to kiss. In front of people. Like Andrew and Paisley. For instance.

She needed Josh.

Tori turned toward the bar and pushed through the people to get back to the bartender.

"Hey!" she called to him.

"What's up?" he asked.

"Can you tell me how to get to Autre?"

Was she going to show up and convince him to be her plus one at this wedding even though he'd stood her up and probably completely forgotten her?

Yep.

Hey, she was going home to Iowa in a few days. What was the worst that could happen?

———

JOSH THREW the rope onto the boat, kicked the cooler out of the way, and stomped onto the deck behind the group of tourists who had just debarked the airboat.

"Thanks so much, Josh, we had such a great time." Barbara, the forty-something who had brought her three kids and husband on the swamp boat tour, handed him a thirty-dollar tip.

He gave her a smile. "Hey, thanks, I appreciate it. Y'all were a lot of fun."

They hadn't been. The boys hadn't shut up the entire time and their father kept insisting on answering their questions, incorrectly, before Josh could. But part of his income was tips, so if he had to push the charm out between gritted teeth, he would. He could definitely use the extra cash tonight. He could drink at his grandma's bar for free, but he couldn't get shit-faced drunk there without a ton of questions that he didn't want to answer about his pissy mood and *why* he was getting drunk. He'd have to buy his own liquor tonight.

"Thanks a lot, Josh." Another of his tour attendees handed him forty bucks.

"You bet, Randy. Great to meet you guys." He clapped the older businessman from Bismarck on the shoulder.

He collected tips and thanks from the rest of the group and smiled through it all. But the second the last person disappeared into the gift shop, Josh dropped his smile and headed back to get the boat ready for the next tour.

They had a busy day ahead and he was determined to just keep his head down and get through it. He could handle the tourists. They paid him. But he couldn't deal with his partners today. His brother Sawyer owned thirty-five percent of the business with Josh and their cousin Owen each owning fifteen percent. The other thirty-five percent had been owned by Sawyer's best childhood friend, Tommy.

Tommy had died about six months ago and his portion of the business was now, legally, his sister Madison's. But Maddie lived in San Francisco and was a silent partner. They sent her cut of the profits regularly, but she didn't give input into the business.

The guys got along great and everyone worked hard. Even more so since Tommy's death. Losing him suddenly had brought them all even closer. Their business was thriving. But working together, and living in the tiny town where their families all also lived, made it hard to even sneeze without fifty-seven people blessing you.

Josh realized that sounded like a *nice* thing but, well...yeah, it was mostly a nice thing. But some days a guy just wanted to sneeze in peace. He did not want to get into what was making him a surly asshole today. And he would be a surly asshole if any of the guys got on his case about anything.

He threw new packages of raw chicken into the cooler as he tried not to think about last night. The gators were active today and he'd found four to feed for his last tour. He'd head down a little more east this next time and see who was swimming around down there.

He stored the cooler and made sure all of the life jackets and headphones were put away properly. Then he propped his hands on his hips and looked around. Shit. There wasn't much more to do before the next tour.

Tori didn't show up at Bourbon O last night.

He couldn't fucking escape the thought. Even with the work. On the airboat, a lot of the time it was too damned loud to talk to anyone. So that left a lot of time in his own head. He couldn't do any educating or "tour leading" until they got down into the areas where the cypress trees and old shacks and gators gave them the real bayou experience. Then people loved to hear the stories and facts and ask questions. And then he fired up the airboat again and it was too loud to hear a thing. Except his own thoughts.

Why didn't she show up? Does she have a boyfriend? Is she

okay? Did she just forget about him? But mostly...did she have a boyfriend?

He wanted her to be healthy, of course. He definitely didn't want to think that she'd forgotten him. But holy shit, the idea that she had a boyfriend was the thing making him downright intolerable. Even for himself.

It had been a *year*. She was gorgeous and smart and funny and sweet. He knew that of the three options—she'd forgotten, she was sick, or she was taken—taken was definitely the most likely.

He stomped up onto the dock. He'd hose the boat off. That wasn't as good as breaking shit, which was really what he felt like doing, or getting drunk—also definitely a preference—but it was something.

Turning the faucet on full blast, he aimed the water at the deck of the boat, hosing off bits of mud and grass.

And still thinking. Dammit.

He'd known that the chances of her being there had been slim. Who met a person, spent six hours together talking, and then agreed to get back together a *year* later with no contact in between?

No normal person.

Sure, every other member of his family would do that. But *normal* people, like Tori Kramer, did not. Tori had been *very* normal. Clearly out of place on Bourbon. Clearly out of place at Mardi Gras. And it had drawn him like a fish to bait. She had so clearly been a tourist on her first trip to the Big Easy, like so many women he met every night, and yet...there had been something refreshing about her. She'd owned not fitting in. She'd been onto his I'm-charming-you-for-tips bit from the minute he'd opened his mouth. And yet, he hadn't been charming her for tips. He'd immediately wanted to make her smile. He'd immediately wanted to be the thing she thought about when she went home and thought back on her trip to New Orleans.

He really hadn't understood why at the time—or in the three-hundred-and-some days since then—but he'd wanted to make her laugh, kiss the hell out of her, and protect her. He'd really wanted to send her back to the farm untouched by the stupid-drunken-what-happens-in-NOLA-stays-in-NOLA experiences that most visitors took home with them. He'd wanted to go to her hotel room and taste every inch of her. But even more, he'd wanted to take her home and introduce her to his grandma.

That's what had made him send her back to her hotel room alone. Twice.

He'd been waiting all his life to meet a girl who made him want to act like a crazy, romantic ass for her. It was Landry family legend that the men all eventually stumbled upon *the* girl that made him willing to throw all pride and sense of self-preservation out the window. When he found her, he married her.

Josh had sent Tori back to Iowa without even having her phone number, not quite trusting the love-at-first-conversation thing that he'd felt happening, but trusting that if she was the one, she'd be back. On Mardi Gras. At Bourbon O.

And then...she hadn't been.

And he was more pissed about that than he really wanted to admit. To anyone. And certainly to the family who would be floored...and would then insist he do something stupid like drive to Iowa to find her.

Which he was already considering.

"Josh!"

Fuck. He pretended that he didn't hear Owen calling to him.

He was really not in the mood for Owen. Owen loved to push buttons and really didn't worry about little things like pissing people off to the point that they took a swing at him. He could admit that he sometimes deserved getting popped in the mouth, but he also had really good reflexes, so it didn't happen as often as it probably should. He was especially dedicated to making sure the people around him didn't take things too seriously. Except work. Owen took their business seriously.

But that was convenient since their business was, after all, showing people a good time. The people who came to the Boys of the Bayou Swamp Boat and Fishing Tours were here to ride around on airboats and pontoons, drink, laugh, see a few things they didn't get to see back home, and make some memories.

Owen especially loved the swamp boat tours full of bachelorette parties. Not because he loved women—which he did—but because he especially loved women who had no business on the bayou in their high-heeled sandals and spray tans. He loved to get them a little dirty. Literally. And wet…though when he said *that* he added, "in all ways a pretty girl can get wet."

It was hard to be in a bad mood around Owen. Unless he was flirting with a girl you were interested in, because Owen had a bad-boy air about him that seemed to always trump Josh's good-guy vibe.

But today, Josh really thought he could be in a bad mood around Owen.

Victoria Kramer had stood him up last night.

His reaction to that fact told him everything he needed to know about how he felt about her. He'd had no intention of sending her back to Iowa untouched this time. Hell, he wasn't so sure he'd had any intention on sending her back to Iowa at all.

Maybe it was better she hadn't shown up. Was he ready to get married? Because he wasn't really able to envision any other way for Victoria Kramer's second trip to Louisiana to end.

"Josh!" That was Kennedy's voice.

Josh finally sighed and turned. If Kennedy was out here, it

was about business. One of the tours had gotten messed up or something. Kennedy was his little sister and she handled all the bookings and scheduling. She'd grown up around the muddy waters of the bayou, but she was *not* an outdoorsy girl. She resented every time she had to come out on the docks.

Which meant she'd probably tried to text or call him. Well, he'd had his phone turned off. Because he wasn't in the mood to talk to anyone.

But when he turned, he realized that was one luxury he was never going to get. Not in Autre. Not with his family. Not only were Owen and Kennedy approaching, but Sawyer was with them as well. What the hell?

Josh reached up and turned his cap backward on his head and took his sunglasses off. "What's going on?" he asked as they got close.

"There's a girl here for you," Kennedy said. She was frowning, but it looked more concerned than annoyed. That was unusual. To say the least. Sawyer, Owen, and Josh had been annoying Kennedy for about twenty-four years now. He wasn't even sure what it would take to make her concerned about any of them.

"A girl?" he asked.

"Yeah." Kennedy looked a little pained. "She was booked on the next airboat tour with Owen but she came rushing in, giving me some story about how she'd just been trying to get here no matter what and she'd booked the tour because our bus picks up at the hotels." Kennedy rolled her eyes. "Apparently Uber seems sketchy to her, and the idea of taking a taxi by herself seemed unsafe and she didn't have another way to get down here."

"A girl booked one of our tours just so she could get a ride down here?" Josh asked.

Their grandpa, Leo, and their cousin, Mitch, drove the buses that went around to the hotels in New Orleans to pick up tourists and bring them to Autre for the tours. They also directed them to Ellie's bar across the street for a pre or post tour cocktail. They both also delighted in using the time to play good old, downhome, Cajun music over the stereo system and to tell the tourists all kinds of crazy facts about living in Louisiana. Like that there is a five-hundred-dollar fine if you have a pizza delivered to someone without them knowing about it and all about the haunted Manchac Swamp Bridge.

"I guess," Kennedy said. "And now she's insisting she needs to talk to you. She's been sitting on the dock waiting for you. Doesn't want the tour with Owen." She was clearly put out by this girl.

"I even went in and introduced myself," Owen said. "She said no thanks."

Josh had to laugh at the look of disbelief on Owen's face over that fact. "Really? She'd rather wait for me than get on a boat with you? I gotta meet this girl." Josh suddenly felt a little better about things. Tori hadn't shown up, but some girl had booked a tour just so she could get to Autre. For him. And she'd been unimpressed by Owen. Yeah, he definitely wanted to meet her.

"Hold on there," Sawyer said. "We're...concerned."

Okay, Owen thought this was funny and Kennedy was probably torn between amused and worried. But very little amused Sawyer these days, so he was obviously firmly in the concerned camp.

"A girl choosing me over Owen isn't cause for *concern*," Josh said. "I mean, come on."

"Not that. She seems a little...off," Kennedy said.

"Off?" Josh asked.

"We're thinking she's either a stalker or she's pregnant with your baby," Owen told him.

Josh froze. "*What*?"

"She's very...jittery," Kennedy said. "She won't tell us what she wants to talk to you about. And even when I told her she could be waiting for three hours in the hot sun, she said fine."

"Three hours?" Josh asked. "Where the hell did you think I was taking that last tour?" Their tours lasted about ninety minutes, maybe a little more if the gators were out and being show-offs, or if they happened to get the boat stuck in some of the lower grassy areas.

"I just told her that to try to get her to leave," Kennedy said. She frowned at Josh. "She said she wasn't going anywhere until she talked to you."

"And you think she's *pregnant*?" Josh asked. "Does she *look* pregnant?" That seemed like something that should be pretty obvious. Though he hadn't had sex with anyone in over a year, so there was no way it was his no matter how pregnant this woman looked.

"She doesn't," Kennedy said. "But it could be early."

"It's not mine."

"How can you be so sure?" Owen asked.

"Because I haven't—" Okay, his brother and cousin knew that he'd been less...promiscuous over the past several months, but since he worked in New Orleans a couple of nights a week, they didn't know for sure that he hadn't had sex *at all*. They were already wondering what the hell was going on. If they knew he'd been celibate for almost a year, they'd take him to the doctor.

Or, if he gave them Tori's name, they'd load the truck up and take him to Iowa.

Either way, they'd realize that this was a big deal. Was he ready for them to all know that Tori was a big deal?

And why was he using present tense when thinking about her? She *was* a big deal? Shouldn't he be thinking in terms of she *had been* a big deal? It was over. She hadn't shown up last night.

"I'm just sure," he finally said. "If she's pregnant, it's not mine."

"Then she really might want to kill you," Kennedy said. "I gotta say, that was my first guess anyway. You made her fall in love and then never called her again or something."

Josh frowned at his sister. "First, your faith in me is overwhelming."

She shrugged, clearly not caring that she might have wounded him a little.

"Second, does she seem homicidal?"

He couldn't say that he'd never pissed a woman off to the point that she might come looking for a confrontation, but he didn't think he'd ever made anyone murderous.

"Not really," Kennedy said. "She's just sitting there with Gus. She didn't want anything to drink. She isn't even on her phone. She's just sitting there on the dock, watching the water."

"She's sitting there with *Gus*?" Josh asked. Gus was the river otter that lived under the far Boys of the Bayou dock. He'd shown up one morning and after about a week of watching him, the guys had decided he'd either gotten lost or was orphaned. The boats coming and going kept a lot of other animals out of the immediate area and the guys let Gus stay because, well, he was cute and he entertained the tourists. He rarely got up *on* the dock though and he didn't sit *with* people. The guys would toss him food and he didn't run from them, but he also didn't get too close.

Kennedy shrugged. "He climbed up on the dock and waddled over to her. He's just sitting there by her feet."

Wow. That was different. "What did *she* do?"

"She didn't freak out or anything," Kennedy said. "She did talk to him a little. And she kept the other people from touching him or getting too close."

"She seems...contemplative," Sawyer said. The oldest of the business owners, he was often the voice of reason, the calm one who naturally took charge. *Quit fucking around* was his favorite phrase and he said it at least once a day to Josh and Owen. Sometimes both at the same time. He was also the only one of them who would use a word like *contemplative*. "Not angry. Maybe a little nervous."

"Nervous?" Josh repeated. Now he was even more curious. "So you're all out here to protect me?"

That was...nice.

"I got a picture of her," Owen said, holding out his phone. "We just wanted to make sure you knew her and to give you a heads-up. Just in case."

Josh stepped closer to Owen's phone. And his heart kicked so hard against his ribs that he felt a little light-headed.

Tori was here.

He immediately started up the ramp to the building.

"Hey!"

"Josh!"

He heard his family calling after him, but he didn't have time to explain to them who Tori was. It was a long explanation. Okay, not really. "A girl I met last year" would have done it. But she was...more than that. And he had no patience or time to try to make that make sense to them. Because it didn't really make sense to *him* and he'd been thinking about it for a year.

He rounded the corner of the building that housed the office, check-in area, restrooms, and gift shop for the Boys of the Bayou.

And there she was, sitting on the scarred wooden benches, amidst the group of tourists that were scheduled to go out with Owen on the airboat.

She was leaning against the building, her long, bare legs stretched out, ankles crossed, watching the water lap at the dock. Gus was lying on his side on the dock at her feet, apparently sunbathing.

She looked so gorgeous that Josh felt a little weak in the knees.

That was completely something his dad or grandad would say. But, for the first time in his life, Josh understood it.

He sucked in a breath and gave himself a second to be sure he wasn't going to rush her. He gripped the edge of the building and said simply, "Tori."

There was a lot of conversation going on around them, but she somehow heard him. She looked up at him quickly. And a bright, sincere smile stretched her mouth immediately. She bounced to her feet, startling Gus. He skittered across the deck and she glanced at him. "Sorry," she told him.

He slipped off the edge of the dock and into the water. Several of the kids on the benches ran to the railing to watch the otter swim away, but Tori's gaze locked on Josh's.

"Hi," he finally said.

"Hi," she returned.

He curled his fingers into the wood under his hand, forcing himself to stay put. Because stomping toward her, throwing her over his shoulder, taking her into the office and slamming and locking the door would be a little much. Probably.

She tucked her hands into her front pockets. Her shorts were blue denim and hit high on her thighs. She wore beat-up blue tennis shoes with no socks. Her top was a simple gray T-shirt that said, *Dogs have owners. Cats have staff.* Her hair was in a ponytail and she didn't have any makeup on.

She looked fucking amazing.

"I know that you obviously didn't want to see me. Not showing up last night should have been—I mean, it *was*—a clear message. So me coming here is pretty...crazy. But I need a favor and I'm really hoping—"

"I was there last night."

Tori stopped. "What?"

Josh let go of the building. "I was there. I went to Bourbon O. Four times."

Her eyes widened. "I was there. It was a little...wild in there, I'll admit. But I went. I asked the bartender about you."

"I don't work there anymore."

"I figured that out."

"That's how you found me here?"

"Yes."

Josh felt his gut tightening. She'd been there. She'd tried to find him. She was now *here*. He took a step toward her. "You were there?"

She nodded. "You too?"

"Definitely."

They just stood staring at one another.

"Wow," she finally said softly.

Josh became aware that everyone around them had gone completely quiet and were now watching them. He glanced behind him. Yep, his family was there too. Everyone looked wildly curious and he knew that his mom, dad, and all of his grandmothers and grandfathers would know about this in roughly fifteen minutes.

He might as well give them a really great story.

Josh stalked toward her. She sucked in a quick, sexy little breath as he got close. Without a word, he bent, and lifted her over his shoulder with a little "Josh!" from her. Then he headed for the office. He stepped into the cramped room with the single desk and stacks upon stacks of files, papers, and catalogs. He slammed the door behind him, locked it, and put Tori back on her feet.

"Wha—"

He covered her mouth with his.

4

G od, she tasted amazing. Better than he'd remembered. And he'd been remembering a lot. Often. Almost every night. That had gotten to him the most. He was never affected by women like this. He'd kissed far more than his share of girls in his life. He'd had some really amazing nights with several of them. And he barely remembered their names. Oh, there were a few whose names he remembered, sure. And he'd had two girlfriends in high school that he'd really liked and still saw around town. But he had never thought about a woman every single night for even a week after simply kissing her, not to mention nearly a year.

Tori gave a soft moan that made him hard and aching in

one second flat. She arched against him, slid her hands up his neck to his head, pushed his hat off, and then ran her fingers through his hair.

Holy shit, that felt good.

Her hands in his hair. That was all she'd done and yet he was two seconds away from putting her up against the wall and driving deep.

Of course, he had to get her shorts out of the way first.

He cupped her ass, pulling her up against his throbbing cock and started walking her backward. She went with it, taking those steps, her lips and tongue moving against his.

When her back was against the wall, he slid his hands up her sides, his thumbs skimming over the outside curves of her breasts. She shivered slightly at the touch. He kept going, for now, not stopping until he cupped her face.

He kissed her long and hot, drinking in her taste and scent. Her hands went to his hips, her fingers hooking through the belt loops on his khaki shorts. She pulled him against her, arching her back, the fly of her jeans against his.

Josh sucked in a deep breath and finally, reluctantly, lifted his head.

"I'm so fucking glad to see you."

"I'm so fucking glad I got on that bus," she said, her voice breathless, her smile wide.

"I hope you're planning to stay for a while. Like all day. And night. And then the next. Four or five."

Her eyes widened. "The next four or five *days*?"

He lowered his head, brushing his lips over hers. "I was thinking more like months."

She laughed softly, her breath hot against his mouth. "So everything I remember feeling last year is still here."

"Definitely still here," he agreed. And stronger. Absence did make the heart grow fonder. He also knew it made memories fade and fantasies grow. But it seemed that neither of those things had happened in regard to Tori. He remembered every-thing—the freckles on her nose, the length of her eyelashes, the reddish-gold highlights in her hair, the way her laugh punched him in the gut and made him hard as steel.

"Thank God," she said softly.

"So that's a yes to the four or five months?"

She laughed again. "Part of me is a very definite yes."

"That's the part I want."

"Well, I can definitely offer you a chance to hang out with me for a few days."

"Done."

"You don't even want to know what for?"

"Doesn't matter."

"Wow," she said again.

Josh brushed his thumbs over her cheekbones. "That's what I was thinking."

She blew out a little breath. "So how do you feel about weddings?"

"Are you proposing?" he asked.

Everything in him felt lighter now that she was here. Things felt...right. It was the most bizarre thing ever, but thankfully he had a whole bunch of people who were going to understand. Not normal people, of course. But all he had to do was walk across the street to his grandmother's bar, pull up a stool, and tell the handful of people who would be there all about meeting Tori, spending eleven months apart, and now agreeing to marry her after being together again for only ten minutes.

They'd all get it.

But Tori grinned up at him. "Not yet," she said, her eyes actually twinkling.

"Ah, better than a no." He didn't remember the last time he'd felt this good. And his life consisted of showing people the swamp, fishing, and pouring drinks. He had it pretty easy and yet, Tori was making him feel a sense of happiness he'd felt only once before—when he'd seen her sitting across the bar from him at Bourbon O that second night she was in New Orleans.

"I have a wedding to go to. Actually, a whole wedding extravaganza," she said. She rolled her eyes. "It's a multi-day thing. It's my best friend's wedding. And I could use...a date."

The way she paused in front of *a date* made him curious. "Just a date?"

She wet her lips. "Well..."

For a moment, he was distracted by those lips. Unable to help himself, he lowered his head again and kissed her. She sure as hell didn't push him away. She fisted the front of his Boys of the Bayou T-shirt and got up on her tiptoes.

The kiss was long and sweet, but eventually, she pulled back. She stared up at him as if a little dazed. He knew the feeling.

"So, this date," he prompted, not moving back out of her space one millimeter.

She smiled, as if she'd forgotten what they'd been talking about before the kiss.

"Right. Well, I need a date, yes. But not just any date. It has to be *you* and you have to be..."

"I'm in. What do I have to be?" There was no way in hell he *wasn't* going to this wedding, and whatever else, with her. A chance to spend a few *days* with her? Hell yes, he was in.

"You have to act like you're crazy about me," she said, softly. Almost sheepishly.

He laughed at that. "I think I can pull that off."

She smiled, but said, "I mean, actually, seriously into me. Like we've got a relationship. Like we've been talking regularly over the past year. Like you're...my...you know..."

"Your you know what?" He loved the blush on her cheeks and the way she was stumbling over her words. Victoria

Kramer clearly didn't realize that he'd do anything she needed him to do.

She blew out a breath. "My boyfriend."

"Done." Could he play her crazy-about-her boyfriend for a few days? Probably too well.

"Yeah?" She looked so sweet and adorable looking up at him as if he was her knight in shining armor.

"Fuck yeah." He softened his voice too. "Tori, I've been thinking about you for almost a *year*. I went to that bar *four times* last night. I've been pissed off and frustrated all damned day that I didn't see you. I've mentally mapped out a route from here to Iowa. Even though I don't even know where in Iowa you're from. I *am* feeling crazy here, and I'd love to get to know you better, and if you're here for the next few *days*, I'm right there with you."

She seemed to need a moment to take all of that in, but she finally let out a breath, in obvious relief. "That's...amazing. Thank you."

"But..." he said, as everything sunk in and he was able to think about something other than how much he wanted to get her naked. Right now. "...why do I need to play the boyfriend-of-a-year role? I mean, I'm happy to," he added. "But sounds like there's more to this story."

She nodded. And winced. "There is."

"Is there an ex who's going to be there or something?" Oh yeah, he'd love that. He'd be happy to show some loser that he never should have let her go...and keep him *far* from her over the next few days.

"Not that, exactly."

"You need to keep your grandmother from setting you up with some guy you have no interest in?" That he could also absolutely do. In fact, if his job here, in any way, involved him keeping her away from other men, he was definitely in.

She smiled. "Not that either. I um... Last night, when I went to the bar and was so excited to see you...I saw someone who reminded me of you and I um...kind of...kissed him."

Josh processed that, and the stupid surge of jealousy he felt. "You kissed another guy last night?"

She nodded. "I thought it was you."

He frowned. "How?"

"He was built like you. And you both have beards. And it was in Bourbon O. And he saw me and clearly recognized me. Oh, and he was wearing a mask," she added quickly.

Okay, yeah, that was important information. That helped a little.

"So, I thought it was you and I...kissed him."

"And what does that have to do with this wedding?" Josh asked, feeling like he was still missing something.

"Uh..." She bit her bottom lip, then squeezed her eyes shut and said, "It was the groom."

Oh. Yeah, that could be a problem.

"You kissed the *groom*?"

She nodded, eyes still shut. "And the bride saw it."

Oh boy.

"So, I need to prove that there is actually a guy that I met last year who looks like Andrew who was supposed to meet me there."

"You told them about me?"

She nodded.

"But they didn't believe you."

"Right."

"So your best friend saw you kiss her fiancé and things are now...complicated."

"Except that my best friend is the groom. Andrew. And the bride hates me. Though, she hated me even before the kiss."

Josh blew out a breath.

"Could we..." She wiggled a finger in the small amount of

space between them. "Maybe get some space here? Or less space. One or the other. But *this* is really distracting."

He grinned down at her and leaned in. "I'm distracting you?"

She nodded. "Very much. I really don't want to talk about the wedding right now. But we probably should."

"You did say that *less* space between us is an option, right?" he asked.

Tori wet her lips. "Either we need to lose our clothes and get this over with so I can focus on the problem. Or you need to move back so I can concentrate."

"Get this over with?" he repeated, his grin growing. "You mean, just strip down and go at it right here and now. Get it out of our system?"

She nodded, her pupils dilating and her gaze dropping to his mouth, then back to his eyes.

He leaned in more, bracing his forearm on the wall over her head. "Well, there are a few things wrong with that. One, there's not going to be anything quick about me stripping you down and going at it. Two," he said as she took in a little breath, "there's no way that first time is going to get you out of my system." He leaned down and put his lips almost against her. "And three, there are a bunch of crazy Cajuns about to break that office door down and demand to know what's going on, so we probably don't have time." He kissed her then, but just as she was melting into him, he pulled back. Hell, he'd waited almost a year for her. A little bit longer was just going to make it all sweeter when he *did* finally strip this girl down. And he was going to. For sure. Soon. It was good she understood that. He stepped back. "So a little more space it is. For now."

Tori took another breath. This was a deeper one, as if she was getting her wits back together. Josh grabbed her hand and tugged her toward the chair behind the beat-up and mostly-covered-with-junk desk. He kicked the rolling chair out, nudged her into it, and then leaned back against the desk, facing her.

"Okay, let's hear this story. Andrew, the groom, is your best friend. You kissed him. The bride saw it and freaked out. You told them you thought he was me, but they didn't believe you."

Tori nodded. She sat with her elbows on the arms of the chair, her long legs crossed at the ankles. "That about sums it up."

"Why wouldn't they believe you?"

"You mean, besides the fact that you weren't there?" she asked, lifting a brow.

He grinned. It seemed like giving her some space brought out some sassiness. He liked her breathless and distracted, but sassy was good too. "You mean, I wasn't there when you were."

She rolled her eyes, but smiled. "Right. Okay."

Josh braced his hands on the desk and leaned toward her. "I *was* there, Tori."

Her expression softened. "I believe you."

Good. She needed to. Though there would be not one single doubt in her mind how much he wanted her and how much he'd wanted to see her last night by the end of their time together.

"Mostly they didn't believe me because I've never kept a real secret from Andrew before," she said. "Well, that's why *he* didn't believe me. Paisley didn't believe me because she's convinced I'm in love with Andrew and want to break up their wedding."

"Do you?" Josh felt it was a fair question.

Tori hesitated. Then nodded.

Josh felt his gut clench. "Are you in love with him?"

Jesus. Even the *thought* of that had his entire body tensing up.

Tori frowned. "No, I'm not in love with Andrew." She paused. "I do *love* him. But I'm not *in love* with him. He's my best friend."

"Yeah, you mentioned that." A couple of times already. The truth was, Josh wasn't so sure he believed a man could be *just* friends with a woman he truly liked. Especially not one as beautiful as Tori. Why didn't Andrew want more from her? That made no sense. Which led Josh to believe that Andrew probably *did* have bigger feelings for Tori. There could be reasons they'd never acted on them, of course. Or maybe they *had* and it hadn't worked out.

He frowned. "Have you guys ever been involved?"

Tori didn't shake her head nearly fast enough for Josh. She did, finally, though. "Not involved. No."

"That wasn't really an adamant denial," Josh pointed out.

And the bride suspected there was more between Tori and Andrew, obviously. Josh knew a lot of women. Sure, some of them were crazy, but he would never scoff at female intuition. His grandmothers, mom, sister, and all the other cousins, friends, and even past girlfriends were all scarily insightful when they wanted to be. Paisley might be onto something here.

"I had a crush on Andrew for a little bit in high school," Tori admitted. "A short one. That never turned into anything. There was a New Year's Eve kiss when we were sophomores. Oh, and one in eighth grade. That was it. I was way more in love with the *idea* of being with Andrew—someone I knew really well, who didn't think I was weird because of..." she trailed off and cleared her throat, "...who didn't think I was weird and who was easy to hang out with. Our families get along. We're from the same place. We both had the same goals. At one time, anyway. In any case, it *seemed* like a good idea for us to be together. But it never happened. My crush went away as soon as I saw Danny Jenkins play football the first time." She grinned up at Josh. "Clearly my feelings weren't deep and abiding."

"You ever kiss Danny Jenkins?" He hated Danny Jenkins.

And Andrew the Groom, too, for that matter. Which was probably stupider than his urge to drive to Iowa to find her.

"Nope." She shrugged. "I learned a lot about football watching him though."

"You're a football fan?" he asked. He liked that about her a lot.

"Definitely. I cheer for the Vikings and I don't want to hear anything about it."

He laughed. "Can I talk about LSU?"

She wrinkled her nose. "Definitely not."

"We'll see. Maybe I can convert you."

"Doubt it."

"But you said you're a football *fan*. That means you'd like to watch *good* football."

She stuck her tongue out at him and he wanted to kiss her so badly that he had to grip the edge of the desk to keep from grabbing her.

He coughed and shifted. "Okay, so, you're not in love with Andrew, but you do want to break up the wedding?"

Tori sighed and slumped down in the chair. "I know that makes me a horrible person."

"Why do you want to break it up?"

"Because I don't like Paisley," she said, fiddling with the bottom of her T-shirt.

"Why not?"

"She's just...not nice. And not what I would expect Andrew to go for. She's so...different from him."

"She's from Louisiana?"

"New Orleans," Tori said with a nod. "Her dad was the mayor and is a senator now and—"

"Paisley *Darbonne*?" Josh asked, straightening.

Tori rolled her eyes. "Yep."

"Oh well...shit." The Darbonnes were practically celebrities. Then he thought about it. "Yeah, I guess she probably is a little different from Andrew, unless he grew up with a ton of money and is used to hanging out with politicians."

"Nope. He's just a small-town boy. His dad is a farmer, his mom is a teacher. He grew up down the road from me. We climbed trees and rode dirt bikes and went swimming in the pond between our places. He was the one I first got drunk with, and he was the one that always stuck up for me when I... embarrassed myself."

Josh studied her face. That was the second time she'd said something like that. She'd also said something about being weird. "How did you embarrass yourself?"

"It's not important."

"It is to me."

She looked up at him and gave him a half smile. "Are you going to tell me *your* embarrassing stories too?"

"Sure. Or my family gladly will. Either way, I promise you'll hear all about me being a dumbass," he told her with a grin.

"Okay." She sat up a little bit. "I'll give you one example. When we were juniors in high school, I found out a guy was catching frogs and blowing them up with firecrackers. So I collected a whole bunch of bugs and snuck into his bedroom and let them loose. He had bugs and flies all over his bedroom, in his sheets, in his clothes and shoes and backpacks."

Josh blinked at her. That was not what he'd been expecting her to tell him.

"Because frogs eat all of those things," she said, her cheeks getting pink. "So if they're not around, there will be more bugs and flies." Her cheeks got even redder. "I thought it seemed like appropriate revenge for the frogs."

Finally Josh nodded. "I agree. Wow. I'll bet he hesitated to do anything like that again. But how is that embarrassing?"

She looked surprised. "Everyone at school found out about it, of course, and thought I was really weird to do something like that just to save some frogs. And that I would go to that much trouble to catch bugs. And that I was willing to catch bugs in the first place."

"No offense, but the people you went to school with sound like dickheads."

She stared at him for a moment, then her face broke into a huge grin. "They were," she said. "But I was...*am*...animal crazy. That's not the only weird thing I've done for something with four legs."

Josh couldn't help but lean over, grab the arms of the chair, and drag her closer. He kissed her softly and said, "You are *really* underestimating my tolerance level for crazy."

She took his face between her hands. "Thank you for going to the wedding stuff with me."

"Well, it's not like it's totally selfless, you know. I figure it exponentially increases my opportunities for more kissing." He kissed her again. "And more than kissing."

"Oh," she said softly. "It definitely does."

"So when do the festivities kick off?"

She winced slightly. "Tomorrow night, actually. Cocktail welcome reception for the family and bridal party."

"Okay. I'll rearrange a couple of tours and be there whenever you need me."

"It's at the Buckworth Plantation. Do you know where that is?"

He laughed. "I do." Everyone knew where the Buckworth Plantation—known locally just as "Buckworth"—was.

"Good. It's there. Starting at seven."

"I'll be there."

She gave him a huge smile and kissed him again, then sat back. "Thank you."

"Not a hardship," he told her, gruffly. He was going to have her all to himself tomorrow night at a fancy cocktail party at Buckworth. Well, sure, it would be a party full of other people, but she needed an ally. A boyfriend. He had all kinds of built-in reasons to sneak off into a corner with her, or pull her into the shadows of the oaks outside.

"Well...I'm going to *really* appreciate it," she said, with a sexy, adorable little smile.

"As in, you'll want to *thank me* somehow?" he asked, dropping his voice to a low rumble.

Her lips parted and she was staring at his mouth again. "Yeah," she said softly.

"Well, honey, I think I warned you that bayou boys are dangerous," he said. "But you walked right down my dock anyway and asked me for a favor. There's no going back now."

"I'm okay with that."

He grabbed her hand, pulled her up out of the chair, and in between his knees. Then he kissed her again, knowing he was never going to get enough of it. It was a deep, hot, slow kiss that seemed to set his nerves on fire from his scalp to his toes.

Then, when she made a needy little sound in the back of her throat, he lifted his head and looked into her eyes. "Really fucking glad to see you," he said.

"Ditto."

Pulling in a deep breath and telling himself he only had to make it about twenty-four hours, he nudged her back and stood. He took her hand and started for the office door.

"I'm gonna send you back to N'Awlins," he said. "And I'll meet you at the Buckworth Plantation tomorrow night. But this time"—he stopped with his hand on the doorknob and looked down at her—"you're giving me your number. I'll text you when I get there."

She nodded. "Perfect."

He opened the door with a smile.

That died on an exasperated sigh the next second.

Owen, Kennedy and Sawyer were on the other side, leaning against the railing directly across from the office.

But it was way worse than that.

His father, granddad, and grandmother were there too.

"Well, finally," Ellie—the matriarch of the Landry family—said, getting up from the bench where she'd been waiting.

———

TORI LOOKED from the older woman up to Josh.

He looked...resigned. He glanced down at her. "Sorry about this. But it was bound to happen. Might as well get it over with."

"Get wha—"

"So not pregnant or murderous?" The beautiful young woman, who had insisted that Josh was going to be out on a tour for the next three hours, pushed away from the railing and crossed her arms.

The woman was dressed in black Converse tennis shoes with shorts and a black cropped tank that left her stomach bare and showed off a swirling tattoo on her upper arm, another peeking out from under the strap on the left, and a gorgeous flowered tattoo that ran up the outside of one of her thighs. Her jet-black hair ended in red tips and she had piercings sparkling up the outside of one ear, another gem glinting from her nose, and a small heart that dangled from her belly button. Her makeup was bold—black eyeliner, purple lips, black nail polish—and she had an equally bold attitude. It was clear she ran the joint.

Come to think of it, she was actually the beautiful young woman who had *lied* to Tori about Josh being out on a tour for the next three hours.

Tori frowned at her.

"Neither," Josh said.

"Wait, *me*?" Tori asked. "You thought I was pregnant?"

The girl shrugged. "Or that you were here to kill him."

"Kill *Josh*?" Tori looked up at him. "Why would someone want to kill Josh?"

"Trust me," the woman in black said. "There are reasons."

"Definitely." This came from the big man who had an equally big, deep voice. He was watching Tori and Josh with a frown. He was good-looking. But *big*. He had to be six-five and looked like he could easily face down the defensive line for the Vikings. He also had a scar on the side of his face that made him look mean. It didn't make him less handsome though. It made him better looking in a rough, warrior kind of way. Tori was *certain* that women found that jagged mark hot.

"But since you're not here for a paternity test or to poison him..." The girl looked at Josh. "You've got a tour."

"You think she'd poison him?" the other guy—the one who seemed like a troublemaker—asked, studying Tori.

"What did you think? She's too little to, like, stab him or something," the girl said.

"But it would be *passionate*, right?" the troublemaker asked. "Emotional. I mean, it'd have to be like a gun or something, right? Nothing as long as poison."

"Unless she really wanted to watch him suffer," the goth girl said, watching Josh contemplatively. As if maybe the idea of him suffering was interesting. Or something.

Tori wasn't sure what to say to all of this. They were kind of...a lot. But Josh seemed to be taking it all in stride. So she said nothing. And watched it all with fascination.

"And now that we've got the no-one's-here-to-kill-Josh thing cleared up," Josh said, dryly. "I need to drive Tori back to the Buckworth Plantation."

"You've got a tour," the big frowny guy said.

Josh frowned back at him. "Take care of it."

"No."

"For fuck's sake," Josh muttered. He shoved a hand through his hair. "Tori, this is my brother, Sawyer," he said of the big guy. "This is my sister, Kennedy." He pointed to the goth liar. "And this is my cousin, Owen."

Owen was also very good-looking. This family had some great genes. Owen wore a Boys of the Bayou T-shirt like Josh's and faded jeans. He had his hands tucked in the back pockets and was just watching everyone with a small half smile. He certainly didn't seem like any of this was strange or unusual. He straightened and gave Tori a slow grin and a, "Nice to meet ya." He didn't seem as put out about her showing up as everyone else did at least.

"This is my grandmother, Ellie," Josh said, gesturing to the woman who had ordered them to the bar. "This is my grandad, Leo."

The older man tipped his Boys of the Bayou cap. They'd already met—he'd driven the bus Tori had used to get down here—but she hadn't known he was related to Josh.

"And this is my dad, Jeremiah," Josh finished.

Josh's dad grinned at her. "Welcome to Autre."

Okay, so two of Josh's family members—and wow, they were *all* related?—were smiling at her. Two—his grandad and grandmother—looked more curious than anything. Only his siblings looked annoyed. That was only one third of them. That wasn't too bad.

"Here is the deal," Josh said, addressing the group at large and then staring at his brother and sister. "I met Tori last year at Mardi Gras. We agreed to meet up again this year if we were both single and still interested. And...here she is." He grinned down at her.

Tori felt a little wave of surprise go through her. They were going to just share this whole story with everyone within five minutes of her meeting them?

Of course, Sawyer, Owen and Kennedy had already seen him throw her over his shoulder and carry her into the office. They had to be wondering about *that*.

Unless that was a typical thing for Josh...

"So, you'll all understand when I tell you that I'm taking a few days off and stayin' glued to this gorgeous girl for as long as she can stand me. Don't expect me to be around much."

Again, Tori was surprised by how matter-of-fact and upfront he was being. And his family looked...intrigued, but not exactly shocked by his honesty.

"Does she *want* you to stay glued to her?" Jeremiah asked.

Ellie swung on him. "Why wouldn't she want him to stay glued to her?"

"I'm just asking the question."

"*She* came *here*," Leo pointed out.

"That doesn't mean she wants him twenty-four-seven," Owen agreed. With what could only be described as a shit-eating grin.

"Yeah, that's *a lot* of Josh," Kennedy said with a nod.

"I want you to give me three good reasons that she wouldn't want to be with Josh constantly," Ellie said, putting a hand on her hip and facing Jeremiah.

"Yes, please, let's talk about all the reasons she might *not* want to be with me," Josh said dryly.

"Well, he's not as funny as he thinks he is," Owen offered.

Jeremiah nodded. Ellie scowled. "He's the sweetest of any of my grandsons."

Owen laughed. "Well, that's true." He looked at Josh. "Total sweetheart."

"Fuck off," Josh muttered.

"See?" Owen said with a grin.

"He's smart," Ellie said.

"He's not smarter than Sawyer," Kennedy said.

"I didn't say he was smarter than Sawyer," Ellie said. "I just said he was smart."

"Yeah, okay," Kennedy agreed.

Josh sighed. Tori felt herself fighting a smile.

"Well, he's a charming son of a bitch," Leo said, shooting his grandson a wink.

"He is. And he's very good-looking," Ellie said.

"For sure," Jeremiah agreed. "No question."

Josh rolled his head and seemed to be just waiting for it to be over. He didn't seem surprised by any of this. Or offended. He looked...*resigned* really seemed the best descriptor. As if he'd been expecting all of this. Or at least something like this.

Tori smiled. "No question," she agreed. And something about all of *this* made him even more good-looking. "And yes, to answer the question, I do want him to stay glued to me."

Josh shot her a surprised look, then a grin. Then he turned a very smug grin on his family. "See?"

Ellie chuckled. "And *she* clearly has good taste."

"I'll bet she does," Owen said, waggling his eyebrows.

"Uh, no," Josh said.

"No, she doesn't taste good?" Owen asked. "I don't believe it."

"No, *you* are not going to be thinking about how she tastes," Josh said.

Ellie elbowed Owen in the side. "Don't be an ass. She just got here."

"We can't just leave it at 'don't be an ass'?" Josh asked.

"Well, asking him to not be an ass ever is pretty unrealistic," Jeremiah said.

Owen didn't seem offended by any of this either.

It occurred to Tori that *she* should maybe be blushing. They were talking about Josh tasting her, after all. And Owen tasting her too. Kind of. Or at least him thinking about tasting her. Or him thinking about Josh tasting her. Or something. She was already confused. But, strangely, she didn't feel embarrassed. She felt...included.

Maybe there was something in the air down here that made

people unabashed. She took a nice deep breath, just in case. Unabashed seemed fun.

"Hey, guys?" Josh asked.

"Yeah?" Ellie and Owen asked.

"How about you all shut the fuck up now?"

Yes, Josh had just told his grandmother to shut the fuck up.

"Okay, so no one's pregnant—yet—so let's go to the bar," Ellie said.

Yet? As in... But Tori didn't have time to think about that any further.

Josh sighed and nodded. "Fine. For a little bit. Then she needs to get back to Buckworth. She's there for a wedding."

"I'll get her back," Leo said.

"Just because we used the word 'plantation,' that does not mean driving her down Old River Road and stopping at every place and telling her all your stories," Josh told him firmly. "And she doesn't want to taste William's rum. Or Bessie's gin. Or Tyler's whiskey." Josh looked down at her. "It's all moonshine. Don't believe anybody who tells you it's actually rum or whiskey. And don't drink any of it. And don't drink anything any of them mix up for you."

"Moonshine?" She felt her eyes widen. That sounded... dangerous. And interesting. Like more fun than Paisley's stuck-up cocktail party at the plantation, for sure. And Tori thought she just might want to hear a few of Leo's stories, as a matter of fact.

Leo laughed at Josh's explanation. "After you have a couple of glasses, you don't care what it's called or how it's made."

Josh shook his head. "Don't drink anything Leo offers you, period. Stick with Ellie." He smiled at his grandmother in a way that made Tori's heart melt a little—a combination of affection and exasperation. "She'll give you the good stuff. The *legal* stuff."

Ellie smiled at her. "Definitely stick with me, honey."

Owen laughed. "But don't get sucked in by that sweet smile. She'll get you schnockered, given half a chance," he said. "She'll just do it with liquor that comes from an actual distillery rather than somebody's backyard."

Tori wasn't sure if she should laugh. Or come up with a really good reason to leave.

"But I can come along and protect you," Owen said, stepping up and putting an arm around Tori's shoulders.

Josh immediately shoved it off. "Take a *big* step back, cousin."

Owen held up his hands and stepped back. "Okay. Just tryin' to help."

"You're never helpful unless you think you can get money, beer, a naked woman, or a laugh out of the deal," Kennedy said to Owen. "And I don't think you'll be getting any of that from Miss Tori here."

"Oh, I bet I can get some laughs out of it," Owen said.

"Just stay away from her," Josh said, looking far less amused and laid-back now.

Was he actually feeling protective of her? Tori kind of liked that idea.

"Doesn't matter." Kennedy stepped between them. "You've got a tour too," she told Owen. "A bachelor party." She gave him an evil grin.

Owen groaned. "That's the fourth one in a row. Why are you givin' *me* the bachelor parties?"

"Because you need to have your hands full to keep you out of trouble. And because the last *bachelorette* party I gave you came back in wet T-shirts."

"There were other parts of them wet too," Owen said with a grin and another wiggle of his eyebrows.

His grandmother elbowed him again but she smiled at Kennedy. "But those girls ended up buying four new T-shirts from us, and not one of them complained, so he did a good job."

Kennedy nodded. "I'm not keeping him away from bachelorette parties because they don't like him."

"Exactly. They love him." Ellie was clearly as proud of and as willing to brag on Owen as she was Josh.

Kennedy gave her cousin a small smile. "I'm doing it because I like picturing Owen trying to rein in a bunch of drunk frat guys who act a lot like *he* does on any given Saturday night, and hosing off the boats when they all get sick from bumping over the bayou in the hot sun."

"You're a wicked woman, Kennedy Landry," Owen said.

"Thank you." Then she turned to Tori. "So I guess *I* will be taking care of the new girl."

"Uh, no," Josh said. "I'd like to keep her in one piece and thinking I'm amazing. At least for a little while." He looked down at Tori. "Don't believe anything Kennedy says about me."

"There are a lot of 'don'ts' around here," Tori said, completely amused.

"There really are," Josh agreed. "I can write all the rules down if you need me to."

"Or you can summarize it by saying, 'fifty percent of the people around here are full of bullshit, and the other fifty percent are cuckoo. You just have to figure out which half is which,'" Sawyer said.

Josh nodded. "Yeah. That." He turned to Tori. "Remember when I told you not to trust anyone with a N'Awlins drawl or a bayou drawl?"

"Yep."

"That goes double down here. Guys *and* girls."

She did laugh now. These people were...yeah, a little crazy. Or something. But they seemed so *happy*. So accepting. So comfortable with one another. Clearly they could do or say whatever they felt and were thinking at any moment. The things they'd said might be nuts, sure, but their love for one another and how much they enjoyed each other was obvious. She felt a little warm just being around them.

"Tour boats," Kennedy said, snapping her fingers and pointing at Josh, Owen, and Sawyer. "Now."

"See ya around, Tori," Owen said, giving her a wink. He started around the building to where the boats were docked.

Sawyer followed him, but turned back and said to Tori, "Stay away from Ellie's rum punch if you want to remember the rest of today. And that's not crazy or bullshit."

He gave her a grin that actually startled her. He didn't seem much like the grinning type. And yes, that scar was kind of hot.

"How do I know that for sure?" she asked.

He chuckled, the sound low and rumbly. "Good girl." Then he disappeared around the corner of the building.

Josh was the last of the guys to go. And even though the rest of his family was still standing there, he moved in close to her and slid a hand to the back of her neck. "Stick with the sweet tea and crawfish pie over there," he told her, "and you'll be fine."

With him this close, she felt heat slide through her in spite of their audience. "Didn't you tell me last year that the crawfish pie and sweet tea would make me forget all about Iowa?"

He gave her a slow grin that was sexy as hell—and mischievous. "Yep. You'll never want to leave."

She mostly forgot, or maybe stopped caring about, their onlookers. She rose on tiptoe and put her lips against his.

He took over in point four seconds. His fingers curled into her neck and he opened his mouth. The kiss was all-consuming and he clearly didn't give a crap about who was watching.

He didn't let her go for nearly two minutes. When he did, her heels thunked back down against the wooden slats of the dock, and she stood staring up at him.

She'd never met a guy like Josh. She was surrounded by

blue collar guys who worked with their hands, didn't mind getting dirty, and who lived near and saw their families on a regular basis. In fact, that described most of the men in her hometown. Elton, Iowa was full of hardworking, family-loving men. Okay, maybe not *full*. But there were several. Still, she'd never felt this way about any of them. And she'd known them all a lot longer than she'd known Josh.

He just seemed so...obvious about everything he felt. Whether he was frustrated or happy or turned on, it was clear and he didn't hold back on expressing it. She loved that.

It was what she loved most about dogs. Most animals, actually. They were very clear about their feelings. If a dog was angry or scared, you knew it. If they were hurt, you knew it. If they were happy to see you, you knew it. Most of all, they were loyal and protective and openly, yes, *unabashedly* loving.

Like Josh was. Or seemed to be. She had to keep reminding herself that she didn't really *know* him. But damn, it felt like she did.

Tori grinned up at him. She'd never liked a guy because he reminded her of a dog, but in this case, it was a very good thing.

"I like that smile," he said, his voice unmistakably affectionate. "Let's keep that right there for the next several days."

Tori nodded. "You keep doing *that* from time to time and I'll be grinning like an idiot."

"Can do. Definitely can do." He hesitated, then took a breath. "Okay, I'm going to go to work. Leo will get you back to the plantation." His gaze flickered to his grandfather. "Eventually," he added. "And I'll see you there tomorrow."

"I can't wait." And suddenly that was true. She'd been dreading all the wedding activities for, oh, about seven months.

"Me too."

"Oh, for God's sake." Kennedy was there behind Tori then, grabbing her shoulders and pulling her away from Josh. "Ellie, she's all yours." She nudged Tori toward her grandmother.

Then she turned Josh and pushed him, much harder, toward the boats.

Josh went, but not without casting a last look over his shoulder at Tori.

Even that made her stomach flip.

"Hoo-ee," Ellie said, wrapping her arm around Tori's waist and starting for the dirt path that led from the Boys of the Bayou tour company building to the road. "I've never seen him like that."

"Who? Josh? Really?" Tori asked, tripping onto the road as she tried to look back over her shoulder.

Ellie laughed as she tightened her hold on Tori. "Really. So I'm going to need your life story."

5

Tori let the other woman lead her across the road to what was clearly a bar. It was a wooden shack, really, but it had neon beer signs in the windows and the sandwich board that sat in the gravel out front said, *Today's Specials: Appetizer-beer, Entrée-beer, Dessert-beer, Soup of the Day-Beer cheese... without the cheese.*

"Do we have time for a life story?" Tori asked as Ellie led her into the building.

In contrast to the bright sunshine beating down outside, the bar was dark and Tori's eyes didn't adjust very quickly. She vaguely took note of a few booths along the wall to her left and the wooden tables and chairs in the middle of the room, but they were all empty at the moment. She also noticed there was a jukebox, three televisions mounted in the corners of the room —all of them off right now—and a short step up to where the long wooden bar sat. The place smelled like beer, smoke, and bayou. And none of that bothered Tori. In fact, she thought it smelled like a place that had been here for a long time. It was the kind of scent that made people feel at home. Like her barn back in Iowa.

"Well, you're what? Twenty-six?" Ellie asked.

"Twenty-eight," Tori told her.

"Ah, well, still I think we can fit in the highlights." The older woman laughed. She pointed at a stool as she rounded the end of the bar and moved in behind it.

Ellie was about six inches shorter than Tori's five-seven. She had bright white hair that was braided and wrapped into a bun on top of her head. Her skin was tan and wrinkled with lines that spoke of a life lived outdoors. She wore jeans, tennis shoes, and a T-shirt that said *I put the SIN in Wisconsin*. In spite of her white hair and wrinkles, she didn't *seem* like the grandmother to four adult grandchildren. She was clearly feisty and had a sense of humor and she seemed to kind of...glow. She just seemed contented and happy and perpetually amused. Tori liked her already.

The stool Ellie had indicated was right in the middle of the long bar. There were three open seats. The rest were filled with men. All of whom watched every step Tori made. Three were about Ellie's age, one was roughly Jeremiah's age, and one was... somewhere in between. With her eye still adjusting to the darker room and with them all dressed in cotton and denim with hats on their heads, it was a little hard to judge ages, actually.

She slid up onto the stool. "You're from Wisconsin?"

Ellie frowned, then looked down at her shirt. She laughed. "No. People who come in often send me T-shirts when they get back home." She pulled the shirt away from her body. "Everybody thinks they're better drinkers than us when they come in here."

Everyone at the bar chuckled at that.

"They don't *leave* here thinking that, of course," she said with a wink.

Tori grinned.

Jeremiah and Leo came in just then and took the seats on either side of Tori. She felt stupidly comforted by that. They were also both strangers to her. She'd known them about twenty minutes longer than she'd known the other men in the bar. Still, it felt like they'd moved in to say she was one of them.

"Everybody, this is Tori," Leo said to the gathering at the bar. "Tori is Josh's. Mind your manners. At least for a few minutes."

Her eyebrows went up. She was Josh's? Wow, that sounded very possessive. And a ribbon of heat curled through her. Damn, since when had she been okay with *belonging* to someone?

Since Leo had said she was Josh's, apparently.

She smiled at everyone as they greeted her with *Hey*s. She felt the need to clarify the information being given. Josh wasn't the one saying she was his. Leo was assuming a lot. "Um, actually, Josh and I don't know each other *that* well. Yet. But he's going to my friend's wedding with me."

"This is the one he's been mooning over for the past year," Ellie said, apparently to everyone, as she passed a glass of... something...to Tori.

"Ah," one of the older men said.

"Makes sense," another said.

"Finally," a third added.

"Mooning over?" Tori asked Ellie, picking up the glass and sniffing. It looked and smelled like sweet tea.

Ellie gave her a wink. "Mooning over."

"He told you that?" Josh had seemed *very* happy to see her a little bit ago, but he'd been talking about her? He was the one who had sent her back to her hotel room, alone, *twice* last year.

"Didn't have to. It's obvious," Ellie said, leaning onto the bar.

Tori suspected Ellie had a stool or some kind of raised platform because the little woman shouldn't have been able to rest her elbows on the bar.

Tori studied her. Ellie seemed sincere. "It was obvious that he was mooning over me? How?" She picked up the tea and took a little sip. It was delicious. And didn't taste spiked. Though Tori had the impression that if Ellie wanted to spike something without you knowing, you wouldn't realize it until you were falling flat on your face trying to walk back to the tour bus.

"I know him," Ellie said. "I know all my kids. But Josh and Owen are easy. What you see is what you get. I always knew when they fell in love, it would be the most obvious thing in the world."

Tori choked as the tea went down the wrong pipe. Jeremiah calmly patted her on the back as she coughed and dragged air into her lungs.

Ellie shook her head. "The *in love* part is a surprise to you?"

"We barely know each other. We spent only a few hours together almost a year ago."

"Well, how long do you think it takes?" Leo asked her.

"To fall in love?" she asked, her eyes wide. "I..." She frowned. "I don't know. But...longer than that." She looked around. "Right?"

"Why?" Ellie asked. "I'm not saying it's always fast, but it sure can be. Some things you can tell about someone right away."

Tori opened her mouth, but then shut it again. What the hell did she know about it? These people were a lot older than her and had seen a lot more life than she had. "Did you fall in love quickly?" she asked Ellie.

Ellie gave Leo a big smile. "Took about fifteen minutes."

Tori hadn't known for sure that Leo and Ellie were together, but now she looked at Leo. "Wow."

He nodded. "She was wearing short shorts and tryin' to pull a big ol' catfish outta the bayou. She was cussing like a sailor and standing up in her little boat and I knew she was about to tip over."

"He came over and steadied the boat, but let me pull that catfish out by myself," Ellie said. "That's when I knew he was a good one. He didn't try to help me or bust in there like he was a big man or say shit like girls shouldn't be fishing out there by themselves."

Leo nodded, rubbing his jaw as if remembering. "It was a big one too. Bigger than anything I'd caught that summer. That was impressive."

"That was when you knew she was the one?" Tori asked, enchanted by the story.

"Nope," he said with a grin. "That wasn't until she laughed. Soaking wet from the bayou and with her catfish swimmin' away."

"What?" Tori asked, laughing without even knowing the details.

Ellie matched his grin. "I offered him a beer as thanks for holding on to the boat. Ironically, he let go of my boat to grab the bottle and the boat tipped and I ended up in the bayou anyway."

"Oh no!" Tori said. "You weren't mad?"

Ellie shook her head. "Nah. I'd ended up in the bayou before. But I'd never had such a good-lookin' guy choking on beer while I did it." She gave Leo a look. "But I did say, 'you realize that you just passed up getting laid for a beer, right?' He looked down at the bottle, then back up at me and, I shit you not, said, 'well, it's not every day you get a free beer.'"

Tori turned wide eyes to Leo. "But it *was* every day that you got a girl?"

Leo wiggled his eyebrows. "Where do you think my grandsons get all of that charm?"

Tori laughed. She was having more fun than she'd had in a long time. Maybe hanging out with people wasn't all bad. She really liked dogs and cats and cows, but they didn't have great falling-in-love stories to share. "So I didn't stand a chance once I met Josh?"

Leo shook his head, chuckling. "Good you realize that. Just give in."

"How long have you been married?" Tori asked Ellie and Leo.

"Oh, we're not anymore," Ellie said, pushing back and moving to refill a glass down the bar.

Tori frowned at her, then glanced at Leo. "What?"

Leo shook his head. "Lasted thirty years though."

"Thirty-one," Ellie corrected him.

Leo nodded. "Something like that."

"No," Ellie said. "Exactly that. One month *past* thirty-one, in fact."

Leo rolled his eyes. "Been divorced for a while now."

Tori felt stunned. And disappointed. "I'm...sorry." She frowned. "But you're obviously still good friends."

Leo grinned at Ellie. "She's still the feistiest girl with the biggest heart I know."

"What happened?" Tori was suddenly completely invested in this story. The entire thing. Maybe she could help get them back together. She frowned a little at that. That was a weird thought to have about two near-strangers. But there was something so genuine and warm here that she was completely enthralled.

"We still had—have—the chemistry," Leo said.

"And the respect," Ellie agreed.

"But we laugh more when we don't live together," Leo said. "So we just tried living apart. But then the taxes got complicated."

"And I wanted to sleep with Trevor," Ellie added.

"And that," Leo said with a nod.

"Trevor?" Tori asked, her eyebrows nearly in her hairline.

"My boyfriend," Ellie said.

Tori leaned in and looked down the bar, wondering if one of these men was Trevor.

"He's not here right now," Ellie said. "He's at work. He's a banker in New Orleans."

"Oh." For some reason that surprised Tori.

"He's a big deal," Leo said. "He ironed out my retirement account and helped us with transferring the business over to the boys. Good-looking guy too."

If it was strange for a woman's ex-husband to be complimenting her new boyfriend, no one else in the bar gave any sign they thought so. Tori nodded, as if she totally understood this.

"And he's twenty years younger than me," Ellie added with a sly smile. "We met five years ago. He was only forty-four when I seduced him."

Tori swallowed hard. "Oh." She had no idea what else to say.

Ellie seemed to realize it and laughed. "If it doesn't make your heart pound, it's not worth doing."

Leo nodded. "No one around here is gonna die of boredom."

"Or with any regrets," Ellie said.

"Wow." Tori took it all in. This was fascinating. And very different from her life. It seemed that most people she knew—her family, certainly—worked hard to keep things from getting too exciting. Pounding hearts meant you were scared or at least stressed. She knew for a fact that her father avoided things that made his heart pound. Steady and solid were Patrick Kramer's favorite words. "The last time my heart pounded was when one of our cows had twins."

She looked up from her glass of tea and realized they were all watching her.

"I'm a vet," she said. "Twins are often a problem for cows. They almost always need help." No one said anything. "Sheep and goats all have twins without much trouble, but cows are different." She paused, and again no one said anything. "Delivering two heads and eight legs out of the same hole can get complicated." She should probably stop talking. "Goats can also have triplets, by the way. I delivered a set last spring."

Finally Ellie reached out and squeezed her hand. "I'm really hoping my grandson made your heart pound harder than birthing a set of twin calves."

Tori managed a smile at that. "Yeah." She nodded. "Yeah, he definitely did."

"Great love stories run in our family," Ellie said.

Tori felt her heart give at least one hard beat right then. They were already talking about a love story involving her and Josh? That was fast. And crazy. And...fun. They were blowing this all out of proportion, but it was making her smile. This felt like a train that she just had to board and hold on tight as long as it was running.

"Ahem." Jeremiah cleared his throat. "You haven't even told her the best one yet."

Tori looked at him. "I'd love to hear it."

"It's about me and Josh's mom," he said. "It's legend around here."

Tori was instantly intrigued. "Legend, huh? This I have to hear."

"I met Hannah at a dance over in—"

"Oh, you don't tell it as good as Cora does," Ellie interrupted. "Cora!" she shouted toward the swinging door behind the bar. "Cora! Get up here!"

"Good God, what the hell are you screeching about?" A woman with short salt-and-pepper curls and a round face came through the swinging door, wiping her hands on the red apron she wore.

"This is Tori," Ellie said, pointing. "She's Josh's."

Cora's eyes got wide. "The one he's been mooning over?"

Tori rolled her eyes but also smiled. Maybe he really had been.

"Yep," Ellie said, happily. "She came to find him today. She's takin' him to a wedding at Buckworth."

"Nice." Cora studied Tori. "You're a beauty."

Tori blushed. "Um, thank you."

"Gus liked her too," Jeremiah added.

Cora nodded. "It's official then. You're a keeper."

"Who's Gus?" Tori asked, again glancing at the other men at the bar.

"The otter," Jeremiah said. "He doesn't come up to people often."

"Oh." Tori had been delighted to see the otter, and when he'd climbed up on the deck and then sat next to her feet, she'd felt downright giddy. Otters weren't something she saw in Iowa.

"Animals are excellent judges of character," Cora said.

Tori nodded. "I agree a hundred percent."

"She's a vet," Ellie said, with a touch of pride if Tori wasn't mistaken.

Cora finally smiled. "And people who love animals are the best kind of people."

Tori returned her smile. "Thank you. And I agree again."

"It was very nice to meet you," Cora said. "How about some crawfish pie?"

Ah, the crawfish pie. Was she willing to risk eating something that would make her forget about home and want to stay here forever? "I'd love to try it," she said, feeling her stomach flip.

It was lunch. It wasn't a major life decision. But...it felt important.

"I called you up here to tell her Jerry and Hannah's story," Ellie said. "I'll get the pie."

"Oh, Jerry and Hannah's story," Cora said, her eyes twinkling. "It's legendary."

Tori laughed. "So I hear."

Cora moved to the bar and leaned in, much like Ellie had. "It all started at the street dance over in Sutton," she said. "I was over there with my husband, Danny, and Jerry and my son, Luke, came over. We were just sittin' there, listening to the music and drinking lemonade."

Leo snorted at that and Cora shot him a look. "What?"

"Lemonade?" Leo asked. "Last time you told this story, it was root beer."

Cora glared at him. "I had lemonade and Danny had root beer."

Leo outright laughed at that. "I knew Danny all my life. No fuckin' way was he drinkin' root beer."

Cora waved that away. "*Anyway*, we were just sittin' there, drinking *things*, and chatting, and all of a sudden Jerry sits up straight and his mouth drops open and it's like he's gone into this trance."

Jerry—Jeremiah—just smiled as Cora told his story, lifting a glass of sweet tea and taking a sip.

"So we all look over and we see this girl. She's really pretty and she's wearing this cute little sundress and she's talking to a group of friends. And then she turns around and *bam*, she looks at Jerry and she does the same thing—her mouth drops open and she just stares." Cora shook her head. "It was the damnedest thing I've ever seen."

Tori looked at Jeremiah. He gave her a wink.

"So Luke nudges him," Cora continued. "Then when that doesn't work, Luke slaps him upside the head, and finally Jerry snaps out of it. But he doesn't say anything to any of us. He just stands up and heads straight for that girl. They danced and talked, just the two of them, the rest of the night."

"Wow," Tori said. "This is like a scene from a movie."

Cora nodded. "It gets better. He starts seeing her every single night. Until this one night, about two weeks later, he comes home, with her in his truck and her suitcases in the back."

Tori looked at Jeremiah again. "You eloped?" she guessed.

He shook his head. He wasn't grinning now.

"He'd gone to see her and found her and her dad out in the front yard. Her dad was drunk and screaming at her. He had her by the arm and was shaking her." Cora's expression had hardened too. "Jerry jumped out of the truck and stomped over there. He shoved her dad away and when the dumbass came at him, Jerry hit him so hard he put him on his ass. He told Hannah she had two minutes to grab whatever stuff she wanted to take but that she wasn't going back to that house. He stood over her sniveling asshole of a father while she packed her bags. Then he put her in the truck and drove her straight to Autre."

Tori knew her eyes were round. Her heart was racing just hearing the story. It was awful and romantic at the same time. "Wow," she said quietly.

Jeremiah gave her a little smile and nod. "Would have done anything for her. Still would."

"So, anyway," Cora said, clearly with more story to tell. "Her dad came after her. With a bunch of their relatives. They came tearing over here in pickups with their shotguns and shit, wanting to start some kind of war."

Now Tori's mouth dropped open. "*Really?*"

"Oh yeah," Leo said. "Dumbasses." The other guys at the bar nodded.

"What happened?" Tori asked. In that moment, she didn't care about anything more than hearing the rest of this story.

"The sheriff called Leo to tell him they were on their way. He didn't want trouble, but he couldn't do anything until something happened. So Leo called a few people and they called a few people, and pretty soon we had all the men in Autre between the ages of sixteen and sixty out on the road right outside the city limits just waitin' for them," Cora said.

"We blocked their way into town," Leo said. "No way were any of the assholes from Martin gettin' in here."

"And that was it?" Tori asked. "They turned around?"

Everyone chuckled.

"Not exactly," Cora said. "There were a couple bloody noses and black eyes and some shot-out truck tires and a few broken headlights before it was all done. But yeah, they turned around eventually."

"I was so fucking glad they came too," Jeremiah said.

Leo nodded.

"You were?"

"Hannah told me he'd been hitting her and her mom for a long time." Even now, all these years later, his hand tightened around his mug of beer. "I so needed a chance to beat the hell out of him. He even swung first so I could justify it all."

"It all?" Tori asked.

"He still doesn't breathe normally out of his nose," Jeremiah said. His tone was dark, and unapologetic. It was the first time Tori had heard anything from any of these people that wasn't happy and teasing.

"And then *that* was it?" Tori asked. "Hannah just stayed here and you got married?"

"Nah, they tried a couple other times. I beat the shit out of her brother and he beat the shit out of me. A bunch of them showed up at my house once or twice," Jeremiah said.

"But that didn't amount to nothin'," Leo said. "We had guys camped out there, watching the place. They didn't get within a hundred feet of the house."

"Guys from Autre camped out at your house to help protect you and Hannah?" Tori asked.

Jeremiah nodded. "Of course."

Of course. He said it so matter-of-factly. As if anyone would have done the same thing. And maybe down here that was true. "So what made them finally leave you alone?" she asked. "I mean, I assume they finally did?"

"The day she turned eighteen, I asked her to marry me. She said of course and we were hitched by sunset," Jeremiah said. "After that, her dad had no claim on her at all."

"Yep, exactly how it happened," Leo said.

Jeremiah gave him a look and chuckled. "Yep. That's what I've always thought."

Tori frowned, looking back and forth between the men. "I feel like I'm missing something."

"Well, there's this *rumor*," Cora said. "That someone snuck into her dad's house the night after the wedding, handcuffed him to the bed, then set their kitchen table on fire. They let him sweat for about twenty minutes, thinking he was gonna die. Then they put the fire out and told him that if anyone in Autre saw him within ten miles of the town, or Hannah, the next time he wouldn't be so lucky."

"That's a rumor?" Tori asked.

"Well, there really was a fire at his house. But he's never been able to name any names. *Apparently* the guys wore masks. But everyone knows he's a crazy drunk and he'd actually set his back shed on fire twice before on his own. So no one's really sure what to think." Cora looked around. "But that man's never been even within *twenty* miles of this town."

Tori also looked around. She got the definite impression that if these men hadn't personally been involved, they knew exactly who had done it. And that they'd all take it to their graves. It was odd to have a read on a whole group of strangers like that, but the loyal-friends-who-felt-like-family vibe was strong here.

"That's a pretty amazing story," she said to Jeremiah. "You were willing to put a lot on the line for a girl you'd just met."

"I would have gotten anyone out of that situation if I could," Jeremiah said. "But..." He shrugged and grinned. "No one and nothing has ever made my heart pound like that woman did... and still does."

"And once you're part of the Landry family, you're part of the Autre family. And vice versa." This came from Ellie as she set a plate down in front of Tori.

Tori thought about her own hometown. There were a lot of people there she knew she could count on. They would help her out if she asked. They'd believe her if she told them she was having a problem. But would they swoop in and literally carry her out of a situation? Would they take a black eye or broken nose for her? Would they line up their pickups on the road, blocking an entire group of people from entering the town for her?

No.

They'd encourage her to go to the police, probably. They'd talk badly about the other people, possibly, over coffee at the diner. They might offer her money. They might even call the police *for* her. But they wouldn't necessarily put themselves on the line, physically, repeatedly, personally, for her.

But, again, she thought that might be normal.

Jumping into pickups and grabbing shotguns and immediately being prepared to actually physically *fight* someone was maybe not the go-to for most people. She didn't think this Montague-Capulet-standoff thing was typical. At least not as the initial reaction to something. It was passionate. That was for sure. And a little over-the-top.

And, dammit, there was something really nice about it. It wasn't rational and it wasn't following any kind of proper procedure. But it got the job done. And there was something about having someone so into you that they'd do whatever it took to help you. Something about having someone on her side with such an ardent group of people on their side, just because of who *he* was.

She thought it said a lot about Jeremiah that the entire town was ready to rally behind him even if he'd been overreacting.

Maybe Landrys just overreacted naturally.

Maybe people from Autre did.

Hell, maybe it was a Cajun thing.

"That is...something," she finally said.

"So now you understand," Ellie said. She handed Tori a fork.

"Understand what exactly?" Tori asked, taking the fork. The aroma from the crawfish pie was making her mouth water.

"Not to be surprised by anything," Ellie said.

"Anything about Josh?" Tori asked. "Or the town?"

"Yes," Jeremiah said with a chuckle.

"All of it?" Tori took a bite of the pie. And moaned. Out loud. She couldn't help it.

Cora looked pleased.

"Any of it," Leo said. "You can be...amazed. But don't be surprised. You've been warned."

Tori took another big bite and thought about the difference between amazed and surprised. Yep, amazed sounded good. She nodded. "I'll try."

"And now you better scoot," Ellie said. "If you're not back to the plantation on time, Josh'll kick Leo's ass."

Tori took another quick bite, not at all prepared to leave the crawfish pie unfinished. The flaky crust and the tender seafood and the spices...she might move down here just for this pie. "He'd fight his *grandfather*?" she asked after she'd swallowed.

"He'll kick his ass at poker," Ellie said with a wink.

"Can he do that?" she asked Leo.

He shrugged. "Yeah. We usually team up to just be sure Kennedy loses, but if I get in Josh's sights, I'll lose a shit ton."

Tori wanted to keep them talking until she could finish the pie. "You guys gang up on Kennedy?"

"That girl needs to be humbled as often as possible," Leo said with a nod.

"And it takes them all teaming up to beat her at poker," Jeremiah said, clearly proud of his daughter.

"It's all you guys' fault she's so feisty," Ellie said pointing at Jeremiah and Leo. "She's terribly intelligent. Then you both and her brothers never *let* her win a damned thing, so she became something even more difficult to beat."

"What's more difficult to beat than smart?" Tori asked, scooping up another forkful. She might regret her fitted cocktail dress later but she didn't care.

"Determined," Ellie said.

"Bloodthirsty," Leo said at the same time.

Tori laughed. She only had two bites of pie left so she asked, "You guys bet big bucks?"

"We bet for chores," Leo said. "Way more valuable than money."

"Chores around the tour company?"

"And more specifically for who has to work with Sawyer," Leo said.

"Sawyer's in charge?" Somehow she could see that. There was something about the guy that seemed very take-charge. And serious. Kennedy might run the schedule, but Sawyer was the go-to guy.

Leo nodded. "He and Tommy were the primary partners. They bought me out about ten years after Danny died." He nodded at Cora. "Cora, Danny, me and El have been best friends since we were kids. Danny and I ran that company for forty-two years together. I did it on my own with the kids and grandkids' help until the boys were old enough to take it over."

That kind of history wasn't foreign to her either. There were plenty of people who had lived in Elton all their lives and grown up together and who passed their farms and businesses down to the next generations. Her dad and his best friend, Dean, had been friends since childhood. Her mom and her best friend, Linda, had known each other since third grade. "It's really nice that you've kept it in the family." She glanced at Cora. "Do you have grandkids?"

A flicker of sadness passed over Cora's face. Then she smiled. "I do. Tommy was a majority partner in the business with Sawyer until he died last summer."

The last bite of crawfish pie felt like lead as Tori swallowed it. "Oh, I'm so sorry."

"Thank you," Cora said. "I miss him every day."

"We all do," Ellie said, wrapping an arm around Cora. "Tommy was one of our bright lights."

Everyone was quiet for a long moment. Then Cora sniffed. "And then I've got Madison, Tommy's sister. Maddie went to live with her other grandparents in California when she was twelve, after her mom died."

Tori set her fork down. Cora had lost a lot of loved ones. "I'm...sorry," she said again. What did someone say to a woman who had lost a child and a grandchild?

"Thank you. It was best for Maddie," she said. "They were able to give her everything. She went off to college and works for an art gallery in San Francisco now." It was clear that Cora was proud of Madison, but that it hurt to have her far away too.

"Tommy being gone is why Sawyer is so damned difficult," Leo said.

He sounded angry, but it seemed more like concern when Tori looked at him.

"He was always the serious, organized one who kept things running, but since Tommy's accident, he..." Leo trailed off, shook his head, and wiped at one of his eyes.

"He doesn't smile much. He worries about everything and everyone. And he's generally a pain in the ass to be around a lot of the time," Ellie said of her oldest grandson. "It breaks our hearts. When it's not pissing us off."

Tori took a breath. This family was a lot. She had the feeling that no one really left Sawyer alone to brood or whatever. Maybe that was for the best. Surely that could be annoying, but being loved so...loudly...had to be nice too.

"So we take turns playing poker for who has to work with him on chores. The boys do the tours and Kennedy takes care of reservations and such, but when it comes to maintenance stuff, Sawyer insists on doing it and that's when you get bitched at the most," Jeremiah said.

"You make Kennedy deal with it most often?" Tori asked.

They all chuckled. "Trust me, honey," Ellie said. "Kennedy's the best one to take it. She's a tough cookie, she's had a lifetime of dealing with her brothers and cousins saying shit she doesn't listen to. Plus, she's his baby sister. He's nicer to her than the rest of us."

Tori shook her head, smiling in spite of the topic of all the loss this family had been through—and it was clear that Cora and her kids and grandkids were a part of this family even if it wasn't by blood. "I'm really...glad I got to meet you all," she said.

"Well, sweetheart, hurry back," Cora said, pushing away from the bar. "Now I better get busy in that kitchen."

As Cora disappeared, Tori frowned. It really might be the last time she saw Cora and the rest. The wedding activities were going to take up a lot of her time while she was in

Louisiana. Josh would be with her—a thought that made her heart flutter—but they'd be at the plantation or in New Orleans. She knew the agenda contained some tours and such for the guests. There was a bus tour of New Orleans tomorrow. There was a paddleboat ride at some point. Maybe on Sunday? She hadn't really looked too far ahead. This had seemed like a deal-with-it-day-to-day kind of situation. And now that Josh would be there, she was feeling a lot more optimistic about all of it.

But she was a little sad to think that she might not see Ellie and Leo and Cora and Jeremiah again. Which was so weird. As was her disappointment over not being able to get to know Kennedy and Owen and even grumpy Sawyer better.

Leo slid off his stool and pulled the keys to the bus from his pocket.

Tori drank down the rest of her sweet tea and then started to swivel away from the bar. But Ellie stopped her. The little woman leaned over the bar and took Tori's face in her hands.

"The regulars around here are already a little crazy, but we can make anyone crazy, given half a chance."

Tori laughed. "Is that a selling point?"

"It is when you realize how damned much fun it is to have people crazy about you and to be crazy about."

Tori swallowed hard. Her parents loved her. Her grandparents, who were all gone now, had loved her. Her aunts and various cousins cared about her. She had acquaintances and classmates she still saw on a regular basis, though more as clients now than friends. But she wasn't sure anyone had ever been *crazy* about her. Andrew was her closest friend, and he'd never done anything really crazy or gone out on any limbs for her. Not that she'd given him any reasons to, come to think of it. She was pretty easy to just *be* around. No craziness required.

But the idea that someone might feel inclined to lose his head a little...that caused some butterflies.

"Thanks," she said quietly, looking into Ellie's eyes. "I had a great time here."

"You're welcome any time." Then the older woman gave her a little kiss on the cheek and let her go.

Tori turned and slid off the stool. Then she looked over at Jeremiah. "It was nice to meet you."

"Well, you have to come back," he said, lifting a shoulder. "Hannah is gonna be *pissed* at all of us that she didn't get to meet Josh's Mardi Gras girl."

Every time she heard *Josh's* in regards to herself, she felt a little flip in her chest. "Where is she right now?"

"Working," he said. "She's a teacher in N'Awlins."

"Well, I would have liked to meet her."

He winked at her. "We'll be seeing you, Tori." He said it with promise.

Finally, she took a deep breath and headed out to the tour bus with Leo.

6

J osh wiped his hands on the thighs of his pants and took a
deep breath.

He was nervous? Why was he nervous?

Maybe because his family had given Tori their entire family
history—and a healthy dose of their nuttiness—yesterday.

They'd told her his mom and dad's story.

That wasn't something a person told a girl he'd just met.

And they'd told her Leo and Ellie's story.

Both stories. Day one. That was a lot to process for someone
he definitely didn't want to spook.

Of course, both of those stories were pretty good.

Okay, his family wasn't really *crazy*. They were just a little eccentric and over-the-top. Especially as a group. The what-the-hell multiplied when all of those offbeat personalities got together.

But now Tori knew that Landrys tended to think falling in love within ten minutes was no big deal and that he'd been "mooning over" her for the past year.

"Don't worry, darlin', she knows you're hoping for something big with her," Cora had told him.

Yeah, great. Let's just tell the girl that he had diamond rings on the brain within an hour of seeing her again. That was totally normal. That wouldn't make her nervous at all.

And, for the record, he did *not* have diamond rings on the brain. Exactly. He wanted to *date her* first. Spend time with her. Maybe dance with her. Definitely kiss her some more. Hear more about her family and her work. Talk about things like their favorite holidays and pizza toppings. Sure, that was kind of boring and didn't really matter. He'd like her whether she liked pepperoni or not. But he was kind of hoping to do this like an ordinary couple who met and liked one another and wanted to get to know one another before he talked her into staying in Louisiana. Forever.

Of course, the fact that he was even thinking about doing that was probably not normal.

But he'd told his family and all of the bar regulars all of that when he'd gone in for food—he had no idea if this cocktail party included real food or just little puffs with spinach in them —before heading to the plantation.

Not that they'd cared that he was annoyed. They all loved Tori—also within a very short period of knowing her, he noted —and wanted him to bring her back soon.

Which, of course, meant that he couldn't.

If he brought her back, they'd for sure bring up diamond rings.

Maybe even one of *the* diamond rings. Yes, in his family,

there were several meaningful wedding rings that had been passed down through the generations. Of course there were.

There was no doubt in his mind that someone would bring up how his great-grandfather had proposed to his great-grand-mother after getting a letter from her intended for someone else, writing three more letters back and forth, and hitching rides all the way to Savannah to meet her. Yep, the first time he ever saw her in person, he proposed. That was definitely one of *the* rings.

Josh shoved a hand through his hair.

Hell, he wasn't sure *he* was going back to Autre any time soon. Mitch was covering for him on tours for the next few days, and his mother was going to be so pissed when they all told her that not only had they met "the girl" that he'd been distracted about for the past several months, but that they'd had an hour of time with her.

Truthfully, he'd love to introduce Tori to his mom. But that was serious. He didn't introduce women to his family. Because, well, the wedding bells in their brains and stuff.

So yeah, hanging out *away* from Autre and dating Tori—at least kind of—without his family debating if *their* wedding should be in his mother's garden or in the Autre Community Church, would be great.

He definitely hoped he had a bed at Buckworth. With a certain gorgeous brunette from Iowa next to him. All night long.

And that was the thought that made him finally open his truck door and head toward the huge front entrance to the plantation in spite of the fact that Tori hadn't answered his *I'm here* text yet.

An honest-to-God doorman in a tuxedo opened the main door for him, and Josh stepped into the foyer of one of the oldest and grandest plantations in Louisiana.

There was, appropriately, a sweeping staircase directly in

front of him and a chandelier hanging overhead. Huge rooms opened off to either side, both full of people. One side had hors d'oeuvres laid out and the other had a live jazz band playing. The atmosphere was fun and lively with a sophisticated edge.

Josh ran a hand over the jacket and button-down shirt he wore. He could dress up. At Bourbon O he'd worn dress shirts and slacks every night. He was happy that Trahan's dress code was more relaxed. And certainly the gators and tourists didn't expect suit jackets. But he had one and he didn't mind wearing it. Once in a while. If it was to play doting boyfriend to a sweet girl from Iowa, then yeah, he'd even put on a tie.

But he had to admit that he was a little disappointed now that he was staying in the foyer of the plantation house. He'd been envisioning a romance movie scene with Tori standing at the top of the stairs, waiting for him, giving him a dazzling smile as she ascended the steps gracefully to where he stood, slack-jawed, awed by how gorgeous she looked. Then he'd take her hand, dip her back, and kiss her, making sure every single person in this house saw it.

A romance movie scene required a heroine though. And Tori was nowhere to be seen.

Josh blew out a breath. He'd gotten here. He hadn't thought beyond this point.

"Well, hi."

Josh turned to see a beautiful blonde smiling up at him.

He couldn't help his own smile. Pretty girls did that to him. "Hi."

"Please tell me that you're groomsman number four," she said.

Josh shook his head. "Sorry, no."

She pouted. "Dang. I'm supposed to walk down the aisle with him and he hasn't shown up yet."

"Sorry to disappoint you."

She smiled and moved in closer. "I'm Courtney."

"Josh. He'll be bummed when he realizes that he missed out on getting to know you ahead of time," Josh said. Yeah, he was flirting. But he didn't mean it. It was just a natural reflex.

"Hi, Josh. Maybe I'm not as disappointed as I was a minute ago."

He laughed. "Well, thanks, but I'm here with someone."

Now the pout looked a lot more genuine. "Really? Who?"

"Victoria Kramer," he said.

Courtney's eyes widened. "Seriously?"

He nodded. "Yep. Why?"

"She's..." Courtney shook her head. "Do you know she kissed the groom last night?"

He laughed. "I heard. *Big* mistake. She thought he was me."

Courtney stepped back and looked him up and down. Slowly. Then she nodded. "Yeah, okay, with a mask on, in the dark, with a few drinks in me, I can maybe see it."

Josh grinned. "I promise you, I'm gonna be sure *that* doesn't happen again."

"So...you're real."

"Completely."

"Well, this is going to be interesting," she said.

"Is it?"

She smiled, but this time it looked more sly than flirtatious. "Everyone thinks she made you up."

"Definitely didn't make me up. I'm real, and I'm here," he said.

"Well, come on then. I'll show you where she is."

"Oh thanks," he said sincerely.

She shot him another of those sly smiles. "No thanks necessary. I'm happy to have a front row seat for this."

"For what?" Josh asked, following her down a short hallway toward the back of the house.

"You'll see," she said.

Josh frowned, but turned the corner after the blonde. And came up short.

There was a little alcove behind the staircase just before the kitchen door. Josh guessed there was a closet under the stairs based on the door that Tori was pressed up against. But all of his attention was on her. Well, and the tall man with dark hair and a short beard who was standing *very* close to her. They were talking in hushed voices, oblivious to anything around them.

Josh had been absolutely right. She looked stunningly beautiful in the sparkly crimson cocktail dress that hugged her body and showed the scantest hint of cleavage. It had short sleeves and ended just above her knees, showing off her tanned, toned arms and legs. She wore heels, too, that accentuated the muscles of her calves and the sexy arch of her foot.

He loved the heels. She looked sexy as hell. But, strangely, Josh thought he preferred the shorts and tennis shoes from earlier. That seemed more her. Though he wasn't sure he knew her well enough to judge that.

"That's Andrew," Courtney whispered to him. "The groom."

The way Andrew and Tori were standing close and talking softly definitely made the whispering seem appropriate. They gave off all kinds of this-is-private-don't-interrupt vibes.

"I figured," he said dryly.

Every male instinct in him made him want to stomp up and grab her away from the guy. But this was more than the groom. Even more than the guy she'd kissed—accidentally—last night. This was her best friend.

Her best friend who had just reached up and tucked a stray curl behind her ear.

Josh felt his fist tighten at his side and he made himself relax.

If anyone was an outsider here, it was him.

What the hell was he supposed to do here?

"Let's give them a minute," he told Courtney.

She lifted a brow. "Really? You don't want to interrupt?"

He definitely wanted to interrupt. But he couldn't do that. Obviously Andrew was the reason Tori hadn't answered Josh's text. She probably didn't even know he was here.

But he sure as hell didn't want to *watch* Tori and Andrew together.

"They're friends," he said. Friends that stood really close together. "If they have stuff to talk about, that's none of my business."

That was completely true. And, in spite of the surge of jealousy he felt—maybe *because* of the surge of jealousy he felt—he needed to remember that.

Courtney was clearly surprised. "It's not your business if your girlfriend is cuddled up with another guy?"

Josh turned away from Tori and Andrew. "They're not cuddled up," he said, feeling a prick of annoyance. They weren't. Exactly. They were talking. Privately.

"I don't know if Paisley would agree with you," Courtney said.

"Well, if you're worried, why don't *you* interrupt them?" he asked.

"The last thing we need is for the *groom* to be pissed at a bridesmaid too."

"Too?"

"Paisley is, obviously, pretty upset with Tori. And the fact that Andrew refused to kick her out of the wedding party."

"The kiss was a mistake," Josh said. Taking her bridesmaid status away seemed like an overreaction.

"Yeah, maybe." Courtney tipped her head. "I mean, I guess now that you're here that seems more likely. But it's not like that's *all* Paisley is upset about."

"She's a bride," Josh said. "From what I understand, brides

are supposed to be upset about stuff." Hell, they made entire TV shows about it.

"I mean about Andrew and Tori," Courtney told him. "Paisley thinks Tori is trying to talk Andrew out of getting married."

Josh felt a tightness in his chest. Was that what they were talking about now? She'd told him that they'd been friends forever and that she'd had a crush on Andrew in high school. There could be jealousy there that had nothing to do with Tori being in love with him. Obviously, if he'd moved from Iowa to Louisiana and now had a fiancée, his time with Tori had been cut way down. Maybe she was just missing him. As a friend.

Josh really didn't know what to do here. Tori had asked him to come. She wanted him here to help convince everyone that she'd meant to kiss *him*. That he was real. And she wanted them to all think that they were more than two strangers that met last Mardi Gras and hadn't been in touch since. She wanted him to play the part of her boyfriend. She wanted him to help her convince everyone that *he* was the guy she had feelings for.

Yeah, he could do that. Definitely. And if *Tori* was one of the people he convinced, then all the better.

"Tell you what," he said to Courtney. "How about you introduce me to Paisley? That will keep her away from this." He jerked his thumb toward where Andrew and Tori were still talking. "And will prove that I'm real and I'm here. That's gotta make her feel better."

Courtney nodded. "Yeah, that's a good idea." She cast one more glance in the direction of the two friends under the stairs. She frowned slightly, but Josh resisted looking in that direction.

Tori had known Andrew her whole life. It made sense that she was comfortable with him in her personal space. And Josh couldn't forget the way she'd kissed *him* in his office yesterday.

She'd let him *in* her personal space too. Very in. And he intended to spend a lot more time there.

He followed Courtney back down the hallway and into the main ballroom of the mansion. A ballroom. It wasn't as big as he would have expected a *ballroom* to be, but it was impressive nonetheless. A domed ceiling, easily twenty feet high, rose above them, and huge murals decorated the walls. The flooring was polished wood and the walls at the two ends of the room were floor-to-ceiling windows looking out over the rolling lands of the plantation. It was gorgeous. And right in the middle, the princess was holding court.

Okay, it was the bride, but she commanded the space as if this were her throne room. People milled around, smiling and congratulating her, sipping from champagne flutes and plucking fancy hors d'oeuvres—he'd been right to eat before coming—from silver trays carried by wait staff in tuxedos. Paisley nodded and smiled at her guests, even hugging a few. She looked completely content at the center of attention. Without her groom by her side.

And she was beautiful. There was no denying that. She was dressed in a white, well, princess dress. The kind that fit her torso and then flared below her waist in huge billowing layers of material. The bodice sparkled. As did the tiara sitting on top of the blonde curls that had been piled up on top of her head.

It was absolutely the opposite of anything the women in his life would ever wear.

Or that Tori would wear.

He didn't know how he knew that. He just did.

Girls who wore tiaras didn't play with river otters.

Not that Tori had *played* with Gus. She knew better. She knew animals. But Gus had picked her out as a friend. Josh felt very strongly that otters would not like tiaras.

"Introduce me to the woman of the hour," Josh said to Courtney.

"Woman of the week, you mean?" she asked with a little laugh.

Fair enough. Courtney led him across the ballroom and they waited for a few seconds as Paisley finished talking to the people she was with. They moved off and Josh stepped in.

He extended his hand. "Hi, Paisley. I'm about to be your favorite person tonight."

The bride arched a perfectly groomed eyebrow, her blue eyes taking him in from head to toe. "Is that right?"

"It is. I'm Josh Landry. And I'm Victoria Kramer's date tonight. And for your wedding."

Now Paisley's eyes widened and she took his hand. "So you're real."

This was, evidently going to be the general reaction to him tonight. "I very much am."

She looked him over again. "I guess you're built a little like Andrew."

Barely. He had way more muscle than Andrew. And, okay, Andrew had an inch or two on him. But he wasn't going to argue. It was good for Paisley to agree that Tori kissing Andrew could have been an honest mistake.

"I promise you that there will be no more accidental kissing with Tori and...anyone else," he told her, letting go of her hand.

"I'm very happy to hear that." She looked at Courtney. "Oh, hey, Court, Sam is here now." She pointed across the room to a man who'd just arrived and was being greeted by other members of the bridal party.

Courtney glanced over then smiled up at Josh. "Groomsman number four."

He grinned and nodded. "It was nice to meet you."

Courtney winked, then turned and headed for the newcomer, and Josh focused on Paisley. Clearly she'd been trying to get a few minutes alone with him. She grabbed his arm and tugged him off to one side. It wasn't like she could really hide out. She was the bride. And was wearing the biggest dress he'd ever seen. And a tiara, for fuck's sake. But Josh guessed that Paisley Darbonne was used to managing a room like this. If she didn't want anyone interrupting them, Josh was sure they wouldn't be interrupted.

Paisley stopped by one of the huge windows and faced him, her arms crossed. "Listen, if you can keep Tori away from Andrew for the rest of this week and through my wedding, I will give you a million dollars."

He blinked at her. It might just be an expression, but he thought it was possible that she really had a million dollars to throw around. "Trust me, I don't need any incentive to keep Tori away from Andrew. Or any other man." He flashed her a grin. They needed to keep this light. He wasn't going to let a soon-to-be-bride hopped up on adrenaline and champagne to talk him into making this a crisis.

"Good," Paisley said. *Not* lightly.

"But," Josh added. "Obviously I can't keep her away from him completely. They're best friends."

Paisley gave a little eye roll. "Whatever."

"You don't think they're close?" Josh asked. He wasn't going to tell her about their little meeting in the hallway that was for sure.

"Well, when you spend eighteen years within a forty-mile radius and around the same twelve-hundred people, I suppose you're 'close' to everyone."

Josh frowned. "Doesn't mean they're not friends." Most of the people he knew did exactly what Paisley had just described. Maybe the radius was a little bigger and when you added in New Orleans and all the tourists in Autre, the population of people they interacted with was bigger, but Autre was a little town, and most people from there stayed pretty close to home.

"I think they're both making a bigger deal out of their relationship than it really is, that's all," Paisley said.

"Why would they do that?"

"Oh, they *believe* they're close. But a lot of this is just nostalgia on Andrew's part." She sighed. "He's been away from home for a year, and now it's sinking in what a big change it's going to be...for good. Then Tori showed up and made him start thinking about everything at home and the past, and he's just getting a little homesick."

Josh frowned. "So you think the solution is just to keep them apart?"

"Yes." She threw her hands up. "Obviously. Tori is the only thing that does that to him. He can see his parents and not get all emotional. We've been back to Iowa a couple of times and he does get nostalgic then, but he's always ready to come back here with me. He *wants* everything down here. He wants the amazing city, the amazing job, the amazing wife." She gave Josh a look that challenged him to disagree that she was that.

Josh held up his hands. "I'm not saying he doesn't."

"Tori is just this person who...doesn't want more. For herself or for him."

"What do you mean?" Tori was a veterinarian. She was clearly bright, and anyone who loved animals got big points with him. Plus his family had loved her. Paisley made Tori sound unmotivated. Or something.

"She's comfortable for him. She likes things back home just as they are. She's not looking for anything new or bigger. Where they come from, everyone meets someone in kindergarten, goes to prom with them, marries them, has three kids, and farms their dad's farm."

Wow. It was really clear how Paisley felt about all of that. "You're afraid he's gonna bail on you, Paisley?" Josh asked. "Really? You think he's getting cold feet now that Tori's here?" That caused a strange twist in Josh's gut.

"I think she represents everything easy and familiar to him."

"His parents don't represent that? Going back to visit his hometown doesn't make him feel that way?"

She shrugged. "For some reason, not the way she does."

"And you think deep down he wants easy and familiar?" Josh didn't like the sound of that. Not only because he meant Andrew might want Tori, at least on some level, but because Tori should be more than easy and familiar to whoever she was with.

Though, he had to admit, familiar, comfortable, reassuring were all good things too. Things that meant *home*. And yes, he did want the woman *he* went home to at the end of the day to be those things.

"I think he's nervous. I challenge him," Paisley said, lifting her chin. "I believe he can do amazing things. I've pushed him. He deserves someone who will help him aspire to greater things. But, just like any challenge in life, sometimes it's a little scary and it's tempting to fall back on what you know. Tori is... like a teddy bear or a pair of worn-out slippers to him," Paisley said. "Comforting. Broken in. She doesn't demand anything of him. But she doesn't see all the things he can accomplish."

A teddy bear or a worn-out pair of slippers. Okay, well, that was a pretty clear stance on things. "Tori deserves to be more than someone's...slippers," Josh said.

"I agree."

He wasn't sure Paisley cared one whit about Tori, but he wasn't going to argue. They were on the same side here. Tori and Andrew weren't good enough for one another.

"So you need to be sure she's otherwise occupied during these days before the wedding so that Andrew sees that she's fine and doesn't feel compelled to spend a lot of time with her or really even think about her much," Paisley said. "I'll keep him focused on our wedding and our future together. We'll get married next Saturday and then Tori can go back to Iowa and Andrew can move on with his life."

Wow, that was cold. Paisley clearly didn't expect Tori and Andrew to be a part of each other's lives going forward. Was she right that they were friends just because there hadn't been a lot of other options in their little town, or were they tight the way Tori believed? Josh had no idea. But he did know that keeping Tori occupied for the next several days sounded like a hell of an idea. Regardless of his feelings for Tori, Andrew was getting married and he needed to have his attention on Paisley. If he was getting cold feet, well, he needed to figure that shit out. And that was on him to work through. Not Tori. And certainly not Josh.

"I'm in," he said.

"Good," Paisley said, almost seeming as if she'd expected his cooperation.

Josh fought a smile. He wondered how often, if ever, people told Paisley no.

"You are hereby invited to any and all wedding activities," she said. "Standing invitation to be wherever Tori is."

"Sounds perfect to me." It really did. He didn't give two shits about Andrew. But he did care about Tori, and being enemy number one of the bride was not going to be a very fun place to be for her. Josh could make that all better.

"And speak of the devils," Paisley said, focusing on something behind Josh. "I swear, that's the last time they go off alone together."

Josh turned to find Tori and Andrew coming into the ballroom together. Tori looked dazzling. She was the one pop of color in a roomful of black and white and dark blues and purples. Everyone was wearing a dark suit or a dress in a dark color. Tori's red dress with the sequins that caught the light and sparkled looked like a jewel.

Andrew was stopped by a cluster of people in the doorway. He smiled and shook hands, looking like the perfect host. Tori, on the other hand, frowned and tugged at the waistline of her dress as if adjusting something uncomfortable.

Josh took a step in that direction, but Paisley put her hand on his arm, stopping him. "He'll be over in a minute."

Right. The princess didn't go to people. They came to her.

And sure enough, Andrew was already extracting himself from his guests and starting for Paisley. He left Tori behind, adjusting the neckline of her dress and looking like she was trying to itch a spot between her breasts without anyone noticing. Well, Josh was noticing because he wasn't taking his eyes off of her. For the next few *days*.

Josh started in her direction again. He didn't care how Andrew and Paisley worked. *He* was going to *Tori*. He passed Andrew on his way to her and didn't even make eye contact with the other man. He was leaving Andrew in Paisley's hands now.

Tori saw him when he got halfway across the room. Her face broke into a huge smile and Josh felt his heart thunk hard against his sternum. That was all he needed to see. If he could keep that look on her face through all this wedding stuff and weirdness with Andrew and Paisley, then he'd feel like he'd done a very good thing.

"Hey," he said, not stopping until he was standing as close as Andrew had been. And there was no alcove or shadows hiding them.

"Hi."

Then she shocked him by taking his hand, tugging him close and going up on tiptoe to kiss him. And it wasn't a short, sweet press of her lips to his. She took the lapel of his jacket in her fist and *kissed* him. In the middle of the ballroom, in front of all of Paisley's guests, in front of Andrew.

The heels she wore put her two inches closer to his mouth and Josh appreciated the hell out of that.

After a moment, he lifted his head, not even close to being

done, but not willing to make *all* of his displays of affection quite this public. "You look amazing," he told her gruffly. Sincerely.

"Thank you. I'm so glad you're here." She was still gripping the front of his jacket, as if she had no intention of letting go. Maybe ever.

Fine with me.

See, it was those kinds of thoughts that should worry him. Not only because he and Tori had really just met, but even more now since Paisley had pointed out that Tori probably wasn't the type to pack up her life and move it to Louisiana. Tori was comfortable in Iowa. Even if she shouldn't be like an old pair of slippers to Andrew, maybe Iowa, or her farm, or whatever, was *her* old pair of slippers. Maybe she was the old-slippers-at-night kind of girl rather than a...new-dancing-shoes-every-weekend kind of girl.

Josh didn't know her well enough to know. Not that Tori and Paisley were especially close either, but he had to assume that hearing about Tori from Andrew, or even just knowing Andrew's background, would lead Paisley to some accurate assumptions.

"I'm glad you're happy to see me," he told her. Very honestly.

She widened her eyes. "Are you kidding? Of course I am. This way I have *one* person here who likes me."

He laughed. "I'm the only one?" But he noticed her serious expression and dropped his smile. "Really? What are you talking about?"

She grimaced. "Apparently kissing the groom is a good way to get labeled a pariah."

"Come on."

"Seriously. And then the red dress..." She sighed. "I'm kind of messing everything up."

"What about the red dress?" He leaned back to take another good look at it. Yeah, he still thought it was sexy as hell.

"You didn't notice?" she asked.

"Notice that you look fucking amazing? Yeah, I definitely did."

Her face relaxed into a smile. "I'm glad you think so. But I'm kind of...bright."

"So?"

She glanced around. "You didn't notice that everyone else is in dark colors? Except for Paisley, of course. She's the one who's supposed to stand out."

Josh looked over to where the bride was talking earnestly to her fiancé. "Well, it's hard to miss Paisley," he said, looking back to Tori. "But you look amazing. They didn't tell you about the dress code?"

Tori lifted a shoulder. "I was just supposed to know, I guess. I never buy cocktail dresses. So, I really just grabbed something I liked and didn't think anything more about it."

"Fuck 'em."

She looked up at him. "You really didn't think anything about me wearing bright red amidst all of this, did you?" she asked.

"Not really."

She smiled. "Because you're used to being around people who are...vibrant and don't mind extra attention."

He laughed at that. "You might have something there." He hadn't really thought about it, but he didn't really blink at someone doing something that stood out from the crowd. Everyone he spent any significant time with did that in one way or another.

"And people who think nothing of making a scene?"

"That too," he agreed. "But you weren't doing that. You just put on a dress."

"Well, Paisley and everyone here doesn't know that." Tori actually seemed embarrassed.

Embarrassed was the last thing this woman should feel about how she looked tonight.

"There have to be people from back home here, right?" he asked. "Andrew's friends and family? Surely they know you well enough to know that you weren't trying to upstage Paisley and that you'd never make a move on a guy who's engaged. Especially right before the wedding, when you're here as a bridesmaid."

She shrugged. "Well, only one guy from high school is coming for the wedding. The rest of the groomsmen are friends from here."

"His mom and dad are here though, aren't they?"

"Yeah."

"And you've known them all your life."

"Yeah."

He reached down and lifted her chin, making her move her eyes from his collar to meet his gaze. "These people know what kind of person you are. They won't believe that it was a mistake?"

She sighed. "I'd like to think so. But they don't really *know* me," she said. "I mean, it's not like we've sat around and talked a lot."

"I thought you and Andrew grew up together?"

"We did. But it was just me and Andrew talking."

"No family dinners with his parents? Holidays? Barbecues?"

She tipped her head. "Is that what you did with your friends' families?"

"Sure. And them with us. We hunted and fished. My buddy Garrett's dad was the one who taught me to pitch baseball. My friend Matthew's mom taught me to shoot a bow and arrow. I helped Sawyer's friend, Carter, train hunting dogs for a couple of years. We were all always in each other's business."

She seemed to be taking that all in. She gave a soft sigh. "That sounds nice."

"But you and Andrew weren't like that?"

"No. When we were little, I always talked him into things that got him muddy or wet, and his mom would get annoyed about him tracking his boots in the house. When we were older, he'd hang out at the farm with me, but his mom thought it was weird that I had so many animals...and stuff..." She swallowed and her eyes went back to the base of his throat where he'd pulled the knot of his tie loose and unbuttoned the top button. "They wanted him to be out for sports and on the debate team and class president and everything. I wasn't into all of that, so I think she just thought our friendship was strange. And she didn't really encourage it."

There was something about that that really bothered Josh. He couldn't put his finger on it, but it made him like Andrew even less. "What kind of stuff?" he asked.

She looked up. "What?"

"You said she thought it was weird you had so many animals...and stuff." He gave her a grin that had gotten phone numbers out of more than a few women over the years. "What stuff? You can tell me."

Tori shook her head. "You don't *really* want to know."

"Oh"—he reached out and snagged two glasses of champagne, handing her one—"but I do."

"You're going to get me drunk so I'll spill my secrets?" she asked, smiling even as she asked.

"Hey, I'm not driving tonight. We can get totally lit up. As long as we can make it upstairs." He assumed her room was upstairs.

"Oh, you're not driving back to Autre tonight?" She asked it with one brow up as she took a sip of champagne.

He grinned and knocked back half the glass at once. "I'm

not. I told you—well, and my family—that I intend to stay glued to your side for the next several days."

She nodded slowly. "Yeah, I guess you did."

He leaned in and put his lips next to her ear. "And I'm happy to try other methods of persuading you to tell me everything about you."

He felt the little shiver that went through her and grinned with satisfaction as he leaned back.

"Well, you can give it your best shot." She tipped her champagne glass back and swallowed the rest of the contents in one gulp. Then she further stole his heart by reaching for two more from the next waiter.

Josh laughed, took a glass, linked his fingers with hers, and tugged her toward the back patio of the house. He wanted some quiet, but they couldn't get too far out of sight of the party. These people needed to know that Tori was very much *with* someone tonight.

7

T ori had never been happier to see someone in her life as she had been to see Josh standing in the middle of the ballroom at the Buckworth Plantation.

She hadn't been lying when she said he was probably the only person who was glad she was there. Sure, Andrew still liked her, but she was pretty sure the strain she was causing with Paisley was making it harder to be glad Tori was here.

This dress. Ugh. It was the last thing she'd ever typically wear. For some reason, though, she'd seen it in the store and thought it seemed perfect for a New Orleans cocktail party. It was bright and fun and different. Just like New Orleans.

Yeah, she'd really miscalculated that one. Elegant parties at plantations were not like the parties in the Quarter. That was for sure.

Tori let Josh lead her to the big French doors on one end of the ballroom and out onto the huge stone patio at the back of the mansion. She hoped every person in that room was watching them go. Damn right, Josh was real. And damn right, that kiss had been real.

It had been a long afternoon. Leo had dropped her back at the plantation after the bridal party luncheon was already over. Everyone had been resting and relaxing in their rooms, so Tori had done the same, more than happy to avoid any interactions with the other bridesmaids or Paisley.

But that meant she'd missed the invitation to have facials with the rest of the bridesmaids. Not that she cared about that, but it was one more way she was ending up left out of things. She was a bridesmaid because of Andrew. But she wasn't welcome among the bridesmaids and wasn't included with the groomsmen. It was...awkward.

Then she'd had to get dressed in what had to be the scratchiest dress she'd ever worn and twist her hair up into an updo that was similar to how she put her hair up underneath the ball caps she wore at work sometimes. This, however, required an exorbitant number of bobby pins that were making her head ache.

But now Josh was here. And he was giving her a great reason to leave the ballroom without looking like a weird introvert sneaking up to her room to be alone.

Come to think of it, sneaking up to her room *with Josh* to very much not be alone sounded like a great idea.

"You know, we could take these glasses up to my room," she said, tugging on Josh's hand.

He shot her a sexy grin. "Well, I want to talk for a little while."

"We could talk up there."

He stopped in the middle of the patio. It was quieter out here. The strains of the music and laughter and conversation were only muted background noise now. It was also dark beyond the light cast from the ballroom, but the patio itself, including the stone benches and the near side of the fountain and the many topiary trees, were all bathed in a golden light intermingled with the occasional shadow.

As Josh moved in close and gave her a hot look that made her toes curl, they stood inside the circle of light like a spotlight. Anyone inside would be able to look out and see them.

"No, I don't think we could go up to your room to talk," he said, his voice low.

"No?"

"Talking won't be the first thing on my mind. And that's probably a good thing to *talk* about." He moved in closer. "I would *love* to spend the night here with you. But I want to be sure you're good with it. I'm sure I can find another room if not."

Oh, he wasn't staying in any other room.

"You can't ask for another room," Tori said quickly. "Everyone has to think we're *together*. Really together."

He nodded. "Okay. I can sleep on the floor."

"I can't make you sleep on the floor," she said. "You're here to help me out. I can't expect you to camp out on the hard floor."

He looked like he was fighting a smile. "Okay, then *you* can sleep on the floor."

She lifted both eyebrows. "I'm not sleeping on the floor."

"You have a bad back?" He did smile now.

"I have a great back."

"You have a really great front too." He laughed at his own joke.

Tori snorted softly. Then leaned in closer and grinned up at him. "There's no way I would sleep on the floor when there's a hot, sexy, funny, *dangerous* bayou boy in my bed."

He was still smiling as he bent, a hot, mischievous look in his eyes. "Ah, a risk-taker. I like that."

"In certain situations," she said with a nod. "What am I risking here, exactly though?"

He lifted a hand to her face. His expression was still playful, but there was a touch of seriousness now. "Me ruining you for all other men."

That shot a bolt of heat straight through her. She swallowed. "Yeah. In that case, I'm feeling especially daring."

He brushed his lips over hers. Tori started to go on tiptoe to fit their mouths more fully together, but he lifted his head before she could really get into it.

"So, let's go talk for a little bit," he said.

The arrow of disappointment was surprising. She sighed. "Okay."

Josh laughed. "That bad an idea?"

"Well..." She shrugged. "No. I guess not."

"You're not a big talker?" he asked.

"Not unless you have four legs and a tail."

"The animals you work on are good listeners?" He pulled her over to one of the stone benches. It was still visible from the ballroom, but from certain angles, they'd be hidden behind a tree shaped like a swan.

"They think I'm brilliant and funny and incredibly interesting," she said with a nod. "At least they've never said otherwise."

He laughed again. "Yeah, you might worry a bit if they start talking back."

Wow, she really loved the sound of his laugh. It was a deep, sexy rumbling that seemed to come from his gut. Sincere and full of pleasure. As if he was just loving whatever was going on at that moment.

After spending an hour or so with his family, that seemed pretty genetic, actually. They all seemed to be really good at enjoying the little moments and details. Sure, they apparently had a legacy of grand gestures and big stories, but it was in the way they teased each other and smiled and relished good food and long-term relationships. It was clear they enjoyed sitting in Ellie's bar, just being around each other, as much as some people enjoyed special events or elaborate parties. Tori thought about the mansion behind her and the grand ballroom and the woman in a tiara—for fuck's sake. Yeah, some people needed *more* to have a good time. But not the Landrys.

"Okay, what do you want to know?" she asked, turning to face him and tucking one leg under her on the bench. They could talk. But they could do it quickly.

He looked at her with a soft smile for a long moment.

"What?" she asked.

"I *really* like the fact that you'd rather go up to your room right now."

"You changing your mind?" She shifted so she could stand right back up.

Their fingers were still linked and he lifted her hand to his lips, kissing it. "Not yet."

Tingles raced from where his lips touched her right down between her legs. This conversation better not take very long. She hoped Josh Landry had some stamina because she wasn't sure one time with him tonight was going to be enough.

"Tell me about the 'stuff' that Andrew's parents think is weird about you," he said.

Oh that. Dammit. Why had she said that? She wasn't embarrassed about her "stuff" exactly, but she was used to people thinking it was all a little odd. And she kind of wanted to wait and be odd with Josh *after* he gave her a couple of orgasms.

"Oh, it's not—"

"Tori." He stopped her with that one word. "Tell me."

Well, crap. Okay. She wasn't going to *lie* to him. He'd come here tonight to help her out with a bit of an odd problem.

"I have a farm," she started. "In addition to my vet practice. Actually, my vet practice—my clinic, anyway—is run out of a building on the farm."

"Okay."

"It was my mom and dad's, it's where I grew up, but my parents moved into town about two years ago, so it's all mine now."

He was still holding her hand and she loved the feel of it. It was big and warm, his skin roughened by working outdoors with his hands every day. She liked that about him. They didn't do the same kind of work, but clearly Josh wasn't afraid to get a little dirty and he didn't buff the calluses off his palms.

She really wanted to feel those hands all over her body. *All* over her body.

It had been a really long time since she'd had sex. A *really* long time. But it was how much she wanted to now that was really nagging at her. She didn't think about sex that much. Now she couldn't seem to stop.

"Tori?"

She focused on Josh's face. Oh right. They'd been talking.

"Why would Andrew's parents think that your farm is weird?"

She wanted to get this talking stuff over with. "Because it's mostly full of special needs animals."

He just looked at her. For several long moments.

"About ninety percent of my animals have some kind of issue. Some have a missing a leg. Or a toe. One of my cats is paralyzed in her back legs. One cat only has one eye. The milk cow doesn't give milk. One of my dogs has PTSD. My chicken is mentally ill. They all have...something going on with them."

He was still just looking at her.

"See? Weird."

"You have a farm full of special needs animals," he said.

It wasn't a question, but she nodded.

"Okay. How did that happen?"

He wanted to know more? "Um...well, technically it started with me refusing to put Frank down when he was born with a cleft palate," she said. "They didn't want him, so I took him home with me and fed him with a tube and took care of him until he was old enough to undergo surgery. Then we corrected the cleft as best we could. He still needs some feeding help but he's one of my best friends."

Tori winced. See, that was the kind of stuff that had gotten her teased for years.

"And Frank is?" Josh asked.

He was looking at her with...affection. That was unusual.

"An English bulldog," Tori said. Josh wasn't looking at her like she was weird. He wasn't even leaning back. In fact, he might have leaned closer. So she took a deep breath and said, "Okay, *officially* this all started when I was eight and found a baby squirrel that had been knocked out of his nest. I nursed him with a little doll's bottle and kept him in my bedroom, hidden from my parents, until he was old enough to release. But he'd never really leave. He kept hanging around, and climbing up to my window and stuff. So I'd let him in at night, and I built him a little house outside and fed him for...a while after that."

"A while?" Josh tipped his head so she would look at him.

She nodded. "About four years."

He was clearly surprised. "Squirrels live that long?"

"Most live about six years—provided they've got food and shelter and predators don't get to them—though they can live up to twelve."

"Wow."

She couldn't help but smile. If he found that interesting, she had all kinds of crazy facts about animals. "I had a raccoon for three years."

Josh's eyes widened. "In your *bedroom*?"

"Only for a week. When she was a baby. Until my mom found out. But then I kept her in our barn."

He finally smiled completely. "What else? How many other animals did you have as pseudo pets?"

"A family of rabbits. Chipmunks. Mice."

He shook his head. "Wow."

"Yeah. And I built them shelters and made them food—"

"*Made* them food?"

Well, she was this far in. "Little cakes made of seeds and things they liked. Stuff like that."

"And you were just a little girl?"

She nodded. "And I thought it was really cool. Until I told about them during show-and-tell and everyone started calling me Cinderella."

"Why Cinderella?"

"After I admitted that I talked to the animals, they teased me about having the birds and mice help me make my clothes and do my chores."

He laughed softly, but it didn't feel mocking. It felt like he was sharing a memory with her.

She could smile about this now. He was acting interested and was being sweet about her story. She relaxed and kept talking. "So that was my reputation growing up. I had dogs and cats, too, of course. And my dad raised all kinds of farm animals. I took care of any runts or anything that got hurt or had any problems. I made a cart for our dog that broke his leg. I've bottle-fed more cats than I can count. We had a mama cow die in childbirth and I took care of the calf. He became like a dog, really, following me around, meeting me by the fence when he knew I'd be getting home from school." She took a long swallow of her champagne. "But that was why I didn't socialize much or go out for things after school. I needed to get home to take care of my animals."

"And you preferred that, didn't you?" he asked. "You never wanted to play basketball or be in the school play."

She looked up. "I really didn't. I always preferred the animals. And my classmates thought that was weird."

"I can't speak for the girls, but I'm guessing at least some of the guys were just jealous that you didn't want to spend time with them."

She laughed at that. "You really can't help the sweet talk, can you?"

He gave her a sheepish grin. "While you were saving the animal kingdom, I was spending time with *my* favorite hobby."

"Girls."

"Pretty much."

She couldn't even fault him. He was so upfront about it. And yeah, sweet. It made her want to tell him everything.

"So, the rest of the story is then the special needs animals I have now. I take on the hurt ones and the ones with birth defects and the ones that just don't...fit. I have everything from chickens to horses to cats and..." She hesitated for a second.

Josh leaned in, his eyebrows up. "Come on...what else do you have?"

She grinned. She kind of thought Josh might like this. "I have a pig who is scared of thunder. I have a very sweet alpaca who loves me to sing to him. And...I have a mountain lion."

Now he was staring at her. Not necessarily in a you're-super-weird way, but in a wow-that's-pretty-cool way. There was a fine line between those two, she'd found.

"So you do sing to the animals," he finally said.

"I do."

"Maybe you are a little like Cinderella," he said, with a grin that made her want to crawl into his lap and do very un-princess-like things to him.

But again, from him it came out completely differently than it had from the kids at school. She was over the teasing from grade school. She remembered it, of course, but she was twenty-eight now. She worked with and lived with animals, and she was completely happy and she'd figured out that she didn't need people to understand her.

But it was nice when they did. Or when they accepted her anyway.

She wasn't the same little girl who'd been teased. She wasn't the teenager who'd gotten comments about how she had to keep her only friends in a pen to get them to stay. She was the woman they all came to or called when their pets or livestock needed help. There was some definite satisfaction in that. And she was pretty damned gracious about it, to be honest. It wasn't the animals' faults that their owners had been jerks as kids.

"And a mountain lion?" Josh asked. "Really?"

"Really. Found him as a cub. He'd been injured badly. Shot, actually. I don't know if it was an accident or if someone shot him on purpose and just left him there. But I operated and nursed him back to health."

"And then he didn't want to leave either, right?" Josh asked. His voice was softer now and a little huskier.

Tori felt a little shiver of pleasure go through her. "I guess not. He kept coming around."

"Yeah. I totally understand why." His voice was even deeper now.

She watched him move closer, felt him slide his hand up her arm, over her shoulder, to the back of her head, and smelled the scent of his aftershave with a hint of champagne as he leaned in.

"So, none of that's weird, Tori," he said softly. "It's all fucking loveable as hell."

Then he kissed her. Sweetly. But hotly. She'd never realized how sexy a kiss that was all lips could be. No tongue, no wandering hands. Just lips. But there was something about it that made her feel desired in a way she'd never felt before.

And she wanted more. So much more. Not just the physical stuff. She wanted to tell Josh about Fergie and Frodo and Fiona, her triplet fainting goats. She wanted to see his eyes widen when he found out she'd had a sloth for a while. She wanted to know about his childhood too. Though she was ninety-nine percent sure that he'd been an outgoing, getting-dirty-in-the-bayou-whenever-possible kind of kid.

But she also wanted more of the physical stuff. Definitely.

Tori shifted, keeping their lips locked together, until she could slide into his lap. She straddled his thighs and soaked up the sound of his groan and the feel of his hands dropping to her hips. Not to move her off his lap, but to press her more firmly against his fly.

He was hard. Really hard. And big. And suddenly the warm feeling he'd caused by actually being interested in her animals turned into hot, licking flames.

She ran her hands up the sides of his neck and into his hair. She loved the way that made him groan too. She wanted to strip him down and rub her body all over him the way Webster did against the catnip-filled dolphin he hid from all the other animals. She hadn't felt this for a guy in a *very* long time.

Finally he pulled back, breathing hard.

She stared down at him.

"Damn. You are so fucking sweet," he told her, his voice gruff.

Tori smiled. "Thanks."

"And I'm not sure how to feel about this, but all of that sweetness makes me want to see just how naughty I can make you. No matter how bad I'd feel the next day about debauching you."

Debauching. *That* was a great word. She wiggled on his lap.

His hands clamped down, keeping her from moving.

"I'm not as sweet as I seem," she told him.

"No?" It was clear he didn't believe her.

"I've punched a couple of guys. I ruined a girl's prom dress with cow poop. I stole...some things one time. And I put my hands in unspeakable places and walk through crap—literally —on a daily basis."

He laughed, almost as if surprised though. "Okay, but let me guess here. You punched the guys over some animals. You ruined the girl's dress because of something with animals. And you stole food or something for animals."

Ah, he was paying attention. She grinned. "Almost. The girl had a couple of dogs that had been together for three years, since they were puppies, and she sold one—just *one* and split them up—so she could afford that dress. And the guys were brothers and their cat had kittens and their dad didn't want them so he told the boys to take them out to the country and dump them."

Josh's fingers dug into her hips. "So you went after them and punched them and saved the cats?"

"I punched them in the parking lot after school," she told him. "Then I went to their house and stole the kittens."

"So those were the things you stole that one time?" His mouth was curving.

She nodded.

"Does it count as stealing if you take something they didn't want in the first place?"

She laughed. "Hey, I'm trying to be a badass here so that you'll debauch me."

His eyes got hot instantly and his smile dropped. His expression was completely serious when he said, "I'm not sure anything could stop me from doing that. Except you saying no, of course."

"There's no way I'm going to say no," she told him sincerely.

He took a deep breath. "Okay, then there's just one more thing I want to talk about."

"I shot a coyote once," she said. She thought that was pretty badass. "And I took a guy's fuel pump out of his car so he couldn't come after me when I let the birds he had caged loose."

"You can shoot?" That definitely seemed to surprise him.

"Yep. I've been hunting all my life."

"You *hunt*?" he asked.

"Yeah. Duck and pheasants mostly, but I've gone deer hunting too."

"But...you love animals."

"Hunting isn't *not* loving animals. It's important where we are to control their populations. Starving to death or getting hit by cars isn't a nice way for them to die either. When I shoot, I know they go instantly. No suffering."

Josh was looking a little awed now. Or maybe it was confused. "And you know cars?"

She shrugged. "The basics. It's a lot easier and cheaper to take care of your own stuff when you can, and we have several kinds of vehicles on the farm. Trucks and a tractor and a bobcat."

Josh shook his head. "Damn."

"You okay?" She couldn't describe his expression.

"Yeah, I just had no idea how much hunting and car expertise would make me want to bend someone over the end of the bed and lick her from head to toe."

That surprised a laugh out of her even as a hot shiver swept through her body. "Maybe because most of the people you know who can do those things are guys?"

"That's probably part of it," he agreed. "My mom and sister aren't really...outdoorsy."

Tori smiled. She was surprised by how much she wanted to meet Josh's mom.

"But Ellie hunts alligators," he added of his grandmother.

Tori felt her eyes widen. "Wow, really?"

"Yep. Claims hers always taste the best."

Tori didn't have a lot of trouble picturing Ellie hunting. "Is alligator good?"

"You'd try it?" he asked.

"Of course. Why not?"

He shook his head. "At this point, I have no idea. I think I'm just getting used to the idea of being with a tomboy. Not sure I've done that before."

Tori wasn't sure she considered herself a tomboy exactly, but no, she wasn't girlie either. "Your grandma is a tomboy?"

"Definitely. Tough girl. She cusses and she whooped us as often, or more, than our parents did. There's nothing that makes her squeamish that I know of. And she's not reckless, but she's also not scared of much."

"And you're not usually attracted to those things?"

"I guess..." He sighed. "Maybe those girls are rarer and I haven't run across many."

Tori didn't think that was it. "Or maybe you don't *talk* to the girls you...spend time with." That was a nice way to put the fact that she was pretty sure Josh was an obvious playboy. Which had always made him sending him back to her hotel alone last year strange. And now he didn't seem in any hurry to get up to her bedroom either. "Maybe you just don't know what things they can and can't do outside of the bedroom."

He seemed to think about that and then nodded, slower this time. "That might also be it." He paused. "Or maybe it's just that I hadn't met *you* yet."

She laughed, even as her heart flipped. "You and that sweet talk."

That he had yet to act on. Now that she thought about it, Tori wondered if she should be concerned. Maybe he couldn't stop thinking about how unsexy her job was or how she was barely pulling off the heels and lipstick tonight or how she'd hidden wild animals in her closet as a kid. The gross, awkward, odd stuff might be finally adding up.

Josh nodded. "Yeah, let's call it sweet talk."

"What else would we call it?" she asked.

"A genetic disposition to fall head over heels ridiculously fast."

This time when her heart flipped, she wasn't sure it went back to its usual position. It felt bigger in her chest. He seemed so sincere. Almost self-deprecating about it. As if he thought that was what was happening, whether he liked it or not. Whether *she* liked it or not. She didn't actually think that Josh was head over heels for her, but she liked the idea that he *liked* her a lot. And thought of all these things about her were fucking loveable as hell. To use his words.

Yeah, she liked that a lot.

"Does this mean we can go inside and get naked now?" she asked. Because she also really liked kissing him. And she really wanted to get naked with him. Before she said anything else about who she was that might make him wonder what the hell he was doing with her.

He gave a half groan, half laugh. "Soon. I have one more thing I want to ask you about."

"Okay." She wiggled on his lap, on purpose this time, loving the way his fingers curled into her hips as if he couldn't take it.

"You and Andrew," Josh said.

Tori tipped her head. "What about me and Andrew?"

"Paisley thinks that you make him homesick."

Tori smiled softly at that. "Oh. That's kind of nice."

"Is it?"

"Isn't it?" she asked. "It's nice to think that he thinks of home fondly and that I remind him of it and his feelings for it."

Josh shook his head. "I think she means that you make him

want something that maybe he didn't know, or remember, that he wanted."

Tori frowned. "I really don't think Andrew wants to go back home. Not for good. He loves New Orleans and his new job."

"Right. Not the job, really."

"Then what?"

He looked at her as if she was being slow.

She frowned. "*What*?"

"You, Tori. She thinks that you're making him want *you*."

Tori rolled her eyes. "Well, that's ridiculous and insecure of her."

"You sure?"

"Of course."

He took a breath. "I saw you two talking in the hallway alone. It looked kind of...emotional."

"You saw me and Andrew?" Tori asked.

"Yeah."

"And you didn't interrupt?"

"I have no right to interrupt," he said. "He's your best friend. You're here for his wedding. You have a history with him. I'm...new."

He was. New. Exciting. Fun. Different. Tori gave him a smile and took his face between her hands. "All the more reason for you to believe me when I say that Andrew was just trying to let me down easy."

"Let you down?"

"He was starting to believe some of the stuff Paisley is worried about. About me wanting him and trying to break them up," Tori said. "He wanted me to know that he cares about me but not *that way*."

"So he believed the kiss too?" Josh asked.

She shrugged. "I don't think he did at first, but then Paisley wouldn't shut up about it. So he felt the need to talk to me about it."

"What did he say?"

"That the kiss was amazing and that he always thought he wanted to end up with a girl like me—not me, of course, but someone *like* me. Someone from back home. He'd always envisioned himself living and working in Iowa. But then Paisley came along and changed everything."

Josh was frowning up at her now. "He said the kiss was amazing?"

"Yeah." She had to admit, even if she hadn't meant to kiss *him*, it was always nice to be told you were a good kisser.

"And he said he'd always wanted to end up with a girl like you, but not you?"

"Well, he didn't say not me. That was implied."

"So he said he'd always thought he wanted to end up with a girl like you. Period. He didn't qualify it?"

Tori gave Josh a look. "He didn't mean me."

"You're sure?"

"Josh, Andrew has had every opportunity to be with me if he wanted to be. And he's never said or done anything about it."

"He's had every opportunity? What's that mean?"

She winced. She hadn't really wanted to confess all of this. But hey, Josh knew about her crazy menagerie and that everyone at the wedding disliked her, and he was still here.

"Well, we've been friends forever. Spent a lot of time alone. But the only kiss was one New Year's Eve."

"And one in eighth grade," Josh said.

"You've been keeping track." She felt a little flutter in her stomach.

He gave her a single nod.

"Well, then..." She blushed in spite of herself. "I wrote him a letter when we graduated, basically suggesting that if we both were still single when we turned thirty, we should just get married to each other."

Tori felt Josh's fingers dig into her hips again, a little firmer this time. "What did he say?"

"He...let me down easy that time too. Said that our friendship meant a lot to him and he wanted to be my friend forever, and that he knew he'd end up with someone like me but he didn't think *we* should get married."

"So you don't think he could have feelings for you now?" Josh asked.

She laughed. "No. Not only has he never before, but clearly he's actually ended up with someone very *not* like me."

Josh didn't look convinced. "I talked to Paisley while you were talking to Andrew. You should be aware that she thinks Andrew is getting nervous about how different his life is going to be now and that you represent...comfort and home."

Tori thought about that. "Well, that makes sense. But he's approaching the biggest day of his life. It's natural to think about all of that. It doesn't mean anything."

"Or maybe the kiss at the bar made him realize he's attracted to you after all and it's got him thinking," Josh said.

For a second, she flashed back to the bar and the kiss with Andrew. He had kissed her back. And he'd known who she was. Yes, she'd surprised him with the kiss, and possibly his reaction could be chalked up to instinct. When someone kissed you, you just automatically kissed back. But she immediately knew that wasn't right. If someone suddenly kissed her without her expecting it, she was certain her instinct would be to push them away. She frowned. "Well, maybe there was a second or two where he realized I'm not gross or something," she said.

Josh gave a soft chuckle.

"But tonight in the hallway was the first time I've even seen him since then. He hasn't been looking for me."

"How do you know he wasn't looking for you?"

"Not one single text asking where I was."

"Maybe Paisley had him busy so he *wouldn't* text you."

"Okay, maybe. But honestly, Josh, maybe it's cold feet, maybe he's feeling nostalgic, maybe he's contemplating everything. He *should* do that. He should walk down that aisle on Saturday, totally sure that's what he wants to do."

"But you don't think he should."

Tori hesitated. She didn't. Paisley was very different from the woman Tori had always pictured Andrew with. New Orleans was a very different place from where Tori had always pictured Andrew practicing law. "That's his decision to make."

"You're not going to try to break them up?"

She took a deep breath. "You're going to help me *not* do that." She smiled. "You're going to distract me and, if necessary, remind me that he's an intelligent guy and that he needs to make this decision."

Josh squeezed her hips. "I'm very happy to keep doing that. As long as you think that's the right way to handle this."

"Definitely. Not only do I need someone to help me keep my head on straight, I also need to prove that the kiss with Andrew was a mistake, and I have to salvage my pride. Show everyone that someone *does* want to kiss my socks off."

"I want to kiss other things off of you too," Josh said, his voice rough. He leaned in and captured her lips.

Yes. This. Lots and lots of this. Tori leaned into the kiss, sliding her hands into his hair and wiggling again. Josh really seemed to want her. Surely she could get him out of these clothes tonight. He was staying here. With her. He couldn't send her back to her room alone.

But she was really going to need him to take the lead here. She was hardly a seductress. She'd lost her virginity to Chad Winer. Yes, a guy whose last name sounded like *whiner*. But he'd done all the work there. She'd slept with a guy in college twice. Again, he'd come on to her. In the biology lab. He'd found her dissection of the fetal pig hot. Which, of course, should have been a red flag. She was proud of her work and loved guys who loved animals. But dissection probably shouldn't be hot on any level. And then there'd been Anthony. He'd been in her class in vet school. And, come to think of it, she'd decided to sleep with him when his hands had been bloody from operating on a dog that had been hit by a car. But that wasn't creepy. That had been because he'd been confidently and competently saving the life of an animal. Of course that was hot. Made sense to her anyway. So she'd slept with him on and off for about a semester.

But it had been a very, very, *very* long time since that semester. And she hadn't even thought of getting naked with another guy since she'd met Josh. A year ago. Without knowing if she'd ever seen him again. Just meeting him and hanging out at a bar for a few hours and a couple of kisses, and he'd ruined her for other men.

Damn. Maybe she *shouldn't* take him up to her room tonight.

But then he tipped his head, deepened the kiss, pressed her down against his hard cock while sliding a hand up her side to cup her breast and brush his thumb over her nipple.

Oh, she was definitely taking him up to her room tonight.

In fact, right now would be perfect.

Tori tore her mouth away and said, "Room 206."

He sucked in a breath. "Yeah."

She scrambled off his lap, hoping that what she lacked in grace she could make up for with eagerness. Josh caught her from tripping with both hands on her waist, then tucked her against his side and started for the door as if keeping her on her heels was just part of his job here.

Instead of the doors back into the ballroom, Tori tried to tug him across the patio to a side door that she knew would let him in on the other side of the staircase. They could get up to the upper floors without having to go through the ballroom.

But Josh wouldn't let her lead.

"Come on. Through here," he said.

"But we can bypass all of this," she protested.

"Why would I want to do that? We want everyone to know that I'm here...and why, right?"

Well...that wasn't a bad point. But the chances of being waylaid were, of course, greater if they were wading through people.

"We can socialize tomorrow," she said. "In fact, it will be required."

His big hand slid down to cup her butt and he said against her temple, "Yeah, but I want everyone to know where I'm spending the night."

She swallowed. "Won't they just assume?"

"I want them to be sure."

He pulled her to the door and swept it open before she could protest further. Okay, fine, but these people didn't really like her anyway, so she didn't have to be overly friendly.

She'd forgotten who she was with though. And it only took about one minute back in the ballroom for her to remember. As much as she loved animals and couldn't walk past one without stopping, Josh loved people. He grinned and said hello to several people standing just inside the doors. He clapped one man on his back as if they were long-lost friends. He tipped his head with his Southern-boy grin to several ladies old enough they could have been his mother. He stuck his hand out to one of the groomsmen with a, "Hey, man," and gave Courtney, one of the bridesmaids, a big wink when she caught his eye from where she was dancing with another of the groomsmen.

"Do you *know* people here?" Tori asked, almost not noticing that Josh had stopped on the dance floor and had turned to pull her into his arms.

"Not really. But they all know who I am," he told her with a conspiratorial smile.

She realized that they were dancing. She narrowed her eyes. "You intended to stop in here to dance."

"I did."

"But...bedroom," she said. Dammit, maybe he really didn't want to go up.

"You need to be here in the middle of everything, showing everyone that you're completely comfortable and happy with everything as it is."

He had a point. To convince Paisley that Tori was *not* trying to ruin her wedding, Tori needed to play the part of a happy bridesmaid.

But...Josh and the bedroom...

"I'll dance for a while if you promise to eventually throw me over your shoulder like you did earlier today and carry me up to bed," she said.

Josh tripped over his next step and came to a complete stop, gripping her tightly.

"I can probably handle that," he said gruffly.

She smiled at him. "Okay, then."

It maybe wasn't a sign of maturity and self-confidence, but the idea of having Josh sweep her out of this room, knowing they were headed upstairs, because he just *had* to have her, while everyone looked on, was appealing.

And yeah, she was glad her parents weren't here to see it. She also kind of hoped Andrew's parents wouldn't tell them. She was twenty-eight and her parents didn't get a vote in who she spent her nights with, of course. Still, she wasn't a scene-causer. Not these kinds of scenes, anyway. There was that one time that she'd thrown a fit about her biology teacher wanting to feed mice to a snake in class. Yes, she'd let the mice loose, but she'd also let the snake loose. And of course the time she'd punched the Nelson boys over those kittens. And she could never forget her dad's birthday when she was ten, or her grand gesture to Marcus Turner on Valentine's Day her freshman year. But generally she didn't stir things up and almost never in any kind of human relationship.

Josh wanted to make her the center of attention? She wasn't sure how she felt about that. But she let him lead her around the dance floor. In her bright red, sparkly dress.

Hey...he could dance? "You dance," she said out loud. Stupidly.

His lips quirked. "I do."

She understood immediately. "Because girls like guys who can dance."

"Same reason I know how to cook," he agreed, spinning her before pulling her back against his chest.

"You do?"

"I don't have to do it often at all. Between Ellie, Cora, and Kennedy, we're all very well fed, but I can. And do...when the occasion calls for it."

"You mean when it will help you get a woman out of her panties faster," Tori said.

He laughed. "Um... yeah."

"Kennedy cooks?" Tori asked. His sister hadn't really struck her as domestic in any way, though she'd only been around the other woman for a few short minutes.

"She's amazing. She learned from Ellie. I think Ellie and Cora are hoping she'll take over the bar, or at least the kitchen."

"Why do you call your grandma Ellie?" Tori asked.

"Because she's one of three grandmas I've got in Autre," he said with a crooked smile. "Growing up, there were four women I considered grandmas. Oh, and there was a great-grandma. It was too confusing to call them all grandma and Ellie isn't really a 'granny' or a 'nanna' so she was always just Ellie."

Tori nodded, loving the feel of just relaxing and letting Josh lead her around the floor. "You don't think Kennedy wants to take over the business?"

Josh laughed.

"What?"

"Your mind works fast and constantly, doesn't it?"

Tori grimaced. "Yeah. Sorry."

"Don't be. I also love that you went right past the part about me getting women out of their panties."

Tori shrugged. "Well, it's pretty obvious that I'm not the first girl to develop a crush on you across a bar."

Josh's eyes softened. "You have a crush on me?"

She laughed. "You didn't know?"

He smiled. "I guess it's just a...sweet...word. Yes, I've had hookups, one-night stands, that kind of stuff. But I've never had...this."

She looked up at him. "This? What is this?"

"I'm not entirely sure." He leaned in, brushing his lips over hers. "But I really like it."

She did too. She put her mouth against his ear. "I like dancing with you, but I liked sitting on your lap even more. And I'd like to do it without clothes on."

He coughed and missed a step in the dance. Tori grinned to herself.

"Are you flirting with me, Ms. Kramer?" he asked.

"I'm not sure. I don't really do that. Am I?"

"I think you are."

"And is it working?"

"You can't tell?"

She shrugged. "You don't have a tail to wag and you haven't butted your head against me. That's how the creatures I spend most of my time with tell me they like me."

He pressed his palm against her lower back, bringing her against his hot, hard body. "I could say something here about your butt and my *head*, but I'm just going to say that there are definitely ways to tell if I like you and I promise, the main one is on full display."

She laughed. "This might require closer examination."

"Well, here's one for instance." He suddenly stopped—in the middle of the dance floor of course—cupped her face, and kissed her. Because he was, obviously, all about the full displays.

And he *kissed* her.

Full, deep, tongue, the whole thing. She was on tiptoe, his hands were in her hair, their bodies were plastered against one another, and there could be no doubt in anyone's mind that this was real. *This* was the kiss she'd been going for the other night at Bourbon O.

After a few long, delicious moments, Josh pulled back, looked down at her, gave her a little wink, then fulfilled his promise by bending and lifting her over his shoulder before striding toward the grand staircase in the front of the mansion that was line-of-sight for eighty percent of the people at the party.

8

They'd just gotten to the base of the staircase when Josh heard, "Hey! Hang on!"

He turned, swinging Tori away from whoever was coming after them.

Andrew.

Of course it was. Well, fuck.

He had Paisley in tow though. The bride didn't look especially pleased, but it was hard to tell what she was upset about exactly.

Josh was making a spectacle. He knew that. It was very intentional. Paisley seemed to be the type to be annoyed by a guy carrying a girl up to bed at her big party. Not so much because it was a tad risqué, but more because it was taking attention away from Paisley. There was an equal chance, however, that she was pissed that Andrew was coming after Tori with clear concern and curiosity.

"Can I help you?" Josh asked Andrew.

"Tori?" Andrew was frowning at Josh, but not addressing him directly. "You okay?"

Josh pivoted sideways so that Tori could look at Andrew. She giggled. "I'm very okay."

"I told you, this is her *date*," Paisley said, grabbing Andrew's sleeve. "This is the guy she was supposed to meet last night."

"Yeah, okay." Andrew scowled at Josh. "This is just...not Tori's style."

"What do you think? He's going to kidnap her in front of all of these people?" Paisley asked crossly.

"Maybe if no one stops them and asks some questions," Andrew replied.

"Not being kidnapped," Tori said. "Everything is good."

"There, see? Everything is good," Paisley said, tugging on Andrew's sleeve.

"I've just never seen you like this," Andrew told Tori.

"Upside down?" Tori asked.

Josh was unable to contain his smile.

"Like *this*. With a guy," Andrew said.

"Maybe the guys she normally hangs out with aren't strong enough," Josh suggested.

"Strong enough?" Andrew repeated with a frown.

"To throw her over their shoulders." Josh put his hand on Tori's ass. Possessively. "Which is too bad. Because this gets her really hot."

He heard Tori gasp softly and she smacked his butt. He laughed.

Andrew seemed to not know what to say to all of this. "Can you...put her down? Please? So I can talk to her?"

"I'm not sure she's in the mood to talk right now," Josh said. In fact, Tori had been trying to drag him upstairs for the past hour or so for some definite *not talking.*

Andrew scowled and Josh realized that he really liked annoying this guy. He'd never been possessive of a woman before, but hell, it fell in with everything else he'd been feeling for the first time with Tori. This was the kind of cause-a-stir-and-make-an-ass-of-yourself stuff his family specialized in.

"Tori," Andrew said. "Please."

Josh heard Tori sigh and knew she was about to capitulate.

"Tomorrow would be better," Josh said, taking a step closer to the staircase.

Andrew folded his arms. "Actually, tomorrow is one of the things we need to talk about."

Paisley caught Josh's eye. She gave him a look that clearly said *fix this.*

What *this* was exactly, Josh wasn't certain. But yeah, okay, he'd do what he could. He opened his mouth to tell Andrew that he was heading upstairs right now and he could just talk to Tori tomorrow, but Tori spoke first.

"Yeah, okay." Tori wiggled. "We can talk for a minute."

Well, dammit.

Josh realized his desire to make a scene had been a miscalculation. If he'd just taken Tori's hand and headed upstairs...or if he'd let her tug him through the side door...they could be naked right now and she'd be saying his name with that breathless moan that made him ache. But he'd really wanted to make a production of this. He figured she would understand the gesture. She'd collected flies and bugs in order to defend frogs, for God's sake. She'd punched two guys for even talking about dumping kittens. She'd covered a girl's prom dress in cow shit. She knew that when you felt strongly about something, you were willing to get a little extreme. Tori deserved to have someone making a scene over her.

Reluctantly, Josh set her back on her feet and held onto her while she got her bearings. Then he tucked a stray strand of hair behind her ear and gave her a smile. "One minute," he told her huskily.

He knew he was doing a hell of a job acting like a guy who was crazy about her. It scared him how easy it was. And how none of it felt like an act. At all.

Andrew was still scowling when Tori turned to face him.

"What's up?" she asked.

"Just making sure this isn't...Valentine's Day 2006," Andrew said.

Josh glanced at Tori and saw her wince. "Wha—" he started.

"No. It's not that." Tori looked up at Josh. "At least, not really."

"It's got some similarities," Andrew said.

It was clear that he and Tori were talking about a shared memory and that Andrew was making a point that was supposed to be just between them.

Josh didn't like that.

"Everything is fine," Josh told Andrew. Firmly.

"It's part of my job to check up on her," Andrew told him, clearly unaffected by Josh's tone. "Tori's not really the red dress and champagne kind of girl."

Josh scowled at him and then glanced at Tori again. She was chewing on her bottom lip.

"She looks fucking amazing in red and champagne tastes great on her," Josh told Andrew. He met the other man's eyes directly. *Yeah, I tasted the champagne when I was tongue-fucking her mouth. Deal with it.* "Everything is fine," he repeated.

"Like I said, I just have to check," Andrew told him.

"I'm okay, Andrew," Tori told him, her voice softer. "But thank you."

Thank you? For interrupting Josh carrying her up to bed? That was not a "thank you" situation.

"I—" Josh started.

"What's going on tomorrow?" Tori asked.

"The tour got cancelled," Andrew said. "Something wrong with one of their buses, I guess. Anyway, the plan has changed. We're going golfing. Do you want to come along?"

Josh almost laughed at the obvious grimace that crossed Tori's face before she covered it. "Um...sure."

She clearly didn't like golf. By the way, shouldn't Andrew know that? But why wasn't she just saying no?

"No, no. I told you she should come to the bridesmaids' brunch," Paisley inserted. "We're meeting with the makeup artist afterward."

"The makeup artist?" Tori asked.

"The woman who will be doing everyone's makeup for the wedding," Paisley said. "She wants to meet everyone to get an idea of coloring and what she'll be doing on Saturday."

"Oh."

Tori didn't grimace this time, but Josh could tell that the idea of a makeup artist was even less appealing than the idea of golfing.

"We talked about this," Andrew told Paisley with a frown. "Tori is here as a part of the wedding for *me*. She doesn't even know the other girls. She can golf with me and my parents and the guys."

"But she's still a *bridesmaid,* Andrew," Paisley said, clearly through gritted teeth.

"I can't believe we can't get this tour rescheduled," Andrew groused.

"I asked, but it's too late," Paisley said, lifting a shoulder. "There wasn't room for such a big group."

"What tour?" Josh finally asked.

"We were going to take the out-of-towners on a New Orleans city tour," Andrew said.

Josh frowned. "One of those big buses that drives around the city to all the famous spots and gives you the history?"

"Yeah. We thought that would be fun for everyone who hasn't been here before," Andrew said.

"But it wasn't really ideal anyway," Paisley said quickly. "It would take them all away from the plantation *all day* and they wouldn't have made it back in time for dinner. And Tori would have missed the makeup consultation," she added with a tight smile at Tori.

Josh was pretty sure Paisley cared less about Tori's makeup and more about her being off with Andrew all day long where Paisley couldn't keep an eye on them. For a moment, he wondered if Paisley would go so far as to cancel the tour and lie about the broken-down bus. Then he realized that yes, she definitely would.

Suddenly Josh had an idea. He didn't really care if it made Paisley happy, but it was the perfect compromise, really. It would get Tori away from makeup lessons and golf, but it would also ensure that Paisley's homesick fiancé had a chaperone while he was spending the day with the reluctant bridesmaid who made him homesick.

"I'll do the tour."

The three of them all turned to look at him at once.

"What?" Andrew asked.

"You would do that?" Tori asked at the same time.

Josh focused on her. "Of course I would."

"What do you mean you'll do the tour?" Andrew asked again.

"I'll take y'all around the city," Josh said. "I can tell you all kinds of stuff. Probably stuff you wouldn't hear on a regular old tour. We can even make a couple of extra stops. We'll get dinner at Trahan's."

"You're going to load us all up in the back of your truck?" Andrew asked dryly.

Josh gave him a big grin. He got it. This meant that *he'd* be there all day, with Tori, and Andrew didn't really like that idea, obviously. "I have a bus, man. And a driver who knows his way around this city in his sleep."

"Leo would drive us around?" Tori asked. "And you'd use one of *your* buses? What about the swamp boat tours?"

"We'll be fine," he told her. "This will be fun. No problem."

And the bright smile Tori gave him made this all worth any shit he was going to get from Sawyer about leaving them short by one bus driver.

"Well, that's very...nice," Paisley said hesitantly. But she did look like she'd relaxed a little.

Yeah, she could rest assured that with Josh around, nothing would be happening between Tori and Andrew. But it really was about making Tori happy. Josh would just have to have Ellie explain to Sawyer why this was important. His grandma would love this.

"It'll be fun," Josh said. "And then, afterward, maybe Tori and I will head down to Autre."

Paisley's eyes went wide. "Excuse me?"

He nodded. "I never get to see her and I want her to get to know my family better. So I'm thinking we should spend Friday down there."

"You're going to introduce her to your family?" Andrew asked, clearly surprised.

Josh gave him a smile he knew was very smug. "Oh, she's already met them. But they can't wait to spend more time with her." All true. Very true. He loved that.

"You've met his family?" Andrew asked Tori.

He thought Josh was *lying* about it? Asshole.

"I have. They're wonderful," Tori told him. Then she smiled up at Josh.

And Josh knew that was completely true as well. Because Tori didn't lie. She might bite her tongue. She might not always say everything she thought or felt. But when she did, she didn't lie.

Man, he really liked her.

"But, she has to be back by Friday night. She has to get her hair and makeup done early Saturday morning," Paisley said.

Josh couldn't help but notice Tori's little shudder. Josh put his arm around her, pulling her up against his side. "We'll figure it out."

"You mean, 'I'll be sure she's back in time,'" Paisley told him with narrowed eyes.

Josh nodded. "Or something."

"Josh—"

"It will be fine," Tori said quickly. "Josh and I understand that this is your big day."

Paisley sniffed, in the snootiest way Josh had maybe ever heard.

"Fine," she finally conceded.

Clearly Tori being out of the way and occupied by Josh rather than Andrew was more important to Paisley than Tori having the perfect hairdo.

"And now, if you'll excuse us," Josh said, looking directly at Andrew. "I'm going to take my date upstairs."

Andrew's jaw tightened and he said nothing.

"Of course. We're so sorry for interrupting," Paisley said. She grabbed Andrew's arm again.

"We'll want to leave early tomorrow," Andrew said, not moved by his tiny fiancée.

"Absolutely," Josh said. "I'm used to late nights followed by early mornings." He bartended in the Quarter a couple of nights a week and was up with chores for the tour company every day. But he was very happy to let Andrew assume he meant those nights went late because of women.

Sometimes they did. But he never spent the night with women. They were almost always tourists or women he knew from the bars in New Orleans. They weren't spend-the-night-and-have-breakfast-with-me women.

He really wanted to have breakfast with Tori. Did she like grits? Because sweet grits were one of his favorite things in the morning and he'd love to make them for her. Of course, he was certain shower sex with Victoria Kramer would easily knock the grits out of the top spot on his list of favorite morning things.

"You'll join us for breakfast?" Andrew asked, directing the question to Tori.

She wiggled, itching a spot on her rib cage and then one on her thigh. "Um," was all she said.

Fuck Andrew if he thought his breakfast was better than whatever Josh was going to be offering her when the sun came up.

"I'll take care of Tori," Josh said, squeezing her waist. "Just meet us out front at nine."

Andrew's eyes narrowed and he looked from Tori to Josh and back. "There will be blueberry muffins."

And fuck Andrew if he thought his blueberry muffins could top Josh's sweet grits.

"Well, you know I love blueberry muffins," Tori said with a little smile. Then she dug her fingernails into that apparently very itchy spot on her side.

Also fuck Andrew for knowing about her love for blueberry muffins. "I'll get you whatever you want," Josh told her.

He wasn't playing a part here. He really wanted to be the guy supplying Tori with breakfast food. That was crazy. He'd never cared a whit about what the women he spent time with ate for breakfast. But it worked into the whole scheme of him being Tori's completely enamored wedding date, so he didn't pull it back.

"I promise my grits are going to be the best thing you've ever put in your mouth in the morning," he told her.

Tori's eyes widened and Paisley actually made a little choking sound.

He didn't rush to amend that he really did mean grits. Besides, after they ate, they could work on some other great ways to start the day. Things that also included her mouth.

"How are you going to give her grits?" Andrew asked. "There's a cook here who is in charge of meals. Not sure she'd just let you take over the kitchen."

Josh gave him a slow grin. "When it comes to making Tori happy, there's no limit to what I can do."

That was a very Landry kind of thing to say. Ellie would be proud. She would also make the grits and send them up in a Thermos with Leo. Really, obtaining sweet grits was the least of Josh's challenges here.

"She really likes blueberry muffins," Andrew said.

Josh almost rolled his eyes. Were they really having a pissing contest over what Tori would be eating in the morning? Seemingly. But Josh knew that it was about more than that. This was about who knew her and who she'd rather have breakfast with.

"Blueberry muffins are great," Josh said easily. "But I'm winning her over to Southern ways, and grits are definitely a part of that."

"You're winning her over to Southern ways?" Andrew asked. "You sure about that?"

Josh looked down at Tori. She was staring at him and Andrew as if she had no idea what was going on or what to do.

"I'm giving it my best shot," Josh said, realizing it was true. He wanted her to love it here. And to stay.

Wow, that had gotten deep fast.

"Tori is an Iowa girl," Andrew said. "Mardi Gras is one

thing, but her home, her *animals*," he emphasized, as if Tori might have forgotten, "are in Iowa."

The animals. Those were always going to be the key to Tori's heart.

Fuck Andrew.

Josh opened his mouth to reply, but Tori spoke first.

"Josh has a river otter."

Pleasure rocked through him at Tori's response.

Andrew frowned. "What?"

Tori nodded. "Josh has a river otter. Gus. He lives by the dock. He's pretty cute."

"You'd leave your cows for a river otter?" Andrew asked. His scowl was deeper now.

And just like they hadn't really been talking about grits and muffins earlier, they weren't talking about otters and cows now.

"We have cows in Louisiana," Josh said. Anything Tori had in Iowa that she loved, he would get her here. He'd get her a dozen cows if that was what she wanted. And *that* was way crazier than wanting to make her grits.

But he didn't miss the way Tori's brow was now furrowed slightly. Dammit. Andrew had her thinking about her regular life and all the reasons she couldn't just pick up and move to Louisiana.

"You don't have *Tori's* cows in Louisiana," Andrew said, clearly feeling a little triumphant at the look on Tori's face.

He'd succeeded in, if not popping Tori's I-love-Louisiana bubble, at least making a small hole that could easily turn into a slow leak.

"My grandpa's best friend has a dog that thinks he's a duck."

Andrew, Tori, and Paisley all looked at him. Josh sighed. Okay, that sounded pretty desperate. But it was true. It was also true that he felt a little desperate to fight Tori's doubts about Louisiana.

He shrugged. "They found him as a puppy, apparently

abandoned, and took him home. There was a duck with babies that wandered around the property and the puppy started following along like one of the ducklings. He slept with them and the ducklings cuddled right up to him to keep warm. Now he's just one of the family."

Tori's big brown eyes were round and full of happiness, and Josh almost laughed at how much that pleased him.

"Really?"

Josh nodded. "I'll introduce you. The dog's name is Duck."

She laughed.

Andrew cleared his throat. "I'm just saying that Fiona and Travis and Bert would miss you."

Yeah, fuck Andrew for knowing the names of Tori's animals too. Okay, sure, Andrew *knew* her. He'd been involved in her life. Great. Josh got it. But that didn't mean anything.

Mostly because Andrew was getting *married* in two days to another woman.

Josh gave him a "fuck you" look and said, "Fiona, Travis, and Bert?"

"The fainting goat, the pig, and the alpaca," Andrew said smugly.

And Josh supposed Andrew had helped with naming one or all of them. Great. They were long-time friends. So what? Josh was the one taking her upstairs. Right now.

"Can't wait to hear all about them," Josh told Tori. And that was also true. He loved listening to her talk about animals. She lit up when she did, taking her beyond beautiful to downright gorgeous. It really got to him. That and her sweet, husky laugh, and the way she was so self-deprecating and yet passionate about the animals, and the fact that she had the biggest heart of any woman he'd been with. Plus a pair of pretty big balls. She'd take anyone on if an animal's well-being was at stake.

What would it be like to have all of that passion and love directed at *him*?

The thought seemed to come out of nowhere, but once it settled, he realized that...he could handle that.

He'd had girlfriends. He'd had women who he liked a lot and who liked him a lot. But he wasn't sure he'd ever had someone *passionate* about him. Maybe it wasn't just about finding someone to make an ass of himself over...maybe he wanted someone who would do the same for him.

He shook that thought off as he took Tori's hand. One thing at a fucking time. He needed to get her away from Andrew right now and get her mind off of Iowa and how crazy and out of the ordinary all of this was for her.

"We'll talk all about Fiona once I've given you another taste of goin' south." Yep that was absolutely supposed to sound dirty and judging by the looks on everyone's faces, he'd succeeded.

He turned Tori toward the staircase and she didn't stop him. Even Andrew, miraculously, kept his mouth shut.

But by the time they were standing outside room 206, Josh realized that he'd lost her. Or at least the mood. Well, fuck.

"Please, tell me I need to run my hands up under your skirt to find the key," he told her, trying to lighten things and get them back on hot, flirtatious ground.

Tori scratched at said skirt. "It's not locked."

He twisted the knob and pushed the door open. He wanted to throw her over his shoulder again, but somehow sensed that was the wrong move here.

Fucking Andrew.

Josh followed her into the room, noting the way she plucked the bodice of the dress away from her waist again and then reached inside the neckline to scratch.

"You okay?" he asked. He wasn't sure what to do here. That was new. He always knew what to do with women in bedrooms. He either kissed them and went from there. Or he moved the big heavy heirloom dresser from one side to the other. That was what happened when he was in Kennedy's bedroom. Other than her, he was never in a bedroom with a woman who he didn't want to kiss.

That definitely included Victoria Kramer. Yet, he held back. What the hell was going on?

"This dress is super itchy." She scratched her hip. "And I swear the underwire bra has dug down to my fifth rib. And I think I have scratches from the sequins."

"Yikes." She hadn't seemed uncomfortable in the dress when she'd been out on the patio with him. "Maybe you should take it off."

"Yeah, I probably should."

That didn't sound flirtatious or seductive though. "Want some help with that?" he asked, giving her one of his you-know-you-want-to-take-your-clothes-off grins. But it felt forced. And there was about six feet of distance between them.

All of this was very out of the ordinary for him.

"This dress was supposed to be strapless," she said.

He wasn't sure why that was important right now, but he said simply, "Oh?"

She chewed her bottom lip and nodded, watching him. "I wanted to get a strapless dress. I found a really gorgeous one that would have been perfect. But I couldn't wear it because I have tan lines."

She worked outside and he knew it got hot in the summer in Iowa. "That makes sense. You probably wear tanks and T-shirts, right?"

Tori shrugged. "I basically have a farmer's tan."

He grinned. "You're basically a farmer."

She actually smiled at that. "I mean, it's been winter in Iowa and hasn't been warm enough really for tanks yet, but I get pretty tan in the summer and the lines never fully fade, it seems."

He took a step forward. "Tori?"

"Yeah?"

"Why are you telling me this?"

She blew out a breath. "I guess Andrew just reminded me that I'm not really a strapless-dress-with-sequins kind of girl. I mean, I remembered that when I went to buy a dress for tonight, but I...forgot. With you. I didn't think about the tan lines. I didn't even feel the itching until we were standing by the stairs."

When fucking Andrew had stopped them.

"You were scratching at the dress when you walked into the ballroom," he said. It was just when Andrew was around, Josh realized. When Andrew was there, reminding her of who she was in Iowa. Or at least who *he* thought she was. Josh wanted Tori to realize that too.

"You noticed that?"

"Couldn't take my eyes off of you the second I saw you," he told her honestly.

She gave him a little smile. "I guess you distracted me from all of that."

That was a good thing. She was comfortable and not thinking about all of the little things like not being a sequins kind of girl when she was with him.

But she didn't look like she thought that was a good thing.

Josh shrugged, trying to act casual. "So, take the sequins off. I mean, naked is about as real-you as you can get, right?" But what he really felt was a bunch of emotions knotting up into a ball in his chest.

She nodded. "Yeah. Complete with tan lines and scratches and a rash."

"I don't care about any of that." God's honest truth right there. In fact, a little of him wanted to see all of those things. Because, for the first time maybe ever, he wanted the woman in the dress to have all of those imperfections, and to let him see them.

Yes, he wanted her. Yes, he found her gorgeous. But he was

used to women who did everything they could to look good and seductive and like hot-weekend-fling material. And he took them up on it. For sure. He wouldn't deny that. He was a breast man. And a leg man. And an ass man. And a bright red lipstick man. He loved it all. But this was more than that.

Tori had told him about her animals and the things that made her feel a little weird. She'd adorably stumbled on her high heels and gotten a rash from the sequins in her dress. She'd lit up when she realized he could dance, which told him she liked to dance and didn't do it often. She'd been clearly delighted when he'd thrown her over his shoulder, which told him guys didn't make a big deal about her or get a little caveman with her...but that she also liked when they did.

She'd let him see little pieces of who she really was. She wasn't here for hot sex with a Louisiana boy so she could go home and tell her girlfriends about her wild New Orleans weekend. Hell, she didn't even really want to be here. Not at the plantation and the wedding, anyway. She was in no way at her best or her most confident and yet, he was getting to see it all.

He liked her more and more every minute they were together and yeah, he wanted to see her tan lines. So fucking much.

"If I take this dress off," she said after a long moment. "I'll be naked."

"Exactly."

"In a *plantation*. In Louisiana. With a hot bartender who I met at Mardi Gras and barely know."

All of those were reasons *to* get naked for the women he usually hooked up with. With Tori, of course, they were reasons she was hesitating. He was going to have to accept that this girl was different from all others in nearly every way.

"So you're saying that there are a lot of things going on here, besides the dress, that are not your usual style," he said.

She nodded. "Exactly."

"And Andrew reminded you of all of that."

She nodded again. "That's kind of his job—part of it, anyway—as my best friend. He reminds me when I need to... dial things back."

Fucking Andrew. He really didn't like that guy. "You need reminded of that?"

"Not as much as I did growing up," she said. "I tended toward things like punching guys in the face and smearing cow shit on girls' dresses. Remember?"

He couldn't help his grin. "I remember. But Andrew didn't approve of those things?"

She shrugged. "He agreed with my feelings about those things and understood why I did them. But those...tendencies... got me into trouble too. I mean, I saved the kittens and got back at her about her dog, but I also had to serve detention at school for the fight in the parking lot and I had to pay for the prom dress."

Josh scowled at that. "They punished you for that stuff? Your parents went along with it?"

"My dad grounded me in addition to the detention, and he was the one who offered to have me pay for the dress."

Wow. Josh stared at her. Okay, he got it. Kind of. People couldn't go around hitting other people and ruining their stuff just because they disagreed with them. But someone should have been on Tori's side. Josh knew he had an entire family, half a town really, that would have had his back.

Josh tried to quell the emotions rolling through him. "So Andrew was the one who talked you out of doing stuff like that?"

She nodded. "When he had a chance. Or he played the part of buffer if it happened before he could talk me out of it. He'd explain my views to people or tell them it wasn't a big deal or at least reassure me that I was justified or whatever."

Dammit. Josh blew out a breath. Fucking Andrew. He'd

been the one, maybe the only one, to have Tori's back. He couldn't totally hate the guy, knowing that.

Well, okay then. "So, he was trying to talk you out of being carried upstairs to bed by a guy you barely know."

She didn't agree as quickly now. "He was just...making sure I knew what I was doing and that I was okay with...any consequences."

"Consequences?" Josh asked.

"He's the one who gives me the worst-case scenario over anything I'm considering."

Josh scowled. "What's the worst-case scenario here?"

"My parents finding out from Andrew's parents. Paisley being mad that we'd caused a scene. A broken heart after our fling is over." She lifted a shoulder. "Stuff like that."

Josh ran a hand through his hair. "And he was trying to kill the mood." That he knew for sure. Andrew might be getting married in a couple of days, but he did not like seeing Tori with another guy. There might be all kinds of reasons behind that, and maybe some were about friendship and protecting her, but Josh was a guy. He knew guys. Lots of them. Andrew's motivations were not purely altruistic. Or platonic.

"He was maybe trying to kill the mood too," Tori said slowly. "Just to be sure I had a chance to think about everything."

Right. Great. Okay, well... "Then I'll sleep on the floor tonight."

Her eyes widened. "No. Ugh." She looked around the room. "No. You can't sleep on the floor."

"Well, *you're* not sleeping on the floor." No way in hell was he putting her on the floor because she'd changed her mind about what was going on here tonight.

She looked back at him, her expression sad and resigned. "I'm so sorry."

"For?"

"Being a cock tease."

He snorted out a laugh. "You're not a cock tease, Tori."

"I am. I gave you every reason to think that you were getting laid tonight." She stepped forward. "*I* was absolutely convinced you were getting laid tonight."

He reached out and took her hand, tugging her close. "You asked me to come to this plantation and be your date for the wedding. That's all you asked me to do. Everything else is just extra."

"Me eating crawfish pie with your grandma? You saving me from golf tomorrow by arranging the city tour?"

He grinned. "Extra. Like a great garnish on the side of a mojito." He loved that she'd sat at Ellie's bar and had her first taste of crawfish pie in the shack across the road that felt like a second home to him.

She laughed. "Playing tour guide tomorrow will be like a sprig of mint and a lime slice?"

It would be. "You do know what I do for a living, right?"

"You charm people into falling in love with Louisiana."

Her expression and tone of voice were full of affection, and the warmth of it was like a shot of whiskey. The really good stuff.

"That's right. And I love it," he said, his voice inexplicably husky. "I love people. I love meeting new people and showing off New Orleans and my home state and our traditions and history. Tomorrow will be fun. And saving people from golf is a truly noble pursuit."

She looked up at him from beneath her eyelashes. A classic seductive move. That Josh knew was completely an accident from Tori.

"I don't feel the itchiness anymore," she said quietly.

So she wasn't uncomfortable when she was around him. That was really good to know.

He leaned in, kissed her on the nose, and said, "I'm gonna

give you a little time and space. I'll run down to my truck and get my bag. Why don't you put your pajamas on, get under the covers, and...we'll figure the rest out when I get back up here."

She thought about that and finally nodded. "Okay."

He let her go and turned for the door. He needed some air. That was a great idea. Air and space. Because something really crazy was going on.

He suddenly didn't want to fuck Victoria Kramer.

But he did want to sleep with her.

Just sleep. Cuddled up. Spooning. With pajamas on.

What the fuck was *that*?

9

Tori did exactly as he'd suggested. She got out of the scratchy dress, examined the abrasions left behind, studied her tan lines, brushed her teeth, and got under the covers.

The one hiccup was the putting-on-her-pajamas thing.

Because she typically slept naked.

So she was now wearing a tank top and panties and wondering what she was going to do with Josh. Not specifically in bed and without pajamas—though that too—but with him in general.

Because she was pretty sure she was falling for him.

Of course she was.

She wasn't good at human relationships. When she did try to have them, she went overboard. So, of course she'd be falling for the guy who was here *pretending* to be her boyfriend.

Just like that stupid red, sparkly dress, she'd taken something basically simple—go buy a cocktail dress for Andrew's party—and turned it into something awkward—a cherry red look-at-me number that upstaged the bride.

And then it had scratched the hell out of her and been uncomfortable all night.

Typical.

Just like Valentine's Day 2006.

Andrew's reminder had come just in time.

She wasn't this girl. She didn't wear sequins and heels. She didn't dance in ballrooms in one-hundred-and-seventy-five-year-old mansions on plantations in Louisiana. She didn't even drink champagne. She definitely didn't have relationships with guys who lived over a thousand miles from Elton, Iowa.

She did, however, apparently, fall for guys that gave her a few grins and said a few sweet things and introduced her to his grandmother.

Of course, that introduction had been an accident.

Yet, here she was blowing it all out of proportion.

With a loud, heartfelt groan, Tori pulled her pillow over her face. Dammit.

She'd gotten caught up. Just like last time with Josh. Bourbon Street during Mardi Gras was another world. So was the Buckworth Plantation. So was a ballroom full of tuxedos and evening gowns and a string quartet. None of this was anything like her real life back home.

And that definitely included Josh.

Even if he wasn't faking one hundred percent of this—because Lord knew that their chemistry was real and he did seem to be sincerely fond of her—the rest of everything they were doing was happening in a setting and amid a bunch of circumstances that were not real life for either of them.

She could not be falling for him. That was ridiculous. Well, not *ridiculous*. It was quite easy to fall for a guy like Josh Landry. He was the quintessential vacation fling. But this was all like a dream. A fantasy. And it couldn't last. She couldn't get hooked on things like being twirled around a ballroom or being thrown over a guy's shoulder.

She was going to go home to her cows, where she wore jeans and maybe two-stepped around the bar down by the highway once in a while. Where girls and guys met—if they hadn't known each other since first grade—went out to dinner and movies and to ballgames and slowly spent more and more time together until one of them asked the other to move in and then eventually announced they were getting married. It was just natural and low-key and predictable. There was no pomp and circumstance. No big surprises. No running through the airport to stop a plane just in time to declare eternal love. People didn't really do that stuff. Grand gestures were generally awkward in the real world. Even on Valentine's Day. Even when the girl was just a freshman in high school and the whole thing was really just sweet and innocent.

Tori groaned louder into her pillow. The embarrassment of that day was still acute now when she thought about it.

She couldn't fall for the grand gestures and being swept off her feet—literally.

Josh really could ruin her for other men. And not just for sex, but for real courtship.

Being with Josh was fun. It made her breathless. It made her heart pound. It made her laugh and feel sexy and feel like her quirks were endearing rather than weird. It had been full of surprises.

That wasn't how real life went.

The two most important men in her life, her father and

Andrew, had taught her that declaring her feelings and making grand statements, not to mention gestures, was generally frowned upon. Andrew had always pulled her back in an effort to protect her. Her father had always discouraged it to avoid embarrassment.

There was a soft knock at the door just before Josh cracked it open. "You decent?"

"Yep." Well, she was covered up anyway.

"Damn." He gave her a grin as he came into the room with a duffel thrown over his shoulder.

He'd stalled. There was no way going to his truck to grab his bag had taken this long. The fact that he realized she needed some extra time made her just like him even more. Crap.

"So, I was thinking," she said, propping up on her elbows, the comforter pulled up to her chin. "We could still share the bed. Even if we're not naked."

She was such an idiot. She'd been talking about having sex with him all night. She'd tried to drag him upstairs. If he hadn't stopped to dance with her, they could be well into round two by now. Or three. Round one probably wouldn't take long. She wanted him. She knew he wanted her. Their chemistry was explosive. A first hard and fast, take-the-edge-off, up-against-the-wall screw would have been just fine with her.

She blew out a breath. If she wasn't going to sleep with him, she had to stop thinking about sleeping with him.

"Yeah, we could do that," he agreed.

"Great. I think that will be...good." It wouldn't be good. It would be torture. She'd probably barely sleep. Josh Landry, the guy she'd been thinking about for almost a year, was going to be lying next to her. In a bed.

"Yep. That will be...good." He glanced toward the bathroom. "I'll just go brush my teeth. I'll be back."

"Okay." She gave him a bright, everything-is-great smile.

The smile died the second the bathroom door shut behind Josh.

This was going to be a long night.

She could change her mind, of course. She could roll over to him, kiss him, run her hand over his abs, and ask him to undress her. He'd do it. She was ninety-nine percent sure.

But did she want to go back to Iowa, to the good, hard-working men in her small town, with memories of a hot night in a mansion with a playboy bartender who would talk dirty to her in a sexy Southern drawl?

That was hardly fair to them.

She'd want to be thrown over their shoulders. She'd want to wear a hot red dress that made them look at her hungrily. She'd want them to kiss her passionately in the middle of a room full of people. She'd want them to tell Andrew that they were taking her to bed and they were going to have breakfast together and that Andrew could just fuck off. No, Josh hadn't said that in so many words, but he'd implied it.

None of the guys at home would ever tell Andrew any of that.

She could never wear that dress in Elton, Iowa. There was absolutely no occasion for it.

And her father would be mortified if anyone kissed her in public, not to mention throwing her over their shoulder.

She heard the water running and felt a flutter of butterflies in her stomach.

From running water? What? She pulled her pillow over her head again and groaned. How could running water be sexy? He was brushing his teeth. Other guys would do that. They'd run water in the next room while she waited in bed. They'd come and join her under the comforter with minty fresh breath.

She heard the door open and she moved the pillow to look over at him.

He smiled at her as he crossed to the bed and she realized

that in that moment, Josh Landry had just ruined watching other men come to bed.

Crap.

Then it got even worse. He started to unbutton his shirt.

Look away. You should look away. Don't let him ruin watching any other man take his shirt off.

She didn't look away.

The slow reveal of tanned, smooth skin, light brown hair, and deliciously defined pecs and abs made her feel a tight, hot coil tighten in her stomach. She wasn't sure she was breathing. She couldn't be distracted by something trivial like taking oxygen into her lungs.

Holy...

The guy was ripped. His abs were absolutely drool-worthy. His muscles rippled mouthwateringly as he shrugged his shirt off and tossed it toward the chair in the corner.

He was right beside the bed now, looking down at her. His expression was hard to read. He looked faintly amused but also pained. He stopped, blew out a breath, then leaned and switched off the lamp on the bedside table. It had been the only light in the room other than the faint glow that trickled through the window from the moon and lights at the front of the house.

It took her eyes a few seconds to adjust so she missed him shedding his pants and kicking them toward the chair. That was probably for the best, but she couldn't deny the stab of disappointment. She felt the mattress dip, however, as he sat down and then twisted to lie back, and she scooted closer to the opposite edge of the bed. She wasn't sure she could handle having even his big toe touch her.

Josh tugged on the comforter and shifted a few times, getting comfortable. Then everything was quiet.

Tori lay still, for some reason trying to quiet her breathing and not wiggle. Maybe he fell asleep quickly. Maybe he snored.

Maybe he wouldn't say anything else charming or sexy or sweet.

"So, tell me about Fiona."

Crap. He'd said something sweet.

"You don't really want to know about my goats," she said lightly.

"I do, actually," he said.

The dark seemed to make his voice huskier. Or maybe it was her imagination. "Really?"

"I do," he said again. "I like hearing you talk about your passions. And it will distract me."

"Distract you?"

"Thinking about how sweet you are will help me *not* think about how fucking good you smell or the fact that you're lying over there in your pajamas."

And that was sexy. "I'm really sorry."

"For?"

"Not...following through on...things."

He gave a soft huff of laughter. "Tori, you have nothing to apologize for. When it happens, I want you all in, feeling every bit of it. If there's even a niggle of doubt, then...we wait."

She felt heat snake through her. She was quite sure she would feel every bit of it. In fact, that was the whole problem. She was sure she'd feel things that she might never feel again.

Thank goodness Andrew hadn't hesitated to interrupt them. She'd been caught up. She'd been in a lusty, fun, excited haze. She'd been throwing herself at Josh. In front of all of Andrew and Paisley's guests. She'd kissed him when she'd first seen him. She'd suggested the over-the-shoulder thing.

But she needed to dial it back now. She just needed a date to the wedding. She needed people here—okay, mostly Paisley —to believe that she and Josh had a relationship. But that didn't mean they had to make a spectacle of themselves. She'd had her heart—or at least her hormones—on her sleeve. Being overly emotional and demonstrative was not always welcomed by people. That was why she stuck with animals. There had never been a dog who didn't want to be cuddled and loved.

Josh was a fun guy from a big, crazy, effusive family. He was going to go right along with all of this for the wedding weekend. And Tori appreciated that. But it wasn't necessary.

She cleared her throat. "Okay, Fiona."

He gave a low chuckle, and Tori had to squeeze her legs together to reduce the sudden tingling between them.

"She's a fainting goat. I got her from a guy in the next town over when he was selling his place and moving to be closer to his daughter. I already had Fergie and I figured he could use a friend."

"And no one else wanted her, right?" Josh asked.

Tori smiled in the dark. "That's what the guy said, anyway."

"So either it was true or someone tipped him off that that was the surefire way to get you to take her."

She could hear the smile in his voice and it made the tingling worse. Or better. Stronger anyway. "Well, whatever the case, I ended up with Fiona in my family," she said. "I would put her and Fergie out in my east pasture. But every day I went out to feed them, Fergie was there by himself. Fiona had wandered off. I found her, every time, down by the fence that ran along my neighbor's property. I had no idea why she kept going to that same place, but getting her back up to the barn was a battle. Then one day when I went to find her, there was this other goat on the opposite side of the fence. Another fainting goat. They were just standing there on either side of the fence grazing together. This kept happening day after day until finally I called my neighbor and told him I thought our goats were in love. Turns out, he'd gotten his goat about the time I did...from the same farmer."

"No way. They knew each other?" Josh asked.

Tori grinned even though he couldn't see her. "Yep. And

they were definitely in love. They'd found each other even after being taken to separate farms and with all that distance between them. I don't know how they knew where the other was, but Don, my neighbor agreed that they should be together and gave Frodo to me."

"So now they're together."

"Now they're together."

They lay there, not talking for several long moments. Tori felt herself relaxing. At least, not feeling like she had to lie totally still. It was...comfortable.

Except for the tingling in her panties, of course.

"Okay, so now tell me about Valentine's Day 2006."

Ah, crap.

And everything had been so nice there for a bit.

She blew out a breath. "I don't want to."

"It was what Andrew said to remind you that red dresses and hot Louisiana bartenders aren't your style."

She laughed. "Not sure Andrew thinks you're hot."

"I don't really care what Andrew thinks of me."

There was no humor in his tone now.

"Fair enough," she said.

"But you care what Andrew thinks of *you*."

She took a deep breath. "Of course I do."

"So him not wanting you to be up here with me, matters to you."

Tori hesitated over that. "Andrew is just looking out for me. But once he makes me think, if I still go ahead with something, he doesn't try to stop me."

"Maybe not when it comes to cow shit and prom dresses," Josh said. "But I'm thinking with another guy it might be different."

Tori felt a little knot form in her gut. "He's got Paisley."

"But you make him homesick."

"There's nothing between me and Andrew. Like that."

Josh didn't reply right away.

Tori licked her lips. "Andrew feels the need to protect me."

"From guys?"

"From myself."

"What's that mean?"

"I tend to be...embarrassing."

Josh blew out a disgusted breath. "Defending animals and taking care of ones that need extra help should not embarrass you."

She shrugged even though it was dark and he couldn't see her. "I don't embarrass *me*." At least, not exactly.

"I think it's only right you embarrass a girl who's willing to sell her dog for a prom dress."

Tori couldn't help but smile. "Yeah, maybe her a little, but mostly my dad. And Andrew."

She could practically hear Josh's scowl. "Really?"

"Yeah. But Andrew sticks around. For some reason, he decided to try to save me from myself rather than ignoring me or not being my friend." She paused. She didn't know if it was okay to be spilling things about Andrew to Josh. But she still went on. "I've always thought maybe my dad asked him to...be there for me. To look out for me."

"Your dad thought you needed that?"

"My dad isn't into making a big deal of things." She hesitated again. Could she also tell Josh stuff about her dad? Her dad and Andrew were the most important men in her life, and it felt a little like she was telling their secrets. Except, they weren't really secrets. People in Elton definitely knew that her dad and Andrew were often embarrassed by her and that they made apologies for her. "When I was little, my dad was the one telling me when things were inappropriate or pulling me back. But when I got older and was at school all day, someone else had to be there reminding me that acting emotionally was not always the answer. That I needed to think and try to keep my cool."

"And that was Andrew."

"It was. I don't know if Dad actually asked him to watch out for me or if Andrew just took it on, but yeah, he was good at reading me. He could tell when I was getting pissed off or upset and always seemed to know what to say." She sighed. "Andrew and my dad are a lot alike. It's possible Andrew just decided he needed to be my guardian."

"So he kept you from doing things like the cow-poop-prom-dress bit sometimes?" Josh asked.

She couldn't help the little huff of laughter that escaped. "Oh yeah. There would have been incidents like that. And just...arguments and things. I was always kind of..."

"Feisty. Passionate. Loving. Empathetic."

Josh's words made Tori suck in a little breath. Wow, he was something. "Thank you," she said softly. "But I definitely let my emotions get the best of me, and I would debate almost anyone about anything I felt strongly about."

"Animals?"

"Definitely. But other stuff too. I would debate about anything from the best Supreme Court Justice to the best superhero."

Josh laughed softly. "Yeah, you'll fit in perfectly at Ellie's. The regulars love nothing more than a great debate."

Warmth swirled through her at the way he said it as if she'd be back at Ellie's. A lot. "They love a debate more than a grand gesture love story?"

Josh's laugh rumbled across the bed again. "Okay, no. Love stories first. Then arguments. But they'll also tell you that all great love stories have great arguments. The fighting means there's passion."

Tori thought about that. She couldn't argue. Nothing got the blood pumping like being really fired up about a topic.

Well, nothing besides maybe lying in bed next to a hot bayou bartender in nothing but a tank and panties.

"Okay, so now...Valentine's Day 2006," Josh reminded her.

It was getting easier to tell him her embarrassing moments. Probably because so far, he'd used the words feisty, passionate, loving, and empathetic. She liked all of those.

Tori blew out a breath. "Okay. When I was a freshman in high school, I had a huge crush on Marcus Turner. He was new and sat behind me in Algebra. He was always very sweet and we talked every morning. Over the course of the first semester, I decided that I really liked him and wanted to date him. Andrew talked me out of it. He told me that if Marcus liked me, he'd ask me out. He never did. But I couldn't shake this idea that he really liked me. So...on Valentine's Day, I decided to let him know that *I* liked *him*."

She felt Josh roll toward her. He was listening intently. She could feel the heat from his body and her palms itched with the desire to reach over and run them across his chest. His naked chest.

She swallowed and balled her hands into fists beside her. "So, having really only dealt with loving dogs and pigs to that point, I, um, misjudged the size of the gesture I made to show Marcus how I felt."

Josh didn't say anything. But she could somehow sense that he was smiling.

"I got my dog, Buck, and my pig, Priscilla, involved."

"Of course you did."

She laughed. "The day before Valentine's Day, I ran home right after school and loaded them both up. Then I waited outside the locker room. He was on the track team. When he came out to go to practice, I sent Buck up to him. He was wearing a big bow and holding a note in his mouth." She smiled, remembering. Yes, it had been embarrassing and

Andrew had *hated* it, but looking back now, she thought it had been creative. And very *her*.

"And the note said Be My Valentine or something?" Josh asked.

"Oh no." She shook her head. "That would have been too plain."

"Of course." He was still smiling.

"It said, 'Doggone it, I like you.'" Tori waited, grinning in spite of herself.

There was a beat and then Josh laughed. "Of course it did."

"And that wasn't nearly enough," Tori said.

"Right, Priscilla had to be in on it too."

"Exactly. I sent *her* in after Buck. The note was hanging from her neck and said, 'I've even been bacon for you.'" Tori paused. "And then I came in carrying a plate of four cupcakes that *did* say Be My Valentine."

Josh started laughing harder this time, shaking the mattress as he did, and making Tori's grin grow.

"I've been *bacon* for you?" he asked. "Seriously? Priscilla wasn't offended by that?"

Tori giggled. "In retrospect, it was a little insensitive. Good thing pigs aren't good readers."

Josh's laugh got deeper. "Okay," he finally said when he took a breath. "Why four cupcakes? There are only three words."

He really did listen to her. Tori loved that about him. "Valentine is a really long word to fit on one cupcake," she said. "It took up two. One with *Valen* and one with *tine*."

"Wow," Josh said, clearly enjoying himself. "What was Marcus' reaction?"

"Oh, he blushed and stammered and said thank you and then..." Tori paused for dramatic effect, "...Priscilla pooped on the floor."

"Noooo," Josh groaned. Then he laughed. "Really?"

"Yes. And I kind of yelled, "No!" and then lunged for her, which spooked her and she took off running down the hall. I dropped the cupcakes. Buck went for the cupcakes. So I went for him. But Priscilla was escaping. It was absolute pandemonium."

Josh was laughing harder now and Tori was as tempted to roll closer to him because of that as she had been just seeing his naked chest.

"Everyone was gathered in the hallway, horrified and fascinated. There was lots of 'ew, gross' and I, of course, ended up slipping on frosting and landing on my butt in front of Marcus."

"Well, at least you didn't slip in the Priscilla poop," Josh offered.

"Oh no, I *landed* in that."

"Oh my God."

She saw Josh run a hand over his face in the dim light. He clearly found this all highly entertaining. As did Tori. Now, thirteen years later.

"Admit it," she said. "You would have been super embarrassed if a girl had done that to you."

"Okay, maybe a little. But I would have loved it too."

She believed him.

"So was this one of the things you ran past Andrew and he tried to talk you out of?"

"No. That was the start of our rule of running everything past him," she said with a grin.

"Did he see this whole thing?"

"Oh yes. He was on the track team too. He came out just in time to see Priscilla come in."

"And he saved the day after?" Josh asked, his tone a little less amused.

"He caught Priscilla and got her in my truck, helped me clean up the hallway, and the next day just laughed at it all and told people that it was hilarious and Marcus should be flattered."

"And that worked? That smoothed everything over?"

"Well, Andrew was really well liked. He was the team captain for basketball and a great student and involved in everything. People still thought I was weird, but they didn't tease me about it. At least not as much as they would have if he *hadn't* stuck up for me."

"Was Marcus your Valentine then?"

"Lord no," she said. "He could barely look at me for the rest of the week. I'm sure he kept picturing me covered in pink frosting and pig poop. It took a little bit, but eventually we got to a place where we could talk awkwardly."

"Well, at least he wasn't a dick about it."

"Oh, I'm sure Andrew told him that he would *not* be a dick to me."

"Sorry," Josh said after a few seconds. "Any girl who's got a pig and isn't afraid to use her to express her affection is someone a guy should want to know better."

Tori felt a little thump in her chest. "That's really sweet."

Josh shook his head. "You're just so fucking adorable."

Tori felt her eyes go wide. Heat and what she could only call affection shot through her. He wasn't appalled like Andrew had been or confused the way Marcus had been. Josh thought she was adorable.

Her eyes had adjusted to the dark room by now, but she didn't need light to find him. Heat poured off of him and pulled her in. She rolled to face him and reached out, placing her hand on his chest.

She felt him tense, as if surprised, but a millisecond later he gave a low groan and flattened his hand over the top of hers.

"Tori." His voice was low and husky.

She said the first thing that same to mind. "I like you so much."

"Ditto," he said roughly.

"And I want you. So much."

"Girl—" He cleared his throat. "That is absolutely mutual too. But we don't have to—"

"I want to."

His fingers tightened around her hand and he pulled in a breath. "Be sure," he said firmly.

Every single thing he said seemed to send pulses of need to her nipples, gut, and between her legs. She wanted him. He was such a great guy. He sincerely liked her. He made her feel smart and sweet and sexy.

Plus he was easily the hottest guy she'd ever been this close to outside of a barn.

Okay, even inside of a barn.

Yeah, she definitely wanted him. This. Now. Right now.

Tori shifted closer, pushing him to his back, and then swinging her leg over to straddle his lap. He was, as suspected, wearing only underwear, and his erection was hard and hot and *big* pressing against the crotch of her panties. "I'm so sure," she said, leaning in to kiss him.

He groaned again, and one hand went to her hip while the other cupped the back of her head. He immediately took the kiss into deep and wet territory. His tongue stroked hers and her clit pulsed as if he was stroking it.

She followed his lead on the kissing, but her hands roamed his chest, shoulders, and abs. The hard muscles and hot skin made her want all of it against all of *her.*

Josh's hand slid from her hip to her ass, squeezing and pressing her down against his hard cock.

"Not fair," he said gruffly against her mouth. "These are *not* pajamas."

"Best I could do," she said breathlessly.

"You forgot your pajamas? Can't say I'm sorry about that."

"No, I usually sleep naked."

He groaned and his fingers curled into her ass. "That's awesome."

"Makes middle of the night calls to deliver colts and calves a little complicated," she said, lifting her head to look down at him. "But I haven't totally forgotten to get dressed yet."

He laughed. "And this way you won't mind at all that I won't let you get re-dressed again after."

"After?" she teased.

"After I run my hands and tongue all over you and make you come so hard you couldn't get dressed again if you tried."

Her eyes widened and her heart raced at the deep, gruff, totally sincere words. "I don't think I would mind you not letting me get re-dressed after *that* even if I didn't usually sleep naked."

Suddenly Josh rolled her to her back, bracing himself above her on one elbow, his other hand still on her ass. "Last chance to say no."

She knew that wasn't true. She could stop him at any point. He might be disappointed but he'd never *not* stop. She loved that she could be so sure of him. "I love Louisiana," she said. "I've got to fully immerse myself in this experience and sample *everything* this great state has to offer."

He grinned down at her. "Iowa," he said.

"What about it?"

"This moment might be the last time you can remember that word."

She laughed, but it was quickly cut short by Josh shifting, and his big, slightly roughened hands gliding up her sides, taking her tank top up and over her head.

And just like that she was wearing only panties in a big bed on a Southern plantation with a guy who drawled, "Holy fucking shit, Tori," when he looked down at her.

His appraisal made her want to arch her back and stretch

like her cats did when she told them they were pretty. And in anticipation of being petted.

But Josh's hands didn't go to her breasts or her hard, aching nipples. He hooked his middle fingers in the top of her panties and skimmed them down her legs, tossing them off the side of the bed.

And just like *that* she was completely naked.

"Damn, girl." There was that drawl again.

Tori felt the aching move swiftly from her nipples to her pussy and she shifted on the smooth sheets. She definitely needed to be petted. If he wasn't careful, she was going to purr too.

"Touch me," she said softly. "Please."

"*Nothing* I'd rather do." He went back on one elbow, lying beside her, and lifted a hand to her face though, cupping her cheek. "You're so beautiful."

He'd called her adorable and sweet, but right now there was nothing about the look in his eyes that was as gentle and innocent as that. He was looking at her like he wanted to devour her.

"Are you a virgin?" he asked, stroking his thumb along her jaw.

She hadn't been expecting that question. "Do I seem like a virgin?" she asked, actually curious.

He hesitated, then gave her one of his grins. "I don't know if there's a good answer to that."

She grinned. "I seem like one, right?"

"Let's just say, I wouldn't be surprised either way?" He definitely made that sound like a question.

Tori shifted her legs on the sheets, wanting his hands on her but knowing they had to have this discussion too. "It's hard to imagine me getting past pig poop to a bedroom?"

He chuckled. "It's hard to imagine these guys you keep describing being smart enough to get you into a bedroom."

She smirked up at him. "That was a pretty smooth answer."

He ran his hand down over her hip, making tingles dance down her leg and up to her nipples. "I would love it if I was your first."

His gruff answer, combined with the heat and affection in his eyes, amped those tingles up. "Damn, now I wish you *were* my first."

"I'm not?"

"Sorry."

"Me too."

They smiled at each other for a long moment.

"But you're the first in a long time," she finally offered.

He ran his hand up and down her hip again, the calluses on his palm sending delicious shivers of desire through her. "How long?"

She wet her lips, trying to lie still and just talk when she really wanted to grab his hand and press it against her throbbing clit. "Uh, a couple of years."

His eyebrows went up. "Yeah?" He sounded hopeful.

She nodded. "Yeah."

He seemed to think about that. "Okay, that's pretty good."

"It's *good*? I haven't had sex in two and a half years, Josh," she said. "How is that good?"

"Two and *a half*?" he asked, leaning in closer, his hand moving again.

"Well, like two and three-fourths."

"Oh, three-fourths. I like that," he told her, his voice low. "I like that a lot."

"You do?"

He put his lips against her neck, brushing them over the sensitive skin and making her nipples tighten further.

"I *really* do. For one, I love the idea that I get to make you hot and needy and wet and then stretch you out in a way you haven't been in a long time," he said roughly against her ear.

She let out a little moan at that, shifting her legs on the sheets again, urging him to move his hand more to the middle.

He didn't. But he dragged his mouth along her jaw to her mouth and said, "And hey, that long period of time makes it a little easier to make you forget about any man before me." He kissed her long and deep. When he lifted his head he said, "Not that I was really worried about that."

A little niggle in the back of Tori's mind told her to be careful here. He was going to ruin her for other men. Not just because he was, well, *him*. But because he seemed intent on the mission.

Of course, that niggle was nothing compared to the rest of her brain and every inch of her body below her brain yelling, *Yes! Do that! Do it all!*

"Hey, Josh?" she finally said, her voice breathless.

"Yes, Tori?"

"I'm thinking about Anthony and his love for dogs and horses and his heroic rescue of a bald eagle during our last year of vet school right now."

Josh pulled back and looked down at her. "Is that right?"

"Yeah. So you might want to get to work here before I start thinking about Chad and his big—"

Josh took her mouth in a deep, possessive kiss and his hand ran down her hip, then up to cup her breast. Tori sighed happily as he ran his thumb over her nipple. That was more like it. She loved his hands on her and she loved, interestingly, the possessive streak he was showing. She liked him a little jealous. It was ridiculous, of course. He had no competition. But if it got him to quench this fire that was coursing through her bloodstream, then she'd use it.

He lifted his head to look down at her as he plucked and rolled her nipple.

"—TV," she said, finishing her thought from before.

"He had a big TV?"

"*Really* big."

Josh grinned down at her, then lowered his head and took her nipple in his mouth, drawing on it hard, making her gasp and arch, before lifting his head and saying, "I'm very happy to show you how many inches a real man has."

She giggled. "Sixty inches?"

He pressed his cock against her hip. "I've got eighty-four, baby."

Honestly, was sex supposed to be this fun? She slid her head up to the back of his head and into his hair. He seemed to love when she did that. "Show me everything you've got."

He growled. "Gladly."

His mouth went back to her nipple and his hand slid down over her belly. He stroked back and forth sending ripples of heat straight to her core. He flicked his tongue over her nipple as the pad of his middle finger brushed over her clit. She tightened her fingers against his head and lifted her hips as her eyes slid shut.

He moved to her other nipple as he pressed against her clit and made a lazy circle over the tight bud.

"You're so sweet," he told her huskily. "I'm guessing you taste pretty fucking sweet too."

Her eyes flew open and she looked down at him as he slid down her body, dragging his lips over her ribs and stomach to the crease where her hip started.

"Oooh," she said softly. "No one's ever done that."

He lifted a brow, his eyes hot. "Don't lie just to make me happy, Tori."

She laughed. "What makes you think I'm not just trying to make *me* happy?"

"Oh, I'm gonna make you happy. Happier than you've ever been," he promised gruffly. "Even if someone else was here first. But I'd be fucking thrilled to find out that no one's ever been smart enough to taste your sweet pussy until now."

10

J osh watched Tori take in a quick breath, his entire body hard and pulsing. This woman. Damn. He *needed* her. This was more than want. More than anything he'd felt before. And he was thanking every last lucky star he had that she was here with him now. Like this. Naked and wanting him too.

But the idea of being the first to give her pleasure? That was shredding him. Whether it was to be the first guy to feed her a Louisiana delicacy or the first to lick and suck her to an orgasm, he was all in here and it was, yeah, tearing him up. In a good way. As if everything he'd ever known or done or felt before was being ripped out and replaced with *her*.

And thank God she seemed to love the dirty talk because he wasn't sure he could hold back if he tried.

"You'd be the first," she told him. "Promise."

"Fuck yes," he growled.

He flicked his tongue over the spot just a few inches from where he really wanted to be. He wanted her all in here too. This might be a first, but he wanted her urging him on. Not because he thought she was hesitating. The way she was breathing hard and gripping the sheets on either side of her told him she was wound tight and wanted this. But he wanted to talk her through it all, have her here, taking every step because, well, it was hot as hell.

"Spread your legs, sweetheart," he said, his drawl deeper now.

Tori complied quickly, nearly kneeing him in the nose. He chuckled as he jerked back to avoid the contact, but that quickly evolved into a groan as her legs parted, showing off the slippery pink folds where he wanted to be so badly it hurt.

"I should probably warn you," he told her.

"Warn me?"

"I haven't been with anyone since I said goodbye to you on Bourbon last year. I'm probably going to eat you like a starving man. Because I am, baby. I am."

He felt her body tense with surprise. He looked up. She was propped on her elbows, staring at him.

"Seriously?" she finally asked. "You haven't had sex with anyone in over a year?"

"Seriously."

"But...why?"

He lifted a shoulder and said honestly, "Because of you."

She stared for another long moment. "Wow," she finally said. Then she smiled, flopped back onto her back, and spread her knees further apart.

He gave a soft chuckle. Then looked back down at her.

"Damn," he said reverently. He ran a hand up her leg as he moved to settle between her thighs. "This might take a while."

"Don't remember how to do it?"

He grinned and gave her inner thigh a light pinch. "I just can't imagine ever wanting to leave here."

"Oh, I—"

Whatever she'd been about to say cut off as he dragged his tongue up the smooth skin of her inner thigh. Yep, absolutely as sweet as he'd expected.

He licked her again, noting how her body tensed. It wasn't as if she might push him away. It was very much as if she was on the verge of coming. Already.

Josh kissed his way over her inner thigh to her pussy, spreading her open and then giving her clit one little lick. Damn it all, she was delicious.

"Oh my...*Josh*."

Oh my Josh. Yeah, he liked that. "Buckle up, Buttercup," he told her with a grin.

Then he licked her harder, up both sides and right over that sweet little nub. He did it again and again as she writhed against the mattress, finally making him lay a hand on her lower belly to hold her still. Then he sucked on her. At first softly, swirling his tongue over her clit, then harder as she started to spiral closer to her orgasm. She was easily the best thing he'd ever tasted and he would never go down on another woman again.

Holy shit. That was quite a thought. He loved oral sex. He loved giving as good as he got and he *loved* blow jobs. But yeah, he couldn't imagine ever being with another woman like this. No one else would ever sound or feel or taste this good.

Dammit. He might just have to move to Iowa.

Hell, men had uprooted their lives and moved everything a thousand miles away for far less than the best pussy they'd ever eaten. And Tori was so much more than that.

That thought hit him as he slid two fingers into her very tight, but very hot and wet channel, sending her over the edge and into a hard orgasm. Her muscles clamped onto his fingers and she bucked her hips, calling his name loud enough that Josh was certain the people next door heard it if they were in their room.

He hoped they were in their room.

He kept his fingers and mouth right where they were, gently working her as she came down from the climax. Then he crawled up her body and took her mouth in a deep kiss, making sure she tasted just how fucking delicious she was on his tongue.

Finally he let her up for air.

Don't propose. Don't propose. Don't propose. He repeated the words until he was sure he wasn't going to say something crazy.

"Holy crap, can you move to Iowa and do that to me every single night?" she asked as she wrapped her arms around his neck and pressed her body against the length of his.

Okay, so *she* could say the crazy stuff. For now. He chuckled, holding her close, willing his heart to stop jackhammering against his rib cage. "Well, dammit, I guess I'm not done."

She looked up at him. "No?" Did she seem eager?

He laughed. "Well, you still remember where you're from."

She grinned. "Oh yeah. I guess I do. The state anyway. The town name is fuzzy. You'd better give me something more."

"You asked for it." He kissed her hungrily, then reached for his pants beside the bed and the condoms—hey, he was an optimist—in the pocket. He pushed himself up to kneeling and started to shed his boxers.

"Oh, let me." Tori was suddenly sitting up and reaching for him.

She was so open about what she was feeling and wanting. He loved that. He loved when it was directed at and about him especially, but he loved that about her in general. It seemed the only time she tamped things down was when Andrew was there, reminding her to dial it back.

Fucking Andrew.

Tori pulled his boxers down and sighed happily as she took in the sight of his cock—his never-this-hard-before cock—for the first time, and Josh forgot about anything and anyone but her.

There was no, "Oh my God, you're so big" or "You're so hot". Nothing seductive. She just reached out and took his cock in her hand, circling it and stroking up and down, watching herself touch him.

Josh felt his balls tighten and he had to grit his teeth against the sensations suddenly pounding through him. It was her touch, of course, but it was also the look on her face and her contented little exhalation. Like she was just so happy in this moment.

She wasn't a virgin, maybe, but she was hardly experienced. She had flirted with him last year at Bourbon O, but she hadn't been trying to seduce him. She'd just been having fun, teasing, enjoying. Which was what had seduced him, he realized. It was just how honest and open she was about how she was feeling and what she was thinking. She hadn't liked the Hurricane. The gin fizz had been okay. She'd really liked the beer. It had all been there in her face and voice. And that was how he'd known how she felt about *him*. And why he'd wanted things to be different with her.

Right now, watching how turned on she was and how much she clearly just liked touching him and looking at him, was the hottest thing he'd ever seen.

Well, maybe second to that moment when she'd first spread her legs.

And when he'd first twirled her on the dance floor.

And when she'd lit up first seeing him on the dock in Autre.

Holy hell, he was falling in love with her.

Like someone had smacked him in the face, it was clear.

And he'd never wanted a woman more.

He handed her the condom without a word—because he was actually a little worried about what he might say—and she tore it open and rolled it on. Then he pushed her back, kneeling between her knees, scooped her butt up in his hands, and positioned himself.

She looked down and watched as he slid into her wet heat slowly, making lust surge through him as strong as all of the other softer emotions.

Josh gritted his teeth as he pressed forward, wanting to take it easy and slow, overriding his body's urges to thrust and pound. But her little moans and the way she moved against him tested every shred of self-control he had. He would freaking go to war for the, "Oh, Josh" she gave him. Not to mention the way her sweet body clamped around his cock like she never wanted to let go.

He pressed all the way in, relishing everything about being balls deep, before pulling out again, also slowly. He moved in and out with long, easy strokes, watching her perfect breasts bounce, her hands grip the sheets, her body take him fully, softening around him, welcoming his length and girth even as her pussy gripped him snugly.

"If I move to that place you're from," he said, teasing gruffly. "I will insist on doing a lot of this too."

She swallowed hard, looking up from where she'd been watching him fuck her. "Where am I from again? I can't remember."

He wanted to grin. He wanted to tease and laugh. But for some reason the light, don't-really-mean-it words wouldn't come. "Too fucking far away," he told her. Then he ran his thumb over her clit, circling and pressing and taking the air from her lungs so that she couldn't respond to that with anything other than a hard, fast orgasm.

She gasped his name, arched her neck, and squeezed his cock with her pussy so tightly that he was only a few seconds behind her, coming hard, shouting her name.

Yeah, he fucking hoped someone was in the next room to hear that too.

It took several seconds for the waves of pleasure to quiet and calm. Josh stayed braced above Tori, breathing hard, watching her gasp for air as well. He was still deep inside her, and he couldn't tell if the aftershocks from the shared orgasm were from her or him.

Finally, he lowered himself onto one elbow and rolled slightly. But he didn't pull out. He couldn't bring himself to separate their bodies just yet. He snuggled her up against him, one of her legs draped over his hip, spreading her open and keeping him fully embedded.

She sighed heavily and seemed perfectly content tucked up against his side.

They just lay there, breathing, for several long minutes. Long enough that he wondered if she'd fallen asleep.

But finally she said, "So *that* was definitely worth waiting a year for."

He chuckled. And agreed a thousand percent. Then he was again hit by emotions that he'd never felt when tangled up in bed sheets with a naked woman. A sense of panic among them. He might have never seen her again. Last year on Bourbon Street she might have walked away forever. She might have decided not to come to Autre to try to find him. Josh felt his heart starting to race and he took a deep breath and then gathered her closer.

"Thank you for coming back to Louisiana. Thank you for coming to Autre," he said, his voice gravelly.

She laughed softly. "I might not have come to find you at the bayou if I hadn't accidentally kissed Andrew."

Josh worked on not squeezing her too tightly at her words. She might not have. What the hell would he have done then?

But then she wiggled her butt against him and gave another of those long, contented sighs, and Josh decided that instead of thinking about what could have been—or what might *not* have been—he was going to enthusiastically embrace his family's love for destiny and soul mates.

Because he was *not* going to be thankful to fucking Andrew for anything.

———

"WE DON'T REALLY LOOK that much alike, do we?" Josh asked Owen. "I'm more muscular for sure, right?"

"Yes, Princess, you're prettier than him," Owen said, lifting his glass of sweet tea and rolling his eyes.

"Fuck off," Josh grumbled, pushing his fork through his seafood pot pie.

They were sitting in Trahan's Tavern, just off of Jackson Square, sixteen hours after Tori had fallen asleep in his arms.

In those sixteen hours, he'd slept, snuck out of bed early to meet Leo downstairs to get the sweet grits and chicory coffee Ellie had sent, been not at all surprised to find Owen delivering breakfast, driving the bus and playing chauffeur for the city tour of New Orleans instead of Leo, fed Tori grits that she'd loved and coffee that she'd been okay with once he added cream and sugar—she'd come around to the chicory, he was sure—and bundled eight people from Iowa onto a tour bus and shown them the Big Easy.

"I think you're more muscular than him," Gabe Trahan said to Josh.

"Thanks, man."

"You've got better hair too," Gabe decided. He'd taken a seat with Josh and Owen after he'd gotten the group's dinner served and was now studying Andrew.

Josh shot Owen a look. "See? *That* is how to be supportive."

"But he's taller," Gabe said. "And he looks smarter than you."

"Excuse me?"

Gabe looked back at Josh and shrugged. "It's probably just the glasses, but he kind of has a polished, college-boy look."

"He *is* a college boy," Owen said. "And a law school boy."

"Fuck off," Josh told them both.

Gabe chuckled. "I think you're okay. After all, his balls are in Paisley Darbonne's pocket, so you've got that."

"Why do you think that?" Josh asked, surprised Gabe even knew who Andrew was engaged to. Of course, it was possible it had been in the local papers, he supposed.

"Andrew and his buddies were in here the other night and I heard them talking," Gabe said with a shrug.

"They were in *here*?" Josh asked. "When?"

"Mardi Gras."

"They were here on *Tuesday*?" Josh had been running in and out of the bar, completely distracted by thoughts of Tori, so it was very possible he'd missed seeing Andrew. Then again, he hadn't known who Andrew was on Tuesday. He could have seen the other man, but not really *seen* him. He could have pushed the groom-to-be a beer or two and never really looked at his face.

"They were. Nice big tab and good tippers," Gabe said.

"But he was bitching about Paisley?" Owen asked.

"Just that she was pissed off about how things were going and that he needed to figure out a way to smooth it all out. And one of his groomsmen asked when anything was going to be about Andrew and Andrew said, 'When Paisley tells me it can be.'" Gabe and Owen laughed at that.

Josh just continued to watch Andrew and Tori together.

Andrew was disgruntled with the wedding planning? He hadn't
known that.

"So you've been showing them the sites, huh?" Gabe asked.
"You know your way around on concrete and not just swamp
water?"

"Oh hell," Owen said. "You give this guy a captive audience
and some stories to tell and he's in heaven. Doesn't matter what
the vehicle is or if the stories are true or pure bullshit."

"I like to fall somewhere in between those," Josh said with a
grin. He couldn't deny that he'd had a great time showing this
group around.

"You showed them Preservation Hall and the Cathedral and
the streetcars?" Gabe asked.

"Yep."

"And you handed out pralines and told them why we call it
Canal Street?"

"Yep."

"And you took them to the World War II museum?"

"Took 'em *by* it," Josh said. "That's a whole day thing to
really appreciate it. But we did stop in at Mardi Gras World."

Gabe grinned. "And they fed them King Cake?"

"You bet."

Mardi Gras World was one of the big old warehouses where
they created and stored a lot of the Mardi Gras floats. It was a
little bit cool and a little bit crazy. The amount of work that
went into the floats was amazing and seeing them up close was
always fun, especially for people who hadn't ever been to a real
Mardi Gras parade. The sampling of King Cake was a part of
the tour at the facility and again, was often a first for out-of-
towners. The Iowa group hadn't really understood the whole
bit about the plastic baby being hidden somewhere in the cake,
but they'd liked their samples.

"We went up and down Canal Street and St. Charles
Avenue," Josh said. He'd showed off the mansions of the

Garden District, talked about the streetcars, and they'd done a loop through Audubon Park where he'd told them about the insectarium and the aquarium and the Tree of Life, the old oak estimated to be between one hundred and five hundred years old and that had a spot in its branches with a view of giraffes. The ones in the zoo not too far from the tree.

"But we gave them a...unique tour too," Owen said.

He and Josh shared a grin.

"What's that mean?" Gabe asked, lifting a brow.

"Well, we told them all about Katrina and a bunch of the stories we know and have heard in here," Josh said. He'd only been fifteen when the hurricane had ravaged the area, but everyone knew someone who had a story and a lot of people loved to tell those stories. The first responders who frequented Trahan's from Engine 29, the firehouse just a few blocks away, had a trove of stories, some that they'd experienced themselves and some they'd heard from others.

Josh knew that some, or even most, of those stories had grown over the years since the storm and that there were some urban legends mixed into the recounting of the hurricane and the aftermath. But the destruction had been very real, the lives affected had been countless, and the effects could still be felt around the city. It was easy for him to get impassioned about it.

"Then to lighten things up, we made a stop at the Museum of Death and the Voodoo Museum," Josh said with a grin. "And ended up outside the LaLaurie Mansion." The famously haunted mansion had a grisly history, and the story of the socialite, Delphine LaLaurie, who tortured and killed slaves in her lavish French Quarter mansion in the mid-1800s, was always good for shock factor.

Gabe laughed. "Good lord, these people are never coming back to N'Awlins after all that."

Josh's eyes went to Tori again. She had to come back. *Had to.* If she had to leave at all.

"And then you brought them in here?" Gabe said, looking around. "If their stomachs are queasy, they won't eat as much."

"They'll drink though, to try to get all that crazy shit outta their heads," Owen said.

"Guess I won't tell them the bar is haunted too," Gabe said, pushing back and stretching to his feet.

Owen chuckled. "Good call."

Josh shook Gabe's hand as his friend, and technically his boss, headed back behind the bar. It never felt like he was really working for the Trahans though. It was more as if he was helping run a business he loved and cared about.

"And we'll take 'em to Café Du Monde after this and they'll forget all about the nasty, horrible stories," Owen said, popping a crawfish into his mouth.

"Thank you for not telling Gabe that plan," Josh said.

The famous café sat kitty-corner across the square from Trahan's and yeah, the Iowans needed a beignet before leaving New Orleans. He'd be shirking his responsibilities as a tour guide if they didn't have one. But the brown butter pecan pie at Trahan's beat beignets hands down. Though Josh would never deny a tourist a plate of beignets and a café au lait at Café Du Monde. And he'd never tell them that Café Beignet was even better. Or that his own grandmother could make beignets so good that they could make a grown man cry. Café Du Monde was simply a must-do.

"So why don't we like Andrew?" Owen asked, taking a huge bite of his blackened redfish, one of the many amazing things on Trahan's menu. Owen was eating for free since he was driving the bus—a deal Leo had hammered out with Sawyer and Tommy long ago—and was taking advantage of it. "He's Tori's best friend, right? Shouldn't you be tryin' to get on his good side if you want back in her panties?"

The mention of Tori's panties made Josh shift on his seat as heat shot through him. "What makes you think I'd be goin' *back*? As if I've been there?"

Owen chuckled. "Because that girl's glowing." He pointed his fork in Tori's direction.

To where she was sitting and talking with Andrew at the end of the bar. Just the two of them. Andrew had been trying to get her alone all day but Josh had kept them moving, spurred on by Tori's obvious interest and delight in the tour as much as a desire to keep them apart. She asked Josh a million questions and was the last one back on the bus whenever they got off. She'd even wanted to go inside the LaLaurie Mansion. Which got a big *hell no* from Josh. Not even a guy who dealt with gators on a daily basis had big enough balls to go inside that place.

Josh watched Tori with Andrew for a moment. "Glowing, huh?" She looked gorgeous to him. He'd been itching to kiss her all day. But he kind of felt that way constantly around her.

"Well, that and the fact that she was looking at you all gaga all day." Owen shook his head. "*No one* thinks your explanation of why we bury people above ground and your history Holt Cemetery is *that* interesting. Trust me. She was thinking about your cock and all the dirty things you did to her last night."

Josh coughed and shifted on his chair. In the middle of the cemetery? But he'd wanted to kiss her there, too, so maybe.

Oh yeah, they'd gone to a cemetery too. The unique below-ground-burial cemetery in New Orleans. Of course they'd found that interesting. It had been a burial ground for the indigent population back in the day and because of the high water tables there were times that caskets would float up. The cemetery was unique for sure and Josh had always found it charming. The grave markers were homemade—PVC pipe, painted wooden posts, and a variety of other things—and trinkets like beads, photographs, stuffed animals and even beer and bottles of liquor could be found in the branches and roots of the huge oak in the middle of the cemetery.

What could he say? There was a lot of morbid-but-fascinating shit in New Orleans.

"But honestly, she doesn't just seem well fucked," Owen went on, as if they were discussing the tour schedule for tomorrow or who's turn it was to scrub the dock. And as if there weren't several other people within earshot. "She was looking at you like you were the most amazing person she's ever met. Like she actually *likes* you. Even in the middle of the murder museum. Which is not hot or romantic in the least. *That's* something." He shook his head. "Freakin' place makes my skin crawl."

"It's the Museum of Death," Josh corrected, thinking about what Owen had said.

"Yeah, well, it's got letters from serial killers in it." Owen shuddered. "That's fucking freaky no matter what you call it."

Yeah, it was. Josh grinned. Tori had clearly enjoyed the whole tour but some of the fun of it—and the inspiration for the stop at the Museum of Death—was how queasy Andrew had looked at the cemetery and the voodoo museum.

Okay, so Tori had been aptly listening to everything he said, but that was kind of just Tori. Wasn't it? Or maybe not. Maybe she did think he was amazing and interesting and charming. Lord knew that standing up in front of newcomers to Louisiana and telling them cool, if slightly twisted, stuff about his home state was one of his favorite things in life.

But man, he loved the idea of Tori being enamored with him.

Owen leaned back in his chair, tipping the front legs up, and lifting his mug of tea again as he looked over to where Tori and Andrew were talking. This was very likely the first time Owen had ever drunk something nonalcoholic inside this building. Trahan's had become a regular spot for drinks and fun when they were all up from Autre. Gabe and Logan Trahan were great guys and poured awesome local beer and the best

Pimm's Cups in the city. But Owen was off liquor and beer while he was driving people around in their tour bus.

"She doesn't look at Andrew gaga," Owen said.

Josh watched Tori. No, she didn't look at Andrew like she was gaga, but she did look like she was completely comfortable with him. It was clear that they'd sat that close and talked that easily many, many times before this. It had been juvenile to try to keep them apart today. Not just because it could only last so long, but because they *were* longtime friends. He'd thought it odd last night that Paisley clearly wanted Tori out of Andrew's life. But now, watching them, it was hard not to wonder if there was something more there. Not because of how Tori was looking at Andrew, but because of how *he* was looking at *her*.

Fucking Andrew.

"Oh shit." Owen leaned forward quickly, thunking the legs of his chair back on the floor. He quickly scooped the last couple of bites of redfish into his mouth, chewing fast.

"What's going on—"

"Logan Trahan, I am here to be impressed. But I'm not holdin' my breath."

Josh froze at the sound of that voice. Then groaned. "No."

Owen swallowed hard. "I can't have her see me eatin' someone else's redfish. If she asks, I had the gumbo and it sucked."

"Eleanor Landry, what the hell are you doin' in my bar?" Logan called to Josh and Owen's grandmother from across the room. "Here to steal my secrets?"

But he wore a big grin and when he met Ellie in the middle of the room, he grabbed her up in a big hug.

"As if you've got *anything* I haven't seen *and done* before," Ellie told him with a huge wink when he set her back down.

Josh sighed. Ellie got along with everyone. Logan got along with everyone. They were kind of the same person in many ways, and when they got together it was loud and the insults flew. Good-natured insults, but still.

Of course, there was no way Ellie had come to New Orleans, to this bar, today, all by herself. Josh wondered how many family members he could expect through the door in the next few minutes.

"It's just not fair that you were born too soon for me to sweep you off your feet but in time for me to know you and see you gallivanting with that other young stud, rubbing my face in the chance I missed," Logan told her.

"Holy shit, boy," Ellie said, laughing. "Does that pretty wife of yours know that you're still out here letting all of that charm ooze out all over the place?"

Logan laughed and nodded. "She does. She finds it hilarious. Claims she's the only one dumb enough to fall for it."

Ellie cackled. "She doesn't strike me as dumb."

"Well..." Logan lowered his voice but definitely not far enough to not be overheard by *everyone*. "I got lucky in the beginning. She was tipsy and then had pregnancy hormones raging and making her horny."

Ellie nodded as if that explained it all. "Yeah, knocking her up was a good move."

"I agree." Logan grinned.

Josh watched as Ellie looked across the room and gave a little wave and blew a kiss to someone. Josh didn't have to look to see that it was Tori. His grandmother's smile for Tori made his heart swell. But of course, he did look. He found Tori watching the whole exchange between Ellie and Logan. And smiling affectionately. That made him want to stalk across the bar and, not surprisingly, throw her over his shoulder.

Then she looked at him and her smile grew and he actually started to stand. Then Andrew leaned in and said something that grabbed her attention and made her frown.

Josh blew out a breath. Okay, he needed to just relax for a minute here.

And then Kennedy walked in, joining the party.

Huh. Just one other family member. A shockingly small number, really. For which he decided to just be grateful.

But it meant that they'd shut the tour company down for the day. And possibly the bar. And, very likely, that Sawyer was pretty ticked off.

"So," Logan asked Ellie, his hands on his hips. "Business so bad down on the bayou you needed to come up here and see what a real bar looks like?"

"Oh, Logan, fuck off," Ellie said with a laugh. "Why don't you put your tight ass back behind that bar and mix me a Sazerac while I talk to my grandsons?"

"Okay, but you better ogle me all the way across the room," Logan told her.

"Count on it." She definitely watched Logan walk away before turning and heading straight for Josh and Owen's table. Kennedy was right behind her.

Ellie didn't take a seat since her drink was being mixed and she would much rather talk to Logan. Or Gabe, for that matter. It was impossible to make Logan blush. Gabe, on the other hand, was difficult, but not impossible, and Ellie took it as a personal challenge to do it whenever she was in here. She also usually put away two pieces of the brown butter pecan pie and then threatened to smother them in their sleep and put them in her gumbo if they ever told anyone how much she liked it. Real grandmotherly stuff, for sure.

"What are you doing here?" Josh asked with a sigh as Kennedy did kick a chair out and take a seat at the table.

"You didn't really think we were going to just sit back and let you take a bus and order up morning grits without us wanting to see this up close and personal, did you?" Ellie asked.

"See what?" he asked.

Ellie grinned. "You goin' all out for a girl."

Josh actually chuckled at that. "No matter how good your grits are, I'm not sure that's going *all out*."

Which got him to thinking. What would going all out for Tori look like? And why hadn't he already done it? Yeah, he'd fallen in love with her in basically one day. Well, a year and one day. But that was plenty of time for a Landry man to lose his heart. And mind.

"It's not the grits," Ellie said. "It's that you're taking care of her. You want to make her happy. And you're using things other than your wangadoodle to do it."

Owen choked on his tea and Kennedy rolled her eyes. "Oh my God, *please* never say wangadoodle ever again."

Ellie grinned. "I have other terms."

"Never mind," Kennedy said. "Wangadoodle might be the least horrifying."

"Is love stick better?" Ellie asked.

"No, it definitely is not." Kennedy pushed back from the table and stood. "I'm going to the bar. To drink. You're driving home so take it easy on the Sazerac."

"Oh, we've got a long day ahead of us," Ellie said, waving that away. "Lots of time to sober up."

Kennedy groaned at that.

"Why are you here?" Josh asked his sister.

"Well, if y'all aren't workin', I'm not workin'," Kennedy told him. "I'm not gonna sit down there and deal with tourists calling, pissed off about rescheduling."

"So we did cancel tours?" he asked. He felt a little bad about that. But a glance in Tori's direction affirmed that he would do it all over again.

"We did." Kennedy shrugged. "But I don't care. I get paid either way."

Josh frowned. "No you don't."

"I do." She reached over and grabbed a stray fry from Josh's plate. "Read my contract."

"You have a *contract*?" Owen asked.

She rolled her eyes. "You two just keep on being the swamp people. I'll happily negotiate my terms with Sawyer. He's a grump, but he's fair and not a flake."

"We're flakes?" Josh asked. But as Kennedy opened her mouth to remind him of all the trouble he and Owen had caused over the years—some unintentional, some...not—he held up a hand. "Never mind."

He didn't want to do any more of the business stuff than he had to. His job was pretty much to charm and inform and up their ratings on the travel review sites. Owen's was all of that plus general maintenance of the boats and equipment. Sawyer, and previously Tommy, had handled the books and business. And apparently their employees. Which included their grandfather, cousin, and sister. Should have been a piece of cake. But negotiating with Kennedy was a no-win situation.

She worked for them because it was a family business and Leo made them hire her. She had a job as long as she wanted it, no matter how badly she might do it. Fortunately, she had a lot of pride and wouldn't do anything less than a great job. Within the very narrowly defined job description she'd agreed to. But she was a ball buster. Which was, of course, their own fault.

She'd been the only girl in a family with two older brothers and about a dozen male cousins. She didn't take any shit and she knew when a man was feeding her a line, probably before he did. She didn't much care what humans of the male persuasion thought of her and she, generally, knew she was smarter than any she came across.

But Kennedy was also beautiful and sharp and confident and pretty interesting. Even to her brothers. She'd gone from a beauty queen trained to look just right and to say and do all the right things, to a goth feminist in rebellion against everything superficial and repressive to girls and women. Needless to say, the guys in her life loved to push her buttons and they were *so damned easy* for her brothers to push.

"Plus, Trevor texted me that he'd pay me one hundred dollars if Ellie didn't kiss anyone, stayed fully clothed, and didn't end up in jail," Kennedy said of Ellie's boyfriend. She gave her grandmother an affectionate-if-put-upon look. "It's a tough gig, but I could use the money." She looked at Josh and Owen. "My 'bosses' are kinda cheap." She even put "bosses" in air quotes.

She moved off to the bar and took a seat next to the single groomsman from Iowa. The guy had been pretty quiet most of the day, but seemed nice enough. He looked over, gave Kennedy a friendly smile, took in her black hair with the red tips, her dark eye makeup and lipstick, her pierced ears and nose, her black tank that showed off a few of her tattoos, black shorts, and short black boots and his smile widened. And Josh was pretty sure Kennedy was about to drink her next couple of cocktails for free.

"So, as I was saying, you're trying to make a girl happy with something other than your…"

Josh saw Owen wince as he himself braced for Ellie's next term for penis.

"…dinglethumper," Ellie said.

Both of her grandsons groaned, which clearly made her happy.

"And I think that's great," she said.

Okay, she had a point. Underneath the cringe-worthy terminology. "Well, thanks," he told her. "Tori is…special."

Ellie gave him a soft, sincere smile. "Finally," she said.

He couldn't help but smile back at that. Ellie wanted everyone she loved to be madly in love. Even her ex-husband.

"Y'all are coming home after the wedding, yeah?" Ellie asked.

That made a knot in Josh's gut tighten. "I don't know how long she's staying."

"Well, then ask her. And then talk her into staying longer," Ellie said. As if it was as easy as ordering a burger.

Josh sighed. It had been just over twenty-four hours since Tori had walked onto his dock. How could Ellie expect that he and Tori would be talking about her staying? But if he asked her that, she'd ask him why it was taking him twenty-three hours longer than it had the other men in his family.

"Maybe a day or two," Owen said. "You can ease her into... everything. You can't just drop that sweet girl into the middle of our craziness."

"Well, she's gonna have to be okay with it," Ellie said lifting her shoulder. "I don't see any of that changing." She looked at Josh. "You've given her a good taste of crazy by now, haven't you?"

If Museums of Death and throwing her over his shoulder in a ballroom full of the rich and sort of famous counted, then yeah.

But his hesitation made his grandmother shake her head. "Oh, boy, you gotta get on that."

"Just blurt out how I feel?"

She laughed. "*Show her* how you feel."

Right. Big gesture. A spectacle. All of that. It didn't count if it wasn't a story everyone in town wanted to tell. Repeatedly.

Damn. What big gesture could he do for Tori? He'd have to come up with something good.

"And what if you scare her off?" Owen asked.

"If you think that's gonna happen, she's not the one," Ellie said resolutely.

But Josh wasn't so sure she'd be scared off. At all. Tori had her own brand of over-the-top. And she'd sure liked being kissed in the middle of the ballroom last night, and spun around the dance floor, and thrown over his shoulder. Just like those animals that needed extra love and attention and someone willing to go a little bat-shit—or cow-shit, as the case may be—crazy for them, didn't Tori deserve that same thing?

The idea of Tori being immersed in his world—and loving it—made his heart pound.

Yes, he needed to get her to Autre, on his turf, away from the plantation and sequins, away from the murder museum and his stand-up-tour-guide routine, to the heart of...*him*. He wanted to show her everything and show her that he was willing and able to be crazy about her.

"So where is she?" Ellie asked, looking pointedly at the empty chairs at Josh and Owen's table.

"Over there with Andrew," Josh said. "The groom. Her best friend from back home."

Ellie found Tori at the end of the bar. "They look cozy."

Yeah, they really frickin' did.

"So, you want me to leave them alone?" Ellie asked.

Josh sighed. Not really, but he should say yes. "Probably." Then again, *he* maybe couldn't interrupt them without being a bit of an asshole, but Ellie could get away with almost anything. "Well...I mean...*maybe*."

11

"Come on, Tori. You don't really know him."

"I'm *getting* to know him." Tori glanced from Andrew to where Josh sat across the bar.

Somehow they'd gotten separated when they'd come into Trahan's. There were a lot of people in here who were happy to see him and wanted to talk. Which didn't surprise her a bit. Josh was a people person. She'd realized it early on, watching him behind the bar last year, but it had been on full display during the tour of New Orleans today. He'd loved every bit of the storytelling, all the questions, the oohs and ahhs from the group. He'd clearly been in his element and if she'd been attracted to him before, it had multiplied tenfold today. It was clearly a case of opposites attract. He had that natural charisma that she was drawn to because she didn't have a bit.

Of course, the night before had been a part of the increased attraction too. She'd obviously thought he was very good-looking before they'd gotten naked together, but all day she'd been finding it hard not to get hot and tingly looking at his mouth and his hands and his ass. Even his voice had been making her panties wet, remembering the things he'd said last night with that hot, gruff tone as he'd made love to her, the deep groans and growls...

"Tori?"

She snapped her attention back to Andrew. Dang. She was incredibly distracted today. The tour had been fun and she'd loved all the weirdness, but she'd also been wondering when she and Josh would be alone again and looking forward to that night. Even in the middle of the Museum of Death she'd been thinking about how awesome he was and how much she wanted to kiss him.

"Yeah?" she asked Andrew.

"Are you okay?"

Horny. But okay. She smiled. "Yes."

"Did you hear what I said?"

"You said that you think I barely know Josh." She understood why he'd think that. They hadn't known each other long. Even less time than Andrew thought, actually. But she believed she did know Josh. He was a what-you-see-is-what-you-get guy. She loved that about him. She didn't have to figure him out. She could easily tell what he was feeling. Very much like a dog. In a very good way.

"I was saying that I don't think it's a good idea for you to think about moving down here."

Tori frowned. She'd confessed to her best friend that things were going well with Josh and that he was the first guy in a very long time that she could see having a long-term relationship with. And how hard that would be if one of them was in Iowa and one was in Louisiana.

"You don't think I should go for something that makes me this happy?"

"You have a business."

"So does he. And it's a lot harder to move a bayou than it is to move a barn." Of course, she wouldn't move her barn. But she could move everything inside it to a new barn. Outside of Autre, possibly. Her heart flipped at that thought.

"I guess this is just...hard for me," Andrew said.

"Hard for you? Why would it be hard for *you*?"

"I didn't know anything about this guy. You've told me *nothing*. Then suddenly you show up here, supposedly in this serious relationship, with this guy you're thinking about uprooting your life for. It's just taking me by surprise and it's tough to adjust quickly."

Tori frowned. "You don't have to adjust to it, Andrew. It's not about you."

The flash of hurt that crossed his face was obvious and Tori felt bad. She sighed. "I just mean, this doesn't change *your* life. And if I'm here, you can get to know Josh and get used to all of this faster. We could go out, the four of us." She did not want to go out with Paisley. Mostly because of Paisley and her obvious dislike for Tori even with Josh in the picture. There was a still a jealous vibe coming from the other woman that Tori couldn't understand. But Tori also thought that she and Josh would want to hang out at places like Trahan's and Ellie's, while Paisley would want something more lavish.

"Yeah, maybe we could do that," Andrew said, though he didn't seem enthusiastic. "You know I just want to take care of you."

She nodded. She did know that. Andrew had always been her main ally. "I know. And you know I love you for that."

Something else flashed across his face with that, but she couldn't quite name the emotion.

She didn't have a chance to think about it more, however, because just then a loud voice proclaimed, "Logan Trahan, I am here to be impressed. But I'm not holdin' my breath."

Tori looked toward the voice, her mouth stretching into a huge grin. "Oh my gosh."

"You know her?" Andrew asked, also watching Logan meet the much smaller, much older woman in the middle of his restaurant and lift her up into his arms for a hug.

"That's Ellie," Tori said, feeling what she could only term as fondness as she watched Ellie. She'd just met the woman the other day but, yes, she was very fond of her. "She's Josh's grandma."

"That's Josh's grandma?" Andrew asked, as Ellie said, "Holy shit, boy," to Logan and asked him, "Does that pretty wife of yours know that you're still out here letting all of that charm ooze out all over the place?"

"It is," Tori said with a nod, still watching the scene. "She's hilarious."

"What's she doing here?"

"I think Ellie kind of has a radar for fun," Tori said.

Ellie looked over and gave Tori a little wink and blew her a kiss. That warmed Tori to her toes. In a different way than Josh did, of course, but dang there was something about these Landrys that made her just...happy. She'd been a little stunned by how Josh's family had embraced her and pulled her into their fold, but she was already eager to experience it again. But she couldn't leave Andrew, and she didn't think her friend would want to join the Landry clan.

Josh looked over and their eyes met, and when she grinned at him, something in his expression became instantly hot and possessive. And yeah, that definitely warmed her. For just a second she thought he was going to get up and come over. But then someone else walked in.

Tori's smile got even bigger. This was highly entertaining. Right up there with the cemetery. "And that's Josh's sister," she said to Andrew.

Andrew looked over and took a moment to study Kennedy. Which is what any straight guy with a pulse would do. She was not only gorgeous, but she carried herself with a way that said, "You can look, but you can't handle this." Her hair, her piercings, her tattoos, her clothes, her...everything...was as opposite from Paisley Darbonne as someone could get.

"Um, wow," was all Andrew came up with as he turned back to Tori.

Tori gave a soft chuckle. That pretty much summed it up. "Josh's family is very...involved in each other's lives. And..."

"Loud and obnoxious?" Andrew asked.

Tori gave him a frown. She didn't know them well, but she felt defensive of his insult of them. "Boisterous, but fun. And loving."

"You're definitely getting in deep here, Tori," Andrew said. "Just slow down a little. Be careful."

"I don't need to be *careful*, Andrew. They're wonderful. And I'm not stupid."

"Of course you're not. But they're...new. And, sure, fun. I get the appeal. Like Cajun food. It's great. In small amounts. But it's spicy and different. Do you really want that all the time, every day?"

Tori shook her head. "Don't *you* like Cajun food?" She knew they weren't talking about the unique blend of unusual meats and spices that were an integral part of Louisiana cuisine.

"Sure. Sometimes."

"Well, I have Josh taking care of me now," she said with a smile. "He finds me adorable. His word. And I know that he'd have my back if I did something that other people thought was weird or something."

"Seems like he's the one doing weird things," Andrew said, almost in a mutter.

She laughed. Andrew had not enjoyed the museums or cemetery today. "He's different. And I love that. He makes me feel comfortable and accepted and...special."

Andrew's scowl deepened and Tori frowned in response. Shouldn't Andrew be *glad* about all of that?

"You're in love with him?" Andrew asked flatly.

The question hit her directly in the chest and she took a quick little breath. "Um...well..." The answer was clear though. And this was Andrew. He was hurt that she hadn't told him about Josh before. So now was a good time to confide in him. "I think I'm falling in love with him," she said honestly.

Andrew blew out a breath.

"What?" She leaned in. "You're not happy for me?"

Andrew looked at her, affection clear in his eyes. "I'm worried."

"You really don't like Josh?"

"It's not Josh I'm worried about, exactly." Andrew shifted on the barstool, also leaning in. "I just think you're...doing your thing."

"My thing?" But she knew what he meant and her stomach dropped. Hell, she'd just told Josh all about "her thing." She sighed. "Okay, you're worried this is Valentine's Day 2006 again." He'd even mentioned it last night.

Andrew gave her an indulgent smile. "You could have just passed him a note or said, 'Hey, Marcus, want to go out sometime?'"

"Yeah." Of course he had a point there. It was the same point he'd made back then too. "But Josh is different."

"When the guys with the kittens were going to dump them,

you could have just *asked* for the kittens. Or offered them ten bucks. I'm sure they would have taken it."

She sighed. "Fine. Okay."

"And instead of filling Carter Langley's car with mud and dog shit and grass, you could have just approached him or even gone to the cops and had them talk to him about taking care of his dogs."

"He wasn't cleaning their pen *at all*. I was showing him how unpleasant that is," Tori said hotly. And she'd do all of that again, dammit.

"You went over-the-top."

"I was trying to make a point."

"Well, *my* point is that this might be another time when you're overdoing it."

Tori felt her heart plummet toward her toes. Was falling for Josh an overreaction to everything? It had only been a day with Josh. Okay, kind of two. And two nights a year ago. But these days had been eventful. Fun. Different. Very different.

Yeah, okay, maybe she was overreacting a little.

Andrew reached out and took her hand. "You know I just want you to be happy, right?"

"I am."

"And safe. I *need* you to be safe. Physically. Emotionally." He squeezed her hand. "I know you've known him for a year, but you haven't been here with him. He hasn't come to Iowa. Maybe you've talked a lot but—"

"How do you know he hasn't been to Iowa?" He would know if Tori had been in Louisiana. She would have called him and hoped to see him.

He hesitated. "Uh—"

"You asked my dad."

He nodded. "Yes."

She wasn't surprised. She was a bit annoyed however. "Why?"

"Because I'm concerned. And curious."

"Great. And now my dad is concerned and curious."

"Of course he is."

"And he asked you to talk to me about all of this."

Tori had always known her dad didn't really understand her. He was a private person, who didn't make a big deal out of, well, anything really, and when *she* got worked up about things, he couldn't relate. Worse, when she made a big deal for *him*, he got terribly embarrassed. Like the time when she was in kindergarten and he'd come to school to have lunch with her. She'd nearly swooned. She'd sat him in the middle of her group of friends and they'd all given him their cookies and pudding cups, and Tori had told every single kid, person, and janitor her dad's name, his favorite baseball team, that he hid watermelon candies in the door of his truck, and that he and her mom went to bed early on Thursdays and moved the furniture around. That had been their explanation to her about the noises and bed squeaking she heard through the wall anyway. He'd never come to another school lunch with her. Or like the time when she was ten and made him his favorite brownies and took them into the diner where she knew he was having coffee with his friends and had all of the guys sing "Happy Birthday" to him and made him blow out the candles. Or the time she'd written a poem for the school talent night when she was a sixth grader and it had been all about him. He'd gotten up and left before she was done. It hadn't been because he'd been upset or didn't like it. She knew that. He was just painfully uncomfortable being the center of attention.

Over the years, she'd learned to pull back on all of that. Really being emotional toward any humans. She'd channeled it all into the animals she loved.

And that he *did* understand. They shared a love for animals and he'd been incredibly proud of her going to veterinarian school. So she'd been content with sharing that with him.

But her displays of passion, and love for the animals that involved punching people and cow poop, concerned him. Those he didn't understand.

And yes, hearing that she was considering moving to Louisiana for a guy she barely knew and that he'd never met, would definitely concern him. He wouldn't understand that for sure. He'd met her mom at the county fair when she was only twelve and he was fifteen, and he'd never dated anyone else since.

"He actually didn't ask me to talk to you," Andrew said. "He knew I'd take care of you."

That should have made her feel good. And for most of her life, it had. Having her dad and Andrew looking out for her had always given her a sense of comfort and security.

But right now, it was making her stomach knot up and her temper spike.

"You've met Josh," she said calmly. "He's great. And he really likes me."

Andrew blew out a breath. "Of course he does, Tori. You're awesome."

That took her by surprise. Of course she knew Andrew liked her and thought she was great. If weird. But he didn't say that often. "Well...thanks."

"You're surprised by that?" he asked.

Clearly it had showed in her face.

"Really? I've been your friend practically all our lives." He seemed almost hurt.

"Yes. Of course. You were protective. But maybe..." She frowned, thinking about it all. "I guess maybe I thought you just always felt a little sorry for me."

There it was. She and Andrew had always gotten along. She'd always appreciated having him on her side. She'd always enjoyed their time together. But she wasn't sure she'd ever felt that it was a soul-deep connection. Their friendship wasn't based on shared interests or passions. It was a way for her do "her thing" without horrible ridicule and his way of taking care of someone. It worked for them, for sure. Andrew accepted her and her craziness more easily than her dad did. But he didn't really get her either.

"Hell, Tori," Andrew said, pulling her attention back to his face and the conversation. "That's what you really thought? That I just felt sorry for you?"

"Hey," she said, squeezing his hand and giving him a little smile. "More than most, I can understand how you can love things that need you."

Andrew frowned and his grip on her hand tightened. "I don't love you because you *need* me, Tori. I love you because—"

"Andrew! I'm so happy to meet you!" Suddenly Ellie was at Andrew's side, beaming up at him.

Andrew was clearly startled as he turned on his stool. "Um, hello."

"I'm Ellie. One of Tori's biggest fans." Ellie gave Tori a bright smile.

That was such a nice thing to say and a surprising way for her to introduce herself that Tori was tongue-tied for a moment.

"Well, it's nice to meet another of Tori's fans," Andrew said, recovering and giving the older woman a smooth smile. "I'm the President of her fan club. Have been for years."

Tori looked at him with wide eyes.

"Lovely." Ellie patted him on the arm. "Though I don't know if you're going to have that position for much longer."

"I can't imagine what would change it," Andrew said, still smiling but with a coolness sneaking into his tone.

"Well, sounds to me like you will soon have your hands full leading a new fan club," Ellie said. "Gosh, tomorrow, right?"

Andrew looked puzzled. "I'm sorry?"

"Your wedding is tomorrow isn't it?" Ellie asked.

"Oh, well, yes."

"And you'll need to be the biggest fan of your lovely new wife," Ellie said.

Andrew cleared his throat. "Yes, well, of course."

Ellie nodded as if she'd expected that answer. "But no worries." She smiled up at Tori. "I think there's someone new to take over with Tori."

This was all so strange. But Tori couldn't help her smile. "You're all so sweet."

Andrew didn't say anything. But he was back to scowling.

"And speaking of your lovely bride," Ellie went on. "I know you need to get back to her. But," she said, turning to Tori. "I want you and Josh to go out with us."

"Go where?" Tori asked, intrigued for sure. Ellie Landry was something even in tiny Autre. In the city of New Orleans? This could only be trouble. In the best possible way.

"The Crimson Stiletto," Ellie said, her eyes twinkling.

"What's that?" Tori asked, already smiling.

"Burlesque club."

Tori laughed. "Oh, wow. I've never been to one."

"It is the *best* time."

"Hey, weren't you banned from the Crimson Stiletto?" Josh asked as he joined them.

Finally.

Tori felt her heart give a little extra *hi Josh* beat. He gave her a grin as if maybe he felt it too.

"Oh, we hashed all of that out," Ellie said, waving his question away.

"You sure? I don't really want to haul you out of there cussing and swinging. Again," Josh said.

Ellie didn't deny that had happened. She laughed. "Nope, not this time." She looked at Tori and Andrew. "My boyfriend's ex works there and we got into it last time I was in there. But once I got him to pay her the five hundred dollars she thought he owed her—which he didn't, but he's a big fancy lawyer so he can spare it—she decided I was a good egg and we get along fine now."

Andrew's mouth opened as if to reply, but then he shook his head and shut it. Tori hid her grin. She thought that maybe a lot of people had that reaction to Ellie a lot of the time. He did look at Josh, though. "You had to carry her out of there?" he seemingly couldn't help but ask.

"Yep, she was halfway across the table with her claws out when I grabbed her." He put his arm around Ellie. "Good thing she's little."

His grandma elbowed him in his side but grinned up at him. "Hey, a girl doesn't get by with calling Trevor an asshole douchebag with me."

"I've heard *you* call him worse. To his face," Josh teased.

"Yeah, but he's *mine*. I can do that."

And, though it was stupid, because they were just goofing around, Tori realized she wanted to say "he's mine" about someone.

No, not just someone.

Josh.

She wanted Josh to be hers.

She looked at Andrew, who was watching the Landrys with a bit of disbelief mixed with amusement. Andrew thought she was being crazy and overreacting. Andrew, who had known her most of her life and had seen her overreact. He was kind of a specialist in this area.

Dammit.

"Okay, okay," Josh said to Ellie. Then he looked up at Tori. "So what do you say? Crimson Stiletto?"

She started to reply but Andrew broke in. "We need to get back to the plantation. But if you want to go with your family, that's no problem. Tori is fine with us."

Josh let go of Ellie and moved in closer to Tori's stool. "Oh,

I'm not going anywhere without Tori. And yeah, *you* do probably need to get back. But she can come out with us."

Andrew took the last swallow of his drink and set his glass down. "Tori is a part of the wedding party. She needs to come back to Buckworth."

"Why?" Josh challenged.

"Paisley wants everyone there tonight," Andrew said with a lift of his shoulder.

"I will have Tori back in time for the wedding," Josh said.

"Not good enough," Andrew returned.

"How about we let Tori decide?"

Josh turned to her as her stomach dropped. Crap. She didn't want to have to choose between them.

"What do you say? We'll have fun and I promise I'll get you back and in bed with plenty of time to spare." He said it with a look in his eyes that told her clearly where he was spending tonight and that she wouldn't be going to *sleep* early. "Owen can take everyone back to Buckworth and Kennedy will drop us off later."

It sounded like fun, no doubt about it. Something she'd never done before. Something she couldn't do in Elton, Iowa. Or maybe anywhere in Iowa to be honest. And she certainly couldn't do it with Josh in Iowa. Or Ellie. Or Kennedy. People she was starting to care for, no matter how reckless or overreactive that might be.

But this was Andrew. Andrew's *wedding*. And Paisley was already put out by them being gone in New Orleans all day. It was kind of Tori's fault too. If Josh hadn't been her plus one, there wouldn't have been an alternative to the tour that got cancelled and everyone would have stuck close to Buckworth today.

"You're here for me," Andrew said, before Tori could reply. "I...appreciate that Josh is here as your date and I don't want to be a jerk, but you're really down here because of me, right?"

"Well, because of your *wedding*," Josh replied pointedly.

Andrew didn't respond to that. "I'd really like for you to come back to Buckworth with me."

Tori frowned. She wouldn't be going back just with him. It would be with the whole group from Iowa. And if she did go back to the plantation, it would because of the wedding activities, not to be *with* Andrew.

She knew that Josh was rubbing Andrew the wrong way. He was concerned she didn't know Josh well and that she was either taking this too seriously and was going to get hurt or make a fool of herself. But she wasn't choosing between these two men. She should be able to have her best friend *and* a romantic interest.

She frowned at Andrew. "Once you're back at Buckworth, you'll be with Paisley. Why do you care if I'm there?"

He cared because he was worried about her being with Josh. Obviously. But why? Clearly Josh wasn't going to *physically* harm her. And yeah, she might get her heart broken, but that was what Skype calls and ice cream and puppies were for. Why was Andrew this adamant about her not getting closer to Josh?

"Do you want to spend some time together later?" Andrew asked. "I'd love that. I can get away and we can...go for a walk or something." He leaned in, suddenly looking strangely earnest. "I'd love a chance to talk more. I think...there are some things that we need to talk about."

That was weird.

She looked at Josh. He met her eyes directly. "Your choice," he said. "I'm going wherever you're going."

"I don't want to keep you from the burlesque show if you want to go," she said.

"There's nothing I want to do more than be with you," he said, and she could see the sincerity in his eyes. "If you want to go back to the plantation, just say the word."

So she wasn't *really* choosing one guy over the other. Josh would come back to the plantation with her. That was probably the best decision. She sighed. "Okay, I should probably go back," she told Josh apologetically. "The club sounds so fun, but Andrew's right. I am here for the wedding stuff."

There was a flash of what could have been hurt in Josh's eyes. She was supposed to have returned to New Orleans for Mardi Gras for *him*. And she would have—of that she was certain—if she hadn't been coming for the wedding. But, well, she *had* come for the wedding. Too.

"We'll go to the burlesque show next time," Josh said, no sign of hurt evident now.

She loved the sound of *next time*. She smiled and nodded. "Okay."

He held out a hand to help her down from her stool. She took it at the same time Andrew grasped her elbow for the same reason and she ended up sliding to her feet awkwardly, in spite of being held on both sides.

Okay, this was all just weird.

Andrew dropped his hold on her after she had straightened and grabbed her purse, but Josh linked his fingers with hers as they started for the door to Trahan's.

"Hey, I'm going to the Stiletto with Ellie and Kennedy," Owen called to Josh.

Josh nodded. "Figured."

Owen grinned and gave him a thumbs-up.

"Owen likes burlesque?" Tori asked.

"Owen likes anyplace he can drink and flirt," Josh said with a laugh. "And now that he's got someone to drive him home, he's happy."

They stepped out onto the sidewalk and waited for the other Iowans to join them.

A brass band was playing up the block and Tori took a step to the corner to look down and try to catch a glimpse. The band was at the end of the street and was coming in their direction. But it was more than a band. It looked like a parade. At the front was a cop on a motorcycle leading the way and clearing a path. Right behind the bike was the band and behind them were what were clearly a bride and groom, carrying parasols and dancing. Following them was a crowd of people, waving white hankies and dancing in the street.

"A wedding parade?" Tori asked Josh as he moved in beside her.

He nodded. "A wedding second line. Huge tradition here. Usually they parade from the wedding venue to the reception."

She smiled at the festive group as they got closer.

"They have second lines for other things too," Josh said. "But the weddings are the ones you'll see most often."

The parade got to their corner and Tori and Josh watched them pass. She was unable to keep from grinning.

"Now *that* is how someone should look on their wedding day," she said, watching the bride and groom dance down the street with their friends and family. "Full of joy and ready to show it off to everyone."

"Agreed."

She looked up at Josh. His voice was a little husky. She smiled. "Why aren't Andrew and Paisley doing one of these?"

He shrugged. "It's not for everyone, I guess."

"Well," she said with a deep breath. "This is totally my style. My mom and dad would hate it, but yeah—" She nodded. "I would love it."

"Me too." He reached up and tucked a strand of hair behind her ear. "And it probably goes without saying that my family would be all in."

She laughed. "Very true."

The rest of their group joined them as the second line passed their corner. Josh gave a brief history of the tradition to everyone and then they headed across Jackson Square to Café du Monde for beignets before walking to the bus that would take them back to Buckworth.

It was a quieter drive back. Everyone was busy eating beignets, and the group was clearly tired after the big day. But they all seemed happy. Josh was driving this time, so Tori sat in the seat behind the driver's seat and rested her head on the window, watching the scenery pass by. Andrew, thankfully, sat back near his parents where they could chat and Tori was mostly left alone.

The drive back was just over an hour and by the time they pulled into the grounds of the plantation, Tori really just wanted to take a shower and maybe cuddle up in that big bed in her room. Without pajamas on. With a big, hot bartender-swamp boat tour captain.

But Paisley was on the porch when Tori stepped off the bus.

And she wasn't, apparently, dying to see Andrew. She came straight for Tori, grabbed her hand, and tugged her into the house and into the torture chamber otherwise known as Hair and Makeup Practice for Tomorrow.

12

J osh watched Paisley drag Tori into the house.

It was almost as if she'd been lying in wait.

As he climbed the steps to the huge front porch, he noticed a half-full glass of lemonade with a lipstick print on the rim next to a white wicker chair.

Yep, she'd been lying in wait. But not for Andrew.

Josh sighed and headed inside. He paused in the foyer, not really sure what to do or where to go.

Andrew and his groomsman had headed off to the back of the house, his parents and their friends had started up the steps, and Tori was God knew where.

Josh went to their room—yes, he was thinking of it as *theirs* and not just Tori's now—and stood in the middle of the polished hardwood floor, looking around.

It was too early to go to bed. Plus he had plans for a certain brunette before he would be even close to ready to sleep. He wasn't that into television. He didn't have computer access or any books with him. And he wasn't really an indoors kind of guy anyway.

He could wander around the property, he supposed. He'd never explored this plantation, but knew that it was one that had multiple buildings on the grounds including original slave cabins that could be toured. There was also an elaborate garden and hedge maze behind the house and a riding stable. The Richardson family, the last to purchase the planation and live in the main house, still owned the plantation and felt it was important to educate about that period of history and the slave experience, as well as remembering the people who had helped build up the plantation. The family still grew sugarcane in the northern fields and at least three descendants still lived in houses on the property.

Or he could go for a run, he thought as his gaze fell on his tennis shoes next to his bag. That sounded good. Though he'd been out in the fresh air all day, he felt strangely restless.

Ten minutes later he was heading down the path at the back of the house. He'd resisted the urge to try to find Tori and see what she was up to. But he thought about her the entire time he ran. Especially when he passed the big barn. And by the time he got back to the house, he really needed to see her.

He still wasn't sure what the absolutely perfect grand gesture for Tori was, but he had found something she was going to love and that was good for right now.

Josh took a quick shower and then went to find her. It had been almost two hours since they'd gotten back from New Orleans. Surely she'd be ready to be done with whatever

Paisley had her doing. He didn't even need to know what that was to know Tori would be over it.

The sound of female laughter greeted him as he stepped off the staircase, and he took an immediate left, heading for one of the small living rooms. One of the *parlors,* if he was being completely accurate.

He stopped outside the door and peeked around the corner. The room was full of women sitting around tables covered with makeup and various mirrors, brushes, and tools. There was a woman at the other end of the room from the doorway addressing the group as she made up Paisley's face. All of the women were alternating between watching her and then looking at themselves in the mirrors and trying to replicate what she was doing. A bunch of Paisley's friends being *required* to look into mirrors? He could probably walk right in, grab Tori, and walk back out without anyone noticing.

Thankfully, Tori was sitting at one of the tables toward the back of the room, closest to the door. He could only see her from the side, but he was happy to see she looked miserable. Well, he wasn't happy she was miserable, but it would make talking her into sneaking out easier. He just needed to get her attention. Still, he didn't want to interrupt the session. In part, because he didn't want to piss Paisley off. But he also didn't want to risk calling attention to he and Tori slipping off. Because *he* didn't want to be interrupted. If he pulled Tori out of the room and Paisley got irritated, she might tell Andrew. And Andrew might come looking for them.

Andrew had had enough of Tori's attention today.

"*Tori,*" Josh tried to whisper. But there was no way she was going to hear him.

He thought quickly and headed back upstairs. In the bottom of his bag were three strands of Mardi Gras beads. He wasn't sure how or when they'd gotten in there, but he'd noticed them when he'd changed clothes. He was back down outside of the parlor door five minutes later.

He waited until the woman at the front turned away and then he tossed a strand of beads at Tori's leg.

He missed.

The beads hit the hardwood floor and slid under Tori's table. No one seemed to notice. Josh blew out a breath and tossed the next strand. This time he hit Tori's shoe, but she simply moved her foot, apparently thinking someone at the table had inadvertently bumped her.

Josh rolled his eyes. This really should be easier. Or he could just wait for her to be done. But he wanted to save her from this. Or maybe he just wanted to see if she'd *let* him save her from this. He hadn't loved that she'd chosen returning to Buckworth with Andrew over staying in New Orleans with Josh and his family. But he understood it. This was her friend's wedding and she needed to be a part of it. And yes, Josh was going to keep insisting to himself that her coming back here with Andrew was all about the wedding and not about Andrew himself. She'd wanted to go to the burlesque club with them more than she'd wanted to come back to the plantation. He was sure of it. Ninety-five percent sure, anyway.

There was something about Andrew that made Josh twitchy, he wasn't going to lie.

At least, not to himself. To Tori? Yeah, he wasn't going to tell her that.

He took a deep breath and with absolute focus on his target —Tori's left lower leg—and a soft underhanded toss, he threw the last strand of beads.

This time he hit her exactly where he'd intended and she looked down. Frowning she bent to pick up the beads—all three strands now lying around her chair and under the table —then pivoted in her seat. Her eyes widened when she saw him in the doorway. He grinned and put his finger to his lips. Then he beckoned for her to come to him.

She glanced toward the front of the room, then back to him. She shook her head quickly.

He nodded. "Please," he mouthed.

She frowned, looked to the makeover instructor again, then back to Josh. "Five minutes," she mouthed to him.

No. Dammit. It was completely irrational, but he wanted her *now* and he wanted her to choose him over all of this hoopla. That she didn't even like.

Aware that he was acting like a toddler, he frowned back at her and shook his head. "Now," he mouthed.

Her eyes narrowed and she pointed at her face. It was only partially made up. He couldn't tell the details but it looked like she had half of her face done in one color and the other half in another, along with eyeshadow and eyelashes on only one eye. He shrugged. "Don't care," he mouthed.

She sighed and turned back to face the table. But just when Josh thought he really was going to have to stomp into that room and throw her over his shoulder again—not that he minded that move—she reached for something in the middle of the table and bumped her glass of champagne. Somehow the glass tipped *toward* her rather than away, dumping what had to have been fifty-bucks worth of expensive champagne into her lap.

"Oh my gosh!" she exclaimed, shooting to her feet.

Everyone in the room stopped talking and peering into mirrors and turned to look at her. "Are you okay?" Paisley asked.

"Yes. Yes. I'm just all...wet and sticky," Tori said. "I'd better...go."

The part of Josh's brain that was, and always would be, a thirteen-year-old boy smirked at the "wet and sticky" line, but he'd pulled himself together by the time Tori got to the door and slipped into the hallway.

"What's going on?" she asked him in a low whisper as she pulled him partway down the hall away from the door.

"I'm rescuing you," he said.

She stopped and lifted a brow. "You're rescuing me?"

"Yeah, you're sick of all of that, aren't you?" He jerked a thumb in the general direction of the parlor.

"Well, yes, but I kind of rescued myself in there, didn't I?" she asked, fighting a small smile.

Josh thought about it, then grinned. "Yeah, I guess you did. But I gave you a good excuse."

"I haven't heard the excuse yet," she said. "How do I know it's good?"

He moved in closer and ran a hand up her arm to her shoulder, then to the back of her neck. He pulled her forward and she took the tiny step that brought her right up against him. "It's *really* good," he said huskily, taking in all the details of her face, from her natural long lashes to the fake ones on the right, the makeup covering her skin, the remnants of some lipstick she must have wiped off. And most especially the way her pupils dilated when she was standing this close to him.

She swallowed. "Now my expectations are *really* high."

"Good." He grinned, then reached up and peeled the fake eyelashes from her upper lid. He rolled it into a little ball and then tossed it into the base of the potted plant to his left. "I like the lighter shade better," he said, running the pad of his thumb over her cheek.

Tori's hands flew to her face. "Oh, geez, I must look ridiculous."

"You look beautiful. And I don't care about this." He ran his thumb over the eyelid that had plum eyeshadow on it. He removed some of it, but not all. This was the good stuff. It wasn't coming off without eye makeup remover. "Plum is not your color."

She laughed softly. "Hey, Josh?"

"Yeah?"

"Thanks for the rescue."

"Any time." And he meant that.

"Now get me out of this hallway and away from all the buffing and blending and brushing."

He laughed too. "Hey, that does make me wonder...you didn't even get all of the eye makeup stuff done? What the hell have you all been doing in there?"

She rolled her half-made-up eyes. "There was this whole skin care preparation routine we had to do before we even started. We're all getting a basket of products delivered to our rooms tonight to use in the morning before our makeup." She looked up at him seriously. "I lost at least two layers of dermis in there. I swear."

He nodded solemnly. "That's terrible. You definitely needed rescuing."

"I really did. Where have you been?"

"I took a run."

"Oh?" She stepped back and looked him up and down. "I appreciate it."

He reached out and pinched her on the ass. "Let's go. I found something while I was out."

"Oh. So we're not going upstairs early tonight? Either?"

He shook his head, as if exasperated—which he wasn't, at all. "I had no idea what a nympho you were."

She grinned. "Me either."

He liked that. A lot.

He grabbed her hand. "Come on. Let me show you this. You're going to love it. Then we'll go upstairs."

"Okay." She sighed, pretending to be put out.

It wouldn't last. He knew her and this was going to be huge.

As he led her out to the back of the house, through the hedge maze, and down the path toward the barn, he realized that he loved thinking he knew her.

"They have a barn?" she asked as the big building came into view outside of the maze.

"Yep. And it's not just for looks," he said.

"What do they have?" Her voice gave away her excitement.

"Horses mostly," he said. "They offer horseback riding to guests and visitors. They have a few carriages and a couple of hayracks."

"We do hayrack rides back home," she said.

"They've got a couple of dogs too," Josh told her, loving the way her walking pace had picked up. He didn't think she was even aware of it.

"Oh my gosh." She sighed. "Yes, I need a dog break."

Yes. He knew it. And there was even more. Josh led her to the side door one of the groundskeepers had showed him earlier when he'd wandered into the barn. He held the door open for her. The barn looked—and smelled—like a barn, and Josh noted with a grin that Tori took a big breath as she stepped inside. The combination of wood, hay, dirt, and animals was a sharp contrast to the air in the mansion that smelled like wood polish and flowers and baked goods. He loved that she preferred this. It wasn't like the bayou smelled what most people would call *good*. But Tori just might not mind.

"Right over here." Josh led her to the third stall on the right. He got in front of her because he wanted to see her face.

He turned as she came around the edge of the stall, and he watched as she scanned the hay and found what he'd brought her to see.

"Oh my God!" She stepped forward and hit her knees beside the mama cat and her six kittens.

Josh felt satisfaction and lust and love—yes, love—flood

him as he propped his shoulder against the wooden post beside him and settled in to watch.

Tori started talking with the mother cat softly, letting the cat sniff her fingers, and reaching out slowly to touch the mother's head first.

"She's clearly used to having people around," Tori said, smiling up at him.

"I talked to the groom a little bit earlier," Josh said of the man who told him he'd been caring for the horses and stables here for over twenty years. "She's basically a house cat but just out here in the barn."

Tori turned her attention back to the cat. "She's clearly well cared for."

"I thought you'd like this."

"I *love* it." She gave him a smile that made his heart turn over in his chest. "Thank you."

"Anything for that smile, Iowa," he told her, noting his voice was gruff.

She looked touched by that and...something else. Something he couldn't quite name. Then she sat down in the hay and reached out for the kittens.

And just like that, he knew that he'd lost being center of her attention for at least a little while. But he didn't mind. He joined her on the hay and they spent the next thirty minutes holding and petting kittens.

He loved animals. Kittens were cute. No one could debate that. But there was nothing like watching Tori with animals. He'd heard her talk about them. He'd heard her stories and seen her face as she told them. But this was even better.

If he could talk her into moving to Louisiana, he was going to have to buy her a farm because he was going to need to keep her supplied with four-legged friends. For her, but also because of what it did to him. He really liked the way this woman made him feel.

"Is this one the runt?" he asked Tori, holding up the kitten he had cradled in his hand.

Tori looked over. She sat cross-legged and had two in her lap, one on her shoulder, and another in her hands.

She smiled. "Yep. But she seems to be doing okay. They're about four weeks old and they're all healthy. She's clearly been feeding."

Josh looked down at the purring ball of fluff in his hands, running a finger over the extra soft fur on the top of her head. Of course, Tori had checked them all out as they'd played. He winced as one of the kittens climbed his sleeve and sank her claws into his shoulder. He reached up and gingerly unhooked her from his shirt. "Now, come on, pretty girl," he said to the kitten. "Holes in the shirt I can deal with, but maybe not holes in *me*." She mewed at him, staring back with her big blue eyes. She was really cute. "Okay, see, then you say something sweet like that." He sighed and put her back on his shoulder. She nuzzled his ear and he patted her head. "Yes, I forgive you."

"Okay, that's it." Tori set all of the kittens to the side and stood.

"That's...what?" Josh asked.

She brushed hay off of her skirt. Then she reached for the ties on the top of her shoulders that were keeping the straps of her dress up. She pulled one loose and the front of her dress fell down, revealing the top curve of one breast.

"I am very in favor of...whatever this is," Josh said, his body throbbing with need instantaneously.

She gave him a soft smile and his cock got even harder. "I want you, Josh. I've wanted you since the first minute we met. Sex with you was amazing. But you and kittens? You *saved* me from wedding makeovers with Paisley...with *kittens*. I've never wanted *anything* like I want you right now." She pulled the other tie loose and her dress fell to her waist. She wasn't wearing a bra. "Right here."

He peeled the kitten off of his shoulder again and set her and her runt sister back in the hay with their mom. "I didn't bring you down here to see the kittens so you'd get naked."

"Which is all the more reason that I really want to get naked with you."

"Here?" He got to his feet, his cock swelling and his chest tight. "You sure?"

She looked around. "Oh yeah." She pushed her dress to the barn floor and stood in front of him in tiny white panties and white sandals. "I'm totally good here. This is my turf."

He stripped his shirt off and tossed it at her feet. "You better put this on."

"You want me to put clothes *on*?" But she picked it up and pulled it over her head. Then she reached underneath and slid her panties down her legs, kicking them so they landed at his feet.

He leaned over and swept them up, tucking them into his jeans pocket. Then unbuttoned and unzipped those jeans as he stepped forward. He knew she'd already figured out why she needed the shirt, but he said, "Don't want your back getting all scratched up." Then he cupped her naked butt in his hands and lifted her. He walked forward until her back was against the stall behind her. "Or splinters in your sweet ass," he said, pressing into her, his cock against her hot center. "When I take you hard up against the wood."

"Yes. Oh my God, yes. Please make me get wet every time I walk by a barn stall."

Well, not something he'd ever thought about doing, but okay. He chuckled. "Can do."

"But, we should go around the corner," she said, breathlessly.

"Around...what?"

"I've thought about barn sex before, but I didn't think about having an audience." Her gaze dropped to the floor behind him.

And the kittens.

Right.

He lifted her and turned them both, carrying them into the next stall. Then he pressed her into *that* wood and took her mouth in a hot kiss. She wiggled against him, gripping his hips with her knees, giving him that little moan that fired his blood and made him need her like air.

He curled his fingers into her ass and ground against her.

She reached between them and pushed his jeans and boxers out of the way. She wrapped her hand around him and he groaned, arching instinctively into her fist.

"This is going to be so good," she said, eagerly.

It was sex in a barn. But...yeah, it was going to be so good.

"Condom in my left pocket."

"My right hand is full."

She squeezed him and Josh had to grit his teeth. "Babe, we can do this two ways. Me balls deep with a condom on, or me coming all over your sweet hand and then getting you off another way. I'm good with either."

Tori jerked her hand away. "Oh no. I want you inside."

He was torn between laughing and swearing. "Condom. Please," he said tightly.

She dug in his pocket, pulled it out, ripped it open, and rolled it on.

He gave a sigh of relief even as anticipation tightened his balls to holy-fuck levels. He pulled her hips forward as he thrust, sliding deep and true.

Balls. Deep.

Tori gasped and sighed and then tightened her arms around his neck. "Yes, Josh."

He tried to move his hands so they were more behind her

lower back between her and the hard wood, but it was difficult to hold her that way.

She wiggled. "Josh."

"Hang on." He tried to get just one hand between her back and the stall and keep one under her ass. "I don't want to hurt you."

"You're not."

"But I haven't started really...doing it yet."

"I'm good. I'm fine. Please start doing it," she said with a soft laugh.

"I just want to be sure to be gentle. And you make me want to...go crazy."

"Josh," she pulled back and looked at him. "I've had my foot broken by a horse in a barn, I dislocated my shoulder falling out of a barn loft rescuing an owl, I've been bitten by...well, a lot of animals...in barns, and I've had my hand—"

He kissed her, cutting that description off, and pulled out then thrust in again.

She gripped his shoulders and her pussy tightened around him.

When he released her lips he said, "Okay, you're a tough girl."

"I am. I can take anything you can dish out in this barn, Josh."

"Sounds like a challenge."

"Totally."

He growled. And then he gave her exactly what she was asking for.

He cupped her ass and thrust deep, pounding into her over and over.

She held on tight, encouraging him with gasps and groans. He felt her pussy tightening around him, the sweet friction and wet heat, heaven on earth.

"You with me, Tor—"

She came before he could even finish the question. Her inner muscles clenched hard and she called out his name. He pounded in and out again a dozen times and then felt his orgasm rip from his balls. He groaned her name, holding her tight, emptying himself inside the condom.

Afterward, he held her against the stall, breathing hard. She was wrapped around him and gave no indication of wanting to let go.

Several minutes passed. Finally they could hear the tiny mews from the next stall over their ragged breathing.

Josh pulled back and looked into Tori's face. He grinned. "I'm going to take that as feline applause."

She laughed. "It was definitely applause worthy."

He kissed. Long, and deep, and hot, and sweet. Then he put her on her feet.

With her eyes on his, she pulled his shirt up and over her head, and handed it to him. He drank in the sight of her sweet, naked body before ducking his head through the shirt. She slipped around the edge of the stall to retrieve her dress.

He re-tucked and re-zipped. And waited.

He could hear her talking softly to the kittens and he smiled and shook his head. She was something. Something he was never going to find again.

He had to figure out an appropriately huge gesture to show her how he felt.

When she finally came back out of the stall, she had her dress and shoes back on.

But not her underwear. Those were in his pocket. And he was keeping them.

Tori stepped up next to him, gave him a huge smile, and slipped her hand into his.

She sighed. "Kittens."

"And hot barn stall sex."

"Not necessarily in that order."

He gave her a look. "You sure? I have the feeling it would take a lot to top kittens for you."

She laughed. "It would. But you did."

And he felt stupidly proud of that.

———

Liquid eyeliner was one of the cruelest inventions ever.

Who the fuck had come up with it? And why did women buy it? Why weren't they writing letters to Congress and protesting in the streets? This industry needed to be shut down.

Tori stared into the mirror. The women who were able to apply it beautifully on the first try were witches. It was that simple.

Feeling frustration welling up, she pulled another makeup remover from the plastic tub by the sink. She wiped her eyes clean. Again. And tossed the remover cloth on the counter with the other eight. Her eyes were bloodshot, the lids were now bright red, she'd lost a few lashes, and worse than looking like she was having an intense allergic reaction to something was the fact that she was going to have to admit that she shouldn't have ducked out of the makeup session early.

Of course, it had been worth it. So worth it.

She was tired today. She and Josh had come back from the barn and had sex twice more before falling asleep. They'd also talked about their day in New Orleans. He'd told her some history of the plantation. She'd told him about the first time her dad had taken her to their shed and showed her the mother cat having kittens in her little red wagon.

Being tired today was worth every bit of that.

But Paisley was going to kill her if she came down looking like this.

Her phone lit up from where she had it propped against the mirror. She'd been watching YouTube tutorials. And ignoring the five missed calls from Andrew. Three last night and two this morning.

Make that three this morning.

Tori didn't reach for the phone. She just stared at the screen that said ANDREW, until it stopped and went black again. She wasn't sure why she was avoiding him. He was probably nervous about today and needed to talk to his best friend.

But she didn't want to answer. She didn't want to listen to his voicemails. Yeah, there were five of those too.

A little notification popped up and again she corrected the number. Six. Six voicemails.

She was avoiding her best friend on his wedding day. What was that?

But she knew. She was mad at him. He'd been trying to talk her out of being crazy about Josh. He'd gotten into her head. He'd made her pull back.

She knew he wasn't *wrong*. She did do this. The overreacting thing. But with Josh it just felt so damned good. In the past, when she'd put her feelings out there, the other person hadn't wanted it. But Josh wanted her. She could feel it in everything he did and said. Even how he looked at her.

Sure, it might be just for fun. Or just for sex. Or the combination of the two that they had going. But even if that was all it was, even if this was temporary, even if this was going to break her heart, it was going to be absolutely worth it.

But she didn't want to talk to Andrew about it. That made her stomach hurt a little. Andrew had always been there for her. He'd protected her. He'd buffered things for her. He'd been on her side.

Now it didn't feel like he was on her side. In the past, he'd been doing it to keep her from being embarrassed. She wasn't embarrassed with Josh. There was nothing about Josh or being with him that made her feel anything but good. Happy. Hot.

Sexy. Interesting. Fun. Why was Andrew trying to talk her out of that?

She looked at the voicemail notifications. Maybe this wasn't about Josh. Maybe this was about Andrew.

We need to talk before the ceremony.

And now he was texting.

She was surprised he hadn't done that before now. Whatever this was, he wanted to literally *talk* about it.

Yeah, this was bigger than her getting involved with Josh.

Shit.

She looked back in the mirror. She had one hour before photos and about two hours worth of work to do here. She didn't have time for a conversation.

But how could she *not* talk to him if he needed her?

"Argh!" She threw the liquid eyeliner tube into the sink and blew out a breath. There had to be an option here. She'd slept past the makeup session with the other bridesmaids. And the hair session. And probably some other session she didn't remember.

She figured Paisley already had a voodoo doll of her and Tori expected to start feeling pain from it any minute.

Then she stared into the mirror again. Maybe *this* was Paisley's voodoo-doll revenge.

"Tori?"

She jumped as she heard Josh on the other side of the bathroom door. She'd left him sleeping in bed two hours ago. It had been the hardest getting-out-of-bed-morning she'd ever had. "Uh, hey. Good morning."

"Mornin'."

Gah, that husky drawl first thing in the morning made her tingly all over even through a wooden door.

"Uh, you okay in there?" he asked.

No. She wasn't. At all. She went to the door and pulled it open. "Nope."

His eyes widened as he took in the sight of her. She was dressed in a silk bathrobe. Her hair was pinned up on one side, but for some reason she couldn't get the other side up properly. And, of course, the eye situation.

But she didn't care how she looked at the moment. Because he was wearing only a pair of jeans that he hadn't even buttoned up fully. His hair was short enough that it didn't really get mussed and he always had the short beard, so he didn't look morning-disheveled exactly, but he did still manage to exude an   I-just-rolled-out-of-bed-and-would-love-to-take-you-back-there vibe.

"What's going on?" he asked, propping a shoulder against the doorjamb.

Tori sighed. She couldn't jump on him. "Pictures are in an hour," she told him. "And this"—she waved her hand up and down her body, indicating, well, everything about her appearance—"is not going well."

He bit his bottom lip, looking very much like he was trying not to grin.

"You can laugh," she told him. "It's ridiculous. Everything about me and makeup is ridiculous."

He reached out, hooked a finger in the tie of the bathrobe, and pulled her close. Then he kissed her, cupping her face, and making her whole body ache even as she felt all the tension melt away.

Worth. It.

Whatever else happened.

He let her go after a few delicious seconds. "We can fix this," he told her.

"This?"

He started backing her into the bathroom. "Yeah."

"*We* can fix *this*?" she asked, waving a hand in front of her face as her butt hit the counter.

He nodded. Then he lifted her up on the counter and stepped between her knees.

"Uh, Josh." Her heart was fluttering, and she was forcing herself to remember that she had to get ready for the wedding. Because she really just wanted to lose the robe and let Josh do... whatever he wanted. "I need to get my makeup on." There, that almost sounded like she meant it.

"I know." He studied her face. Then he leaned in...reaching for something behind her. He straightened with a tube of concealer and a wedge sponge in his hand. He uncapped the tube, as if he actually knew what he was doing, and reached toward her face.

Tori jerked back. "What are you doing?"

"Applying your makeup," he said simply. "Concealer first, set with powder, then foundation, *then* eyes."

She waited a second, waiting for him to laugh. He didn't.

"You know how to do makeup?"

"I do."

She laughed. "Really? Just looking at a lot of girls with makeup on doesn't really make you an expert, does it?"

He gave her a little smile. "Tori, I know *lots* of things about girls."

"Yes, I'm aware."

"But not all of those girls are girls I've gotten naked with."

She narrowed her eyes. "What do you mean?"

"I'll have you know," he said. "That I did makeup *and* hair for not one but *two* Miss Louisiana Teens." He shrugged. "One was a *past* winner and was going back for an award ceremony, but I still did her hair and makeup."

Tori realized that she hadn't blinked for several seconds. "Excuse me?" she finally managed.

He grinned. "My sister was a beauty pageant contestant for years. Mom is a past beauty queen. So when Kennedy was little and Mom was working, she taught me and Sawyer to do it all so we could help out. And it took both of us," he said, shaking his head. "She loved the competitions, but she hated getting her hair done. One of us would hold her and the other would do her hair. We got really good at being really fast. The girl was a biter."

Tori choked out a laugh. She didn't know which thing surprised, or delighted, her most. "*Kennedy* was into beauty pageants?" She thought about Kennedy's dark eye makeup and lipstick, her tattoos and piercings, and most of all, her I've-got-my-own-rules-for-everything attitude.

"'Til she was thirteen," Josh said with a nod. "When she decided she'd had enough of all the bullshit and decided to take her hair and makeup skills, and her love of making an impression, in a new feminist direction."

Tori had to admit that Kennedy's look was very polished and clearly deliberate. It probably did take mad makeup skills to get all of that right. "Did she win any pageants?"

"Oh yeah," he said with a nod. "She's competitive as fuck."

"Wow." Tori looked at him thoughtfully. "So you really know what to do with a makeup brush, huh?"

"*And* a hairbrush."

She shrugged. "Go for it."

Having him working on her face and hair required him to stand *really* close to her. Which was great. She loved it in fact. His body heat, his scent, his confident but gentle touch, his hard chest and abs...it was all *very* good. His absolute focus and attention to the job at hand and not even letting one finger drift anywhere it wasn't supposed to wasn't as good.

She was completely horny and frustrated by the time he finished lining her eyes with the stupid liquid liner. As if it was the easiest thing in the world.

"Stop wiggling," he told her.

"Can't."

"And stop looking at me like that," he said, his gaze on her eyebrows as he shaped them.

He was *shaping her eyebrows*. She blew out a breath. "Like what?"

"Like you're imagining me hiking up this robe and sliding deep right here on the counter."

Her body flushed and her lungs stopped working for a second. "You don't even have to kiss me and mess up my makeup."

He huffed out a short laugh. "I'm not fucking you without kissing you."

"Why not?" That seemed like an unnecessarily restrictive rule.

"Because I really like kissing you."

"But the fucking—"

"Don't say fucking." Now he was frowning.

"Why not?"

"Because that makes me think about it. And how I couldn't do it facing you. You'd put your cheek against mine or something at some point. Or I'd forget myself and grab your hair. But that if I put you on your feet and turned you to face the mirror, I could fuck you without touching your face or hair *and* I'd get to see your face when you come."

She got hot and wet and...pissed...instantly. "That's really mean," she said, breathless in spite of being annoyed. "I can't walk down that aisle all wet and achy, knowing it's going to be *hours* before we can—"

He pulled her off the counter and turned her swiftly. *Yes.* She braced her hands on the counter as she watched him pull a condom from his pocket, push his jeans down, and roll it onto his big, hard cock.

He reached for the tie on her robe and met her eyes in the mirror. "You've got a point." Her robe fell away, revealing her naked body to him.

She smirked at him. "Yeah, I do."

"I still need to finish your hair," he said.

"Then you'd better hurry up with this."

He bent his knees and thrust into her, making her gasp and grip the edge of the sink. He pulled out and then thrust again. Hard, deep, and fast.

She pressed back into him, arching her back, and they both groaned as he went even deeper, hitting that magic spot inside her. They hadn't done it with him behind until now and, man, they'd been missing out.

"Josh, yes," she managed to get out between gasps.

"So. Fucking. Sweet." He held her hips tightly as he pounded into her.

She was so close, so fast. Then he reached around and found her clit and she went soaring. He was right behind her, growling deeply, and coming hard, holding her to him.

13

They didn't have a lot of time for recovery, and Tori could swear she could still feel the bolts of hot lightning shooting through her as she made her way down the staircase in her bridesmaid's dress, her hair and makeup perfect, with three minutes to spare.

It might have been the sex on the counter. It might have been the way Josh looked her over once he'd zipped up her dress and said, "Holy shit, Tori. You're fucking gorgeous." It might have also been the way he'd leaned in a whispered, "If you think there's any way that you're *not* getting hay all over that dress later, you're crazy."

She swallowed and stepped off the bottom step. She just

had to get through photos, a wedding ceremony, and the first half of the reception. After the customary dances and toasts and cake cutting, surely they could duck out.

But that was going to be *hours* from now. Of course he'd be at the ceremony and reception with her, but she had at least a few duties left ahead of her. And even looking at him in a suit after last night and that morning might just make it impossible to get through the rest of the day without pulling him into a storage closet or something.

"Tori, you're finally here," Paisley greeted her. She inspected Tori's makeup and hair, making sure to push a couple of the bobby pins in a little tighter. Tori winced and told herself that bobby pins in the head were better than actual pins in a voodoo doll. Then Paisley gave her a nod that clearly said, "Fine, you're passable but I'm still annoyed with you."

Tori sighed and joined the group near the rose bushes. At least all of her horny thoughts about Josh had been overridden.

The wedding pictures took forever, and twice Andrew had pulled Tori to the side only to get interrupted by the photographer or Paisley. Obviously the groom was needed in most of the photos, so finally Tori promised they'd talk as soon as the photo session was over. He had an earnest, restless look about him and Tori found herself concerned as the session drug on.

Of course, before they could get a second alone afterward, someone dragged him off for something else.

Tori sighed. She was going to be doing that a lot today, she suspected. Okay, so she needed to get through the ceremony, half of the reception, and a conversation with Andrew before she could be with Josh alone again. Fine. She could do that. It would all be great.

And she kept thinking that.

Right up until she'd walked down the aisle. She'd caught Josh's eye in one of the near-the-back pews, gotten a quick wink, paused at the end of the silk runner lining the aisle to give Andrew a smile, and pivoted to take her place several feet down from the center to make room for the long line of brides-maids to come.

But she felt a hand on her elbow before she could take a step toward her position. She turned back, stunned to find that Andrew had grabbed her arm.

"Tori, we have to talk."

She felt her eyebrows rise nearly to her hairline. "What are you doing?"

"I have something I have to say."

She glanced quickly at the congregation, then at the minister, then back to Andrew. "*Now*?"

"Yes. Now. No, actually last night. But you weren't answering the phone. And then this morning. But you still weren't answering your phone. But then—" He sucked in a deep breath. "Okay, I should have said this a long time ago. A *long* time ago. But I didn't know... I never realized. And then—"

Tori forgot about everyone around them. Andrew looked like he was about to hyperventilate. She put her hand on top of his on her arm. "Breathe," she told him softly. "It's okay. We'll talk right after."

But he was shaking his head before she finished. "No. It can't wait. It has to be now. Or never." He looked physically pained.

She frowned. This was her best friend. The one person who'd always had her back. She hadn't cared who was looking on when she'd brought a dog, a pig, and cupcakes to school for Marcus Turner. She sure didn't care about the pews full of strangers that were watching this.

Which was a good thing because the organ had stopped playing and the other bridesmaids were clustered at the back of the church, watching, as if hesitant to come any closer to... whatever this was.

Tori took a deep breath. "Okay. Tell me."

"I'm in love with you."

Tori froze.

The entire church was completely quiet. Silent. Not even a gasp.

She felt her eyes widening as Andrew stared at her.

"*What*?" she finally half-whispered, half-choked.

He nodded. And stepped forward. She stepped back.

"I'm in love with you, Tori."

"But...you're doing this *now*? Like *this*?" She glanced into the congregation and saw a sea of stunned expressions. But she couldn't see Josh.

Or Paisley. She winced. Paisley wasn't at the back yet. They could still fix this. Maybe. Possibly.

Oh God.

"I have to do it now," Andrew said. He stepped forward again and reached for her hand. "I've always loved you. But I didn't realize it was...*love* love. I always knew you'd be a part of my life and I guess I got comfortable with that. But now I'm realizing it's all going to change and I...don't want it to. I love you. I want you in my life. Every day. All the days."

Tori stared at him. This man's face was as familiar as her own. She'd known him through every life phase. Every major milestone. And yet, right now, she didn't know who she was looking at. Andrew was *in love* with her? No. That didn't feel right.

"I can't believe you're doing this here. Now. Like this," she said. Her voice sounded tight. She wasn't sure if she was fighting back tears or hysterical laughter or what exactly.

"I wanted to do it before," he said. "But," he went on, squeezing her hands, "this is good. I'm glad about this now. This is how I should do it. This is like you bringing Marcus cupcakes. This is like all the times you've worn your heart on your sleeve. This is me putting it all out there."

Oh...God.

"Andrew, I—"

"*What in the hell is going on?*"

The screech came from the back of the church. From the woman in white who had just pushed her way through her bridesmaids.

Paisley had arrived.

Now there were gasps from the pews. Everyone turned to watch her, people started talking, and the bridesmaids crowded into the aisle behind her.

"What the *fuck,* Andrew?" Paisley demanded from halfway down the aisle.

The gasps got louder and the minister dropped the Bible he was holding.

Tori jerked her hand from Andrew's hold as the bride came storming up the aisle, her veil streaming behind her, murder on her face.

If her finding them kissing in Bourbon O had been an eight on the oh-shit-this-is-bad scale, this was now a fifteen.

"Paisley, I'm sorry—" Andrew started.

"No!" the bride said firmly, coming to stand right in front of them. She glared up at Andrew and actually stomped her foot. "No. You're *not* doing this. I *asked* you after you kissed her. I gave you an out. You said no. You said you didn't have feelings for her. You're not doing this *now.*"

"I do love her. I don't want to do this to *you,*" Andrew said. "But I had to make a grand gesture for Tori. She knows me. She knows what this means. She knows that I'd never do it this way if I wasn't serious."

Holy crap. This was...awful.

Tori shot a look at the door behind the groomsmen that would lead out of the sanctuary. She could just take off running. It wasn't like anyone was going to tackle her or anything.

She loved Andrew. She really did. But this was crazy.

She looked back at her friend. Her dear friend. A man who, a year and a half ago, could have said this and she would have fallen into his arms. Because he was a good man. Who cared about her.

But she deserved an *amazing* man. Who *understood* her. Who *loved* her.

She'd had a taste of that now. Josh got her. He didn't protect her from her emotions and passions and instinct. He appreciated it all. He liked her *because of* all of that instead of in spite of it. He encouraged it all.

She wasn't in love with Andrew. She couldn't be. Because she was in love with Josh.

"I can't believe that—"

"I have something to say," Tori said loudly, interrupting Paisley. The other woman rounded on her and Tori took a quick step back, holding up her hands in defense. "Hang on."

Did she like big gestures? Yes. She'd been suppressing them because of Andrew and her dad, but yes, a big, grand gesture with her emotions spilling out all over and making a mess of cupcake frosting and pig poop was definitely her thing.

And she'd found a guy she could do that with.

That felt amazing. The idea that she could let it all hang out. That her passions and love and affection and joy didn't have to be channeled only toward her animals.

She stepped forward. "Andrew, I do love you. You're like a big brother to me. You're a lifelong friend. You're someone I will always care about. But I'm not *in* love with you."

"You don't want me to marry Paisley," Andrew said.

Tori glanced at Paisley. "I don't. But not for *me*." She looked back to Andrew. "For *you*. I don't think you belong together."

"You *bitch*," Paisley hissed.

Tori shrugged. "Sorry. But you *both* deserve to be with someone who really appreciates you. Who makes you feel special. Who gets you in a way no one else does. Who loves all of the things that make you quirky and weird and different from everyone else." She looked out into the congregation but couldn't see Josh through the crowd of people craning their necks and holding up their phones to be sure they didn't miss a moment of the drama. "I've found someone like that." She took a deep breath and turned to fully face the church pews. "Josh Landry, I am in love with you. I know it's been fast and maybe that seems crazy. But walking into that bar last Mardi Gras was the most important thing I'd ever done. Until I walked onto your dock a couple of days ago."

There was a beat of silence. Then the congregation all started shifting and turning to look around, trying to find Josh.

Even the minister went up on his tiptoes, peering into the crowd.

But there was no response from Josh. He didn't stand up. He didn't call out, "I love you too!". There was no big, hot Cajun stalking up the aisle to throw her over his shoulder and carry her off into their happily ever after.

Because he wasn't there.

It took her a couple of minutes to realize it. But it became painfully clear when she finally saw his seat between the shifting bodies between there and where she was standing.

It was empty.

Josh had left.

He also hadn't heard a word she'd just said in front of four hundred some odd people. On videos that would soon be uploaded to the internet.

Tori felt a cold trickle of hurt and humiliation go down her spine. Her stomach knotted. He'd just *left*?

"Tori."

She looked over at Andrew. His expression was one of sympathy and concern.

"He's not here."

No. No, he wasn't.

Because Andrew had just declared his feelings for her. In front of a church full of people. People who were here to see him marry someone else.

And Josh thought she would choose Andrew.

Her chest hurt as she thought about that. She hadn't told Josh how she felt about him. She hadn't floated the idea of her moving to Louisiana. She hadn't let him in on all of those thoughts because they seemed crazy and too fast and too spontaneous. She'd convinced herself—with some help from Andrew—that she was overreacting.

Maybe she had been. Maybe he didn't feel the same way. Maybe this whole scene had convinced him he was in over *his* head with this pretend-boyfriend-wedding-date thing and had gotten the hell out of here before everything went nuts.

More nuts.

Or maybe he was trying to be chivalrous. Maybe he thought ducking out and giving her the chance to really be with Andrew if that was what she wanted was the right thing to do.

Heck, she'd chosen Andrew over Josh before. More than once. She'd stopped Josh from carrying her straight up to her room two nights ago because Andrew had been concerned. She'd come back to the plantation because of Andrew yesterday rather than going out on the town with Josh and his family.

Josh didn't know that she'd been ignoring Andrew's calls and attempts to get her alone to talk. He didn't know that in her heart she'd definitely chosen *him* already.

He didn't know that right now, here, in front of everyone, that she'd declared her feelings for him.

Because he wasn't here.

Damn, this was even worse than cupcakes and pig poop in the high school hallway.

A lot worse.

————

"You just *left*?"

Ellie was staring at him like she'd never seen him before.

"What the hell, boy?" Leo added. "You just walked out? Without saying anything to her?"

"Andrew is her *best friend*," Owen said, jumping to Josh's defense. "He's been taking care of her all their lives. At her father's request, by the way. He knows her. He's been there for her. And now he stood up in front of everyone, including his parents, and *God*, and said that he loved her and wanted to be with her. He called off his *wedding* for her." Owen paused and looked up and down the bar. "Josh couldn't just storm up the aisle and say 'me too.' That's weak. He needs something better than that."

Josh clapped his cousin on the back. "Thanks, man."

Owen had summed it up pretty well. Actually, almost word for word what Josh had said to him when he'd slammed into the office, his tie hanging loose, his heart pounding, a tiny kitten tucked inside his suit jacket.

"I think you're an idiot," their grandmother informed Josh.

Josh had expected that reaction from her. But for just a second—and certainly not for the first time in his life—he wondered what it was like to have a sweet grandmother who baked cookies and knitted socks.

"I need something more. Something huge," Josh said. He frowned at his family and friends. "Come on. You all are supposed to be the experts here. I need a plan. A *good* plan. A *big* plan."

Could he have stomped up the aisle? Sure. Could he have shouted *I love you, Tori* from the back of the church? Of course. But...dammit...Andrew had done the in-front-of-God-and-everyone thing. Josh had to top that. He felt more for her than

Andrew did. Josh was absolutely positive. So that meant that Josh had to do more to show her.

Yes, he'd left. He'd heard what Andrew said, saw Tori's shocked expression, flashed back to her agreeing to go back to the plantation with Andrew rather than out with him, and he'd decided that he'd never wanted to one-up another man as much as he wanted to outdo Andrew.

Tori deserved to have two men fighting over her, trying to win her over, making asses of themselves.

Andrew had done his part.

Now it was Josh's turn.

No pressure.

Thinking hard, Josh stroked the head of the kitten who, surprisingly, didn't seem upset about being in a bar or surrounded by strangers. After taking a stool, Josh had pulled her out of his jacket, set her on top of the bar, Ellie had brought her some finely chopped fish, and the kitten settled right in. Now she was sleeping in the crook of Josh's arm.

Taking a detour past the barn to get her had been purely spontaneous. But last night Tori had said they were definitely old enough to leave their mother and...hell, he'd wanted a souvenir, he supposed. And no, Mardi Gras beads or even her panties, which were still in the pocket of his jeans, weren't enough. He'd needed something more. Something uniquely Tori. Something *alive*, warm, loving. Just like her.

God, he really needed to come up with a grand gesture and then fucking *do it*. He was tired of sitting around and being in love with Tori and not telling her. Not showing her. Not shouting it to the world.

But no, storming up the aisle at Andrew's wedding was *not* how Josh's gesture was going to go down.

Something had to *happen* here. This was all much less dramatic than he'd expected. He'd envisioned showing up in

Autre, telling everyone what happened, and having them all pile into cars and head back to the plantation with him.

Of course, he had no idea what came after that.

That was why he was here, asking them for input.

But instead of storming the plantation or hiring a skywriting plane or heading to Iowa so they would all be there when she got home, he was sitting on a barstool, petting his new cat, and listening to his grandparents tell him he was an idiot.

"Look, you're all into big gestures," he finally said. "The girl you keep is the one you're willing to make an ass out of yourself over, right? Well, Andrew made an ass of himself for her. Bigtime. He risked everything. Now come on. Give me something good."

"But you just *left*," Ellie said again. "Good God. What do you think Tori's thinking right now?"

"What was I supposed to do? You don't *warn* people that you're about to make a big gesture. That's part of what makes it big," Josh protested. The truth was, he'd acted on instinct. He'd seen what Andrew was doing, he'd thought, "oh *hell* no," and he'd stormed *out* of the church, intent on sweeping Tori off her feet.

Eventually.

After he'd figured out how.

And hopefully before she decided that him leaving her at the church with Andrew was a sign he didn't want her.

Fuck.

Okay, walking out had been stupid. He hadn't thought about that until he'd passed the Welcome to Autre sign. His need to outdo Andrew had been all that had been driving him.

So, yes, he'd fucked up. But he'd hoped these people would help him fix it.

"I'm freaking out, okay?" he finally said. That was the bottom line. He'd never felt like this. Felt this *much*. He didn't know how to express it in an appropriately huge way. "I was watching her walk down that aisle and thinking how much I loved her and how I couldn't wait to tell her. Then Andrew stops everything and tells her *he* loves her. That's a big deal. He knows about all her public spectacles over the years. He's talked her out of some of them. So doing that, so publicly and humiliatingly, was a big deal for him. Stomping up that aisle, making a big deal out of it all in front of everyone is very much something *I* would do. But Andrew doing that? That was...something."

From Andrew it meant more.

"That was *Andrew's* big gesture. His big moment. I wasn't going to...use that too," Josh finished weakly. Because that really was weak now that he thought about it. What the hell? He wasn't willing to tell her how he felt because Andrew told her first?

Ellie rolled her eyes so big he was afraid they might get stuck at the back of her head.

Cora, however, reached out and smacked Josh upside the back of *his* head. "It's not a competition."

"It's not?" he asked, rubbing the spot. "Really? Two men love her and want her? How is that not a competition?"

"Because there's only one real choice," Cora said. "The one *she* loves."

"This isn't pie, boy," Leo said. "You can't love two people equally like you can love both pecan and rum raisin."

"But you didn't even *tell her* that you love her and want her," Ellie said, giving him a harsh frown.

"She didn't tell *me* that she loves me either," Josh pointed out.

"And *that's* the big gesture," Ellie said, pointing her finger at his nose. "Taking the risk. Putting it all out there because of how *you* feel even if you're not sure how she feels."

That hit Josh right in the chest. Tori never shied away from defending her animals—or any animals—just because someone else might think it was weird or not understand or because the consequences might not go her way. She dove in, driven by *her* heart.

"Shit," he said, blowing out a breath. "Why did I walk out of there? That was stupid."

"Finally," Ellie said.

"Thank God," Cora agreed.

"So what's the plan?" Leo asked.

Josh sighed. "That's where *you* all come in."

"What if she and Andrew got hitched?" Owen asked. "You might be too late."

"No way would they get married like that," Josh said. If he'd thought that was a risk, he wouldn't have walked out. No, he hadn't given that a conscious thought, but his gut—his heart—would have never let him walk away if he thought he couldn't get her back. He just needed to do it right. "Her parents aren't here. And those are all Paisley's friends and family, really." He shook his head with a little chuckle. "No way would Paisley have let them use *her* flowers and shit to get married."

Ellie leaned in. "I have only one word for you."

"Love?"

"Iowa."

Iowa. Right. *Iowa.* He'd go to Iowa. That was a big gesture. That would show her how he felt. He'd find her farm and he'd...

He slid off the stool, still cradling his kitten. "Anyone know where I can get a cow? Preferably one with special needs?" Yes, he was going to give Tori a cow.

Everyone looked at one another, clearly confused.

"No, wait. A pig." Hell, maybe he'd make her cupcakes too. Recreate that moment but this time with a much better ending.

"You want a *pig?*" Owen asked.

"Or a goat. That would probably work," he said. At this point that wasn't really the most important thing he supposed.

"Special needs?" Leo asked.

"Like missing a leg," Josh said. "Or lactose intolerant or something."

"Can cows be lactose intolerant?" Owen asked. He looked around. "I'm seriously asking. That's really weird."

"I know a guy who has peacocks," Cora said.

Josh paused. "Really? Peacocks?"

"Yep. That's kind of unusual, right?"

He shrugged. "Yeah. Do they have any...phobias?"

"Do the peacocks have any phobias?" Cora asked.

"It's a long story," Josh told her.

"I have no idea." She also glanced around. "Who would even know if they did?"

Josh smiled. "Someone very special would." Hell, he'd gamble with the peacock. He'd take it to Tori and just hope it needed to be fed by hand or sung to at night or something.

"I'll call the guy," Cora said.

"Thanks." Josh started for the door. He needed to pack. And get a...peacock carrier. Or...something.

He almost ran Kennedy over when he yanked the door open.

"There's a girl here for you," Kennedy told him.

Just the way she had the other day when Tori had shown up on the dock.

Josh's heart thunked hard in his chest. "Oh yeah?"

"Yeah." Kennedy crossed her arms and narrowed her eyes. "And strangely she doesn't look homicidal this time either. Even though you ran out of that wedding and left her there like a big jerk."

Kennedy had taken Tori's side immediately. Though she had paused for a second to be impressed with the photos he'd sent of Tori's hair and makeup for the wedding.

Josh sucked in a deep breath. She'd come after him. Again. "Where is she?"

"The dock," Kennedy said. "And you should know that Sawyer has now seen her breasts. Naked."

Josh started to move past her but stopped at that. He looked at his sister. "Excuse me?"

Kennedy looked a little smug. "She came by Uber. And she marched down that dock to where Sawyer was tying up the boat. She tossed him a strand of beads, he turned, and she pulled her shirt up. For him and the entire boat of frat boys he'd just brought back from a tour."

Josh's eyes widened. "*What*?"

Kennedy frowned. "She thought he was you. She was making a big *gesture*, Josh. She took an *Uber*. She came after you. *Again*. And she said this whole thing about how Mardi Gras was the best day of her life and how she wants to make every day Mardi Gras, but she needs you for that...or something. She kind of cut off in the middle of it when she realized it was Sawyer bending over on the dock and not you."

Josh felt his smile spreading. He was madly in love with that woman.

Who had just made a big gesture for him.

"Where is she now?"

"Main office."

He started in that direction.

"Hey, we have a tour coming in!" Kennedy called. She'd need the office to process their payments.

"No we don't," he told her.

"Yes, we do!"

"Figure it out, Ken."

"You have a *house*, you know. With a bedroom."

"It's three blocks away," he called back as he crossed the road.

"Exactly! Only *three blocks away*!" Kennedy called.

"Too far!" He rounded the corner of the tour company's building and yanked the door to the office open.

Tori was sitting on the stool behind the main counter.

"You *have* to stop mistaking other men for me," he said, pulling the door shut behind him and locking it.

"Maybe you need to start being where I expect you to be when I come looking for you," she said, giving him a smile that clearly said she was thrilled to see him and relieved. Relieved that he wanted to see her.

He was a dumbass. He never should have made her doubt that he wanted her. Not even for the two hours it had been since he'd left the church.

"Yeah, I do," he said with a nod. "I need to be there for you. Every time. I'm sorry I left."

"I am too. I made this whole big speech about being in love with you."

Love rocked through him. "In front of everyone?"

"Yep. It's on YouTube and Facebook if you want to see it."

"I definitely want to see it." He took a step toward her.

"My hair and makeup look amazing in it."

He grinned. "I'll bet." He stepped up to the counter. "But I'd really rather hear it in person."

"I'm in love with you, Josh. I want to be with you. And I know that's crazy and it's fast, but it's true."

"Even though I left? I walked out? I did it because I was hell-bent on upstaging Andrew's big gesture and I came back here to get everyone in on it. But I shouldn't have left."

She blinked at him. "You did? You were planning a grand gesture?"

"Damn right I was. I was so wrapped up in making it huge and something people around here would call epic and making the story something everyone would tell over and over again that I just walked out and came straight down here."

"You knew I'd still want to see it?" she asked.

"You would have *definitely* wanted to see it." He gave her a grin. Hell, he still didn't really know what it was going to be, but he would make it larger-than-life.

She smiled back. "But now you don't have to do it. Because *I* did it."

That made his chest ache. "You did. And then..." He didn't want to hurt her feelings, but this was a really important part of all of this. "Your big speech in the church, that gesture, it failed again. In front of everyone. But you still got in an Uber and came down here to try again. Even though I walked out and you didn't know why."

"I..." She seemed to be thinking about that. Then she shrugged. "Yeah I guess I did. I mean, if I'm willing to make an ass of myself over dogs and cows, I'm definitely willing to make an ass of myself, repeatedly, over you."

Josh felt this throat tighten. He cleared his throat. "Thank God for that. Since I can't seem to get *my* act together. Though it's not because I don't want to," he added hurriedly.

She grinned at that. "Well, this was low risk." She gave him a wink. "This is a safe place for me. I knew I could do it again if I did it here. In Autre. I feel good here. I know that you think this place is crazy and weird, but I *fit* here and I knew I could come do this and everyone would love it and be behind me. No one would think I was nuts. No one would make me apologize. No one would make me replace any prom dresses...so to speak."

Everything in him ached then. She was amazing and she'd found her place. And it was here. With him. And his family.

He resisted the urge to grab her and pull her over the counter and into his arms. Barely. "Well, I know Sawyer loved this big grand gesture."

She laughed. "That makes it an even better story, doesn't it?"

It did. But he growled. "No. You being naked for any other man ever again for any reason? No."

Her expression softened. "Thank you for wanting my crazy."

He shook his head. "I'll tell you who's crazy—your dad and Andrew. The two men who didn't let you be your amazing self, who didn't *see* you, who didn't want you to be exactly who you are." He took advantage of her being speechless and leaned in. "I want every single bit of you. I'm in love with you too. I've never met anyone like you and I can't imagine not being with you."

Her eyes widened. "Really? You're in love with me too?"

"Yes. Of course. Who wouldn't be in love with you?" he asked with a little laugh. "I was waiting for the right gesture, the right chance to come along to really show you. But, I should have just said it."

Her eyes got a little shiny and she sniffed. "I know that Landrys are big into grand gestures. But I don't think you even realize the gestures you've made. There have been so many. And they add up. They really do. All the little things you've done *all* matter. The kittens, the makeup, the wanting to just *know* me. Accepting me just exactly the way I am. You don't try to dial me back or make excuses for me. You just..." Her voice got softer. "You just love me. And that's the greatest gesture of all."

God, he needed her. In every way. Right now.

He started to lean in so he could kiss her for the next three days straight, but just then the kitten mewed. Tori's eyes flew to the little ball of fur in the crook of his arm.

"Oh my God, is that the runt from the barn?"

She hadn't even *seen* the kitten until now. She'd only seen *him*. That was when Josh knew, without a doubt, Victoria Kramer really did love him. He grinned and nodded, handing the kitten over. "I needed to bring something home that was...you."

Tori cuddled the kitten up to her face, but her eyes were locked on his. "I have never wanted to tear your clothes off more."

He laughed. His little nympho. "There's nothing wrong with her though. No special needs. Sorry."

Tori sniffed and slid off the stool. She came around the edge of the counter to stand directly in front of him.

He lifted a hand and cupped the side of her head.

"It's okay that's nothing's wrong with her," Tori said.

"I can get you some peacocks," he said. "But I'm not sure there's anything really wrong with them either."

She laughed. "That's okay too." Her eyes twinkled a bit. "I would love some peacocks though. That's really cool."

"You don't need crazy animals? I mean, we can move yours down here." Of course they'd move hers down here.

She nodded. "Okay, but—" She lifted her shoulder. "Maybe it's time for me to try taking care of some crazy *people*."

Love, lust, and a happiness he never imagined washed through him. Letting people in. Being crazy *about* them and risking that it wouldn't always be reciprocated. *That* was a grand gesture from Tori.

Of course, it *would* be reciprocated. She'd have so much love she wouldn't know what to do. But being willing to take that risk was exactly what they both needed.

They kissed, long and sweet, but couldn't press too close together because of the kitten. Josh lifted his head, grinning. He desperately needed to press close to her. Very, very close. He took the kitten from her and moved to open the door. As expected, Kennedy, Owen, Sawyer, Ellie, Cora, Jerry, and Leo were outside, leaning on the railing, waiting.

He handed the cat to his sister, gave them a grin, and then

shut the door again, locking it. He turned back to Tori, ignoring Kennedy's, "Dammit, Josh!"

"Now about the Mardi Gras beads and naked breasts I heard about..."

"Well, it's not really Mardi Gras anymore," Tori teased, even as she pulled one of the strands of beads from her pocket and tossed it to him.

"Oh, darlin'." He stripped off his shirt, flashing her in exchange for the beads. Then he tossed them back to her. "For us, every day is Mardi Gras from here on out."

EPILOGUE

Three months later...

"Andrew called."

Josh rolled his eyes. "Don't care."

Tori gave him a grin and handed him Chuck, the kitten that he'd brought in to have her check over. "Chuck is perfectly healthy."

"Awesome." Josh lifted the little cat and looked him in the eye. "Welcome to the family, bud."

It was the third cat he'd brought home in two months, including Bernie, the kitten from the plantation, and Jax, the ten-year-old cat he'd found in the shed at the back of their new property. The farm had come with several outbuildings and they were still going through them all and finding all kinds of treasures—and junk. The cat had clearly been living out there for some time, but he'd taken to being in the house—and on Josh's lap—quickly.

Josh and his new cat obsession was potentially going to be a problem.

But for now, Tori just grinned as she cleaned up the exam table.

"He said that he doesn't think he and Paisley are going to get back together," she said.

"Still don't care." Josh gave her a frown. "And no, he can't come to the crawfish boil on Friday."

The last time Andrew had come down, he'd drunk three mason jars full of moonshine and passed out in the Boys of the Bayou office. He'd slept through the first four tour groups of the next morning. Right there in the middle of the floor with tourists stepping over and around him.

"Oh, come on," Tori teased. "You know you have nothing to worry about."

Josh scoffed. "I'm not worried. I know exactly where your sweet ass is going to be every night. I just don't like him."

Tori loved when he said stuff like that. And yeah, there was no question where her ass, and the rest of her, was going to be. Right here. In Autre, Louisiana. With Josh Landry. She'd only been here for three months and she already felt like she was home.

She took Josh's hand and they headed for the house. She already had a veterinary practice built up. That amazed her. But the nearest vet prior to her arrival had been thirty minutes away. And well, she was a Landry—kind of—and that meant that everyone in and around Autre trusted her implicitly.

They put Chuck in the house with Jax and Bernie and then headed into town and to the tour office. Which really only required them walking out their front door, turning left, and walking a few blocks. Their farm was on the edge of town with their property stretching back behind the house nearly to the county line, but their front yard was on the last street of Autre.

Josh had two tours later on, and Tori was going to stop by a couple of houses to check on patients. But first, Sawyer had wanted to meet with everyone.

Owen, Sawyer, and Kennedy were already there when Josh and Tori came through the door.

Tori didn't have much to do with the tour company but she sometimes filled in for Kennedy at the desk if needed, and she still felt like a part of everything. There wasn't much that went on in this family, this business, or even Ellie's bar, that wasn't common knowledge in the family.

"We have a situation," Sawyer said without even waiting for Tori and Josh to find a seat.

"What's goin' on?" Owen asked, tossing a peanut into his mouth.

"We're comin' up short on money," Sawyer said bluntly. "We're barely making ends meet and that means that we have to put off some new purchases, and the expansion we talked about last year isn't going to happen. At least not right now."

Owen and Josh shared a look. An unhappy look.

"Are bookings down or something?" Tori asked. She'd owned her own business since graduating with her degree but hadn't needed to advertise or seek out patients. Everyone just brought their animals in to her, and everyone in Elton could get her cell number from her mom or dad simply by stopping them at church or running into them at the café.

"Business is good," Sawyer said. "But we're down a man. That means more of my time spent on the business side and more time all of us have to spend on maintenance and repairs and that means less time on tours."

Everyone was quiet for a long moment. That was the

general reaction any time anyone mentioned Tommy, the fourth partner who had died eight months before, even indirectly.

Finally Josh said, "What do we need to do? Hire someone?"

"Maybe," Sawyer said. He shoved a hand through his hair. "But there's more."

"Like what?" Owen asked.

"Maddie."

Owen froze with his hand partway through the motion of tossing more peanuts into his mouth. "What?"

Sawyer nodded. "Maddie. She wants to sell her portion."

Owen set the jar of peanuts down hard and crossed his arms. "Why?"

"She doesn't want it," Sawyer said.

"She doesn't *want* it?"

Sawyer blew out a breath. "Why would she want it?" he asked flatly.

"What's that mean?" Owen asked, clearly annoyed. "Her brother *gave* it to her."

Owen was the laid-back Landry. The fun guy. The flirt. The charmer. Tori wasn't sure she'd ever seen him scowl like he was now, and she'd definitely never seen him agitated like this.

Oh, she so wanted to know who Maddie was and what was going on. She settled in to watch.

"The last time she lived here she was sixteen," Sawyer said. "She doesn't feel connected to the town or the business."

"You mean she doesn't feel connected to *us*," Owen said.

"Well, how the hell would she?" Sawyer asked, clearly exasperated. "She's been living in California for the past twelve years."

"Fine," Owen said. "Then she can give it to us. Whatever."

"Yeah, well, she isn't going to *give* it to us," Sawyer said. "We have to buy her out."

"What's going on?" Tori whispered to Josh.

"Maddie is Tommy's little sister," Josh told her. "He left her his portion of the business when he died. She owns thirty-five percent of Boys of the Bayou."

"Oh." Well, yeah, damn. "And she doesn't want it?"

"Guess not." Josh didn't look happy. "But damn, this isn't a good time for us to be trying to buy someone out."

"Son of a bitch." Owen paced to the door and stood staring at it, his hands on his hips.

Tori gave Josh a puzzled look. She'd never seen Owen act like that.

"Owen and Maddie are..." Josh said, "...complicated."

"There's a history there?" Tori guessed.

"You could say that. There's, um..." Josh lowered his voice. "There's a chance that Maddie might be hesitant to come back to Autre, in part, because of Owen."

Tori looked over at Owen and wiggled. She wanted to know *all* of this history.

"So you need to get your head on straight," Sawyer said to Owen. "She's coming to town."

Owen swung around. "When?"

"Should be here next week. She's stayin' for thirty days. That's how long we have to come up with a solution per the partnership agreement."

"We have a partnership agreement?" Josh asked.

"Well..." Sawyer shoved a hand through his hair. "There's a couple of notebook pages that Leo and Kenny wrote up when they first started the business."

"But that doesn't apply to us, does it?" Josh asked.

"According to George, it's legally binding," Sawyer said of their lawyer. "He was, apparently, there when they wrote it up."

"Let me guess," Josh said. "They wrote it up at the bar over jars of whiskey after being out fishin' all day."

"Almost," Sawyer nodded. "They were at the hunting cabin. But there was definitely whiskey and fishing involved."

Everyone chuckled at that. Except Owen. He was frowning at the floor, seemingly lost in his own thoughts.

Maddie was more than Tommy's little sister, it seemed.

"What's it got in it?" Josh asked.

"What to do if one of the partners steals money from the business. How to settle disputes that arise between the partners. That kind of thing," Sawyer said. "It's a bunch of stuff they agreed to do before either of them could dissolve the partnership or sell off their portion." He rolled his eyes. "Apparently Leo and Kenny acknowledged they were both hotheaded, stubborn asses and put some contingency plans in place in case one of them got pissed off over something stupid and thought about messing with the business."

Josh grinned. "What would they do if one of them stole money from the business?"

"The other one got full ownership of the baseball card," Sawyer said.

Josh laughed.

"Baseball card?" Tori asked. "Did they write that up when they were twelve?"

Josh nodded, grinning. "Leo and Kenny, especially together, did act like they were twelve a lot of the time. But they both had some really valuable cards. Stuff they'd actually hung on to since they *were* kids. They were constantly trying to win one away or trick the other guy into giving something up. But they had a Willie Mays rookie card that they bought together back in 1952. They've always co-owned it even though over the years they each tried everything to get the other to let it go. It's worth thousands now. They'd even talked about selling it to start the business, but in the end they just couldn't do it."

Tori grinned at the story. That sounded just like Leo. A little crusty on the outside, but with a heart of gold underneath.

"Does this agreement give you a good way to settle the idea of Maddie selling?" Kennedy asked.

"Well, I'm not sure how *good* it is," Sawyer said. "But it does say that whoever wants out has to give the other partner thirty days' notice. And that during those thirty days, the partners have to keep working together."

"Maddie doesn't work here," Owen said shortly.

"Not at the moment, no," Sawyer agreed.

Owen blew out a breath. "She's coming here, for a month, and will be working here with us every day?"

Sawyer gave a short nod. "Pretty much."

"And then? What happens at the end of thirty days?" Owen asked.

"Well, then either she keeps her portion because we've convinced her she wants to be a part of it all. Or..." He sighed. "She sells."

"To a stranger?" Kennedy asked. "We can't bring a stranger into the business."

"No fucking way," Owen said.

Tori could see the tension in all of them. The idea of someone who wasn't part of this tight-knit clan coming into the business seemed strange even to her. Tommy and Maddie weren't blood relation to the Landrys, but because of the life-long friendship between the Landrys and Allains, they were one big family in all the ways that counted.

"I fell in love with your family and this town in about ten minutes," Tori said, encouragingly. "I can't imagine how she could spend thirty days here and not want to be a part of it."

Sawyer, Josh, and Kennedy all looked at Owen.

Owen frowned. "What?"

"*You* have to behave," Sawyer told him.

"What do you think is going to happen, exactly?"

"What I *know* is going to happen is that you're going to be nothing more and nothing less than the charming good-old-boy you are to every tourist with tits," Sawyer said firmly.

Owen *was* charming and sweet with every female Tori had

ever seen him with. Well, maybe not Ellie *all* the time. But she usually started it. So why the warning from Sawyer?

"You will not fight with her," Sawyer said. "You will not fight anyone *over* her. And you will *not* kiss her."

Tori's eyes were wide by the time Sawyer was done with his list. Oh, yes, there was a *gooood* story here.

Owen opened his mouth to reply, but seemed to think better of it and snapped it shut. He blew out a breath. Finally he said, "Fine."

"You sure?" Sawyer asked.

"It's been twelve years," Owen told him. "I'd like to think that I have more self-control than I did when I was seventeen."

"I'd like to think that too," Sawyer said. "But I seem to remember patching a hole in the wall of this very office that was about the size of your fist after she was here for Tommy's funeral."

Tori looked at Josh. He just sighed.

"Look, we don't need her to *move* down here or anything," Sawyer said to the group as a whole. "She can own it from San Francisco. But we need to be sure she sees and feels everything Tommy loved about this place. And—" Sawyer paused and took a deep breath. "Everything he loved about *us*. We have to make it too hard for her to let go of this."

Kennedy nodded. "Yeah, okay." She looked at the rest of them worriedly. "We can do that. Right?"

"Sure," Josh said. He didn't seem convinced.

"Of course," Tori added. *She* had fallen in love with Autre, the Landry family, and the Boys of the Bayou easily.

"I sincerely doubt it," Owen said bluntly. "She's a city girl now."

"Well, we've got thirty days to remind her that she's really a bayou girl deep down," Sawyer said. He looked at Owen. "Pull yourself together."

Owen flipped him off.

Tori grinned. Whatever this was, it was going to be very interesting.

———

Thank you for reading *My Best Friend's Mardi Gras Wedding*! I hope you loved Josh and Tori's story!

There's lots more to come from the bayou!
Up next is Owen and Maddie's story in ***Sweet Home Louisiana!***

Grab it now!

**Learn more at www.ErinNicholas.com
under the BOOKS menu!**

And if you loved the Boys of the Bayou, you'll also love the **Boys of the Big Easy**! Sexy New Orleans guys who are also single dads!

Check them out HERE!

MORE FROM ERIN NICHOLAS

The Boys of the Bayou

My Best Friend's Mardi Gras Wedding
Sweet Home Louisiana
Beauty and the Bayou
Crazy Rich Cajuns

———

The Boys of the Big Easy

Easy Going (prequel novella)
Going Down Easy
Taking It Easy
Nice and Easy
Eggnog Makes Her Easy (Christmas novella)

———

And if you loved Erin's Boys of the Bayou and Boys of the
Big Easy
check out the **Billionaires in Blue Jeans series!**

Diamonds and Dirt Roads
High Heels and Haystacks
Cashmere and Camo

ABOUT THE AUTHOR

Erin Nicholas is the New York Times and USA Today bestselling author of over thirty sexy contemporary romances. Her stories have been described as toe-curling, enchanting, steamy and fun. She loves to write about reluctant heroes, imperfect heroines and happily ever afters. She lives in the Midwest with her husband who only wants to read the sex scenes in her books, her kids who will never read the sex scenes in her books, and family and friends who say they're shocked by the sex scenes in her books (yeah, right!).

Find her and all her books at
www.ErinNicholas.com

And find her on Facebook, BookBub, and Instagram!

CPSIA information can be obtained
at www.ICGtesting.com
Printed in the USA
FSHW020458050419
56990FS